She wasn't safe

Somebody had recognized her. If this Captain McAllister was determined enough, he could find a way, legally or not, to get her fingerprints. The life Nell had built so carefully could collapse, like a house carried down the crumbling bluff by a mud slide.

A terrible sound escaped her, a shuddering cry.

I have to run. I can't be here when he comes looking for me again. I can't.

She sank down, right there inside the door, her back to it, and let her purse and the books fall. Her breathing was loud in the silent apartment.

What if he meant it? What if she could trust him?

What if she couldn't?

Nell drew her knees up, hugged herself tight and rocked.

The most insistent voice in her head was the one that whispered, *Am I Maddie?*

Things are not as they seem in Angel Butte, Oregon. Read on to find out how Colin McAllister can help Nell unravel the mystery of who she is in this first book of a captivating new series from reader favorite Janice Kay Johnson!

Dear Reader,

Why do some places feel like home and others never do? I lived in central Oregon for only three years when I was a child, but writing this trilogy, The Mysteries of Angel Butte, felt like a homecoming to me. I've only been back to Bend, where my family lived, a few times as an adult, but the first thing I always notice is the smell. I think it might be the ponderosa and lodgepole pines, maybe the volcanic soil, but that part of Oregon smells different to me than anywhere I've ever been. I can roll down the car window and feel amazing, just breathing it in.

My memories of those years are vivid, too. My dad was a college professor who worked as a naturalist during summers. He set up the first interpretive center at Lava Butte, a volcanic cinder cone not far from Bend. Like Maddie, the heroine in this first book, I'd often go to work with him during the summer. I was happy feeding the chipmunks that lived in the crater and looked pretty darn healthy considering all the stuff tourists fed them! My father was a runner; we lived only a few blocks away from Pilot Butte, the smaller cinder cone that is right in the middle of Bend (needless to say, the model for Angel Butte in my stories), and Dad ran to the top nearly every day. Quite often, I'm not that interested in the setting for my books, but this was different from the very beginning. The town may be fictional, but I was writing about home, in a very real sense.

Of course, to my recollection no skeletons were recovered from beneath the cinders at either Lava Butte or Pilot Butte while we lived there, but think what a great place to hide a body that would be! Both the first two books in this trilogy have characters haunted by their memories of growing up in this town. Tapping into those memories turned out to be easier than I could have imagined, even though they were far darker than mine. I'd say enjoy your visit to Angel Butte—but really I'd like to keep you awake tonight, wondering if you dare go home....

Best,

Janice Kay Johnson

PS—I enjoy hearing from readers! Visit me on Facebook or write me c/o Harlequin, 225 Duncan Mill Road, Don Mills, ON M3B 3K9, Canada.

JANICE KAY JOHNSON

—

Bringing Maddie Home

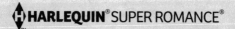

HARLEQUIN®SUPER ROMANCE®

Recycling programs
for this product may
not exist in your area.

ISBN-13: 978-0-373-60808-9

BRINGING MADDIE HOME

Printed in U.S.A.

ABOUT THE AUTHOR

The author of more than seventy books for children and adults, Janice Kay Johnson is especially well-known for her Harlequin Superromance novels about love and family—about the way generations connect and the power our earliest experiences have on us throughout life. Her 2007 novel *Snowbound* won a RITA® Award from Romance Writers of America for Best Contemporary Series Romance. A former librarian, Janice raised two daughters in a small rural town north of Seattle, Washington. She loves to read and is an active volunteer and board member for Purrfect Pals, a no-kill cat shelter.

Books by Janice Kay Johnson

HARLEQUIN SUPERROMANCE

SIGNATURE SELECT SAGA

*The Russell Twins
**A Brother's Word

Other titles by this author available in ebook format.

PROLOGUE

SHE AWAKENED TO darkness, pain and nausea. Had she fallen? Somehow she knew she wasn't in bed. She reached out blindly to explore and found an unyielding surface close above her. Movement and a rumbling vibration made her body sway from side to side. She flailed all around her, finding the walls of a box. Terror swelled in her, more powerful than the nausea.

I'm in a coffin. They're burying me alive.

Before she could scream and hammer on the lid, consciousness slipped away.

The next time she surfaced, it was to the taste of bile in her mouth and the awareness that her stomach was heaving. Too late to get up and run for the bathroom. All she could do was fling herself onto her side before throwing up. Her head hurt so bad. She banged into something as she rolled. And it was dark. So dark. The surface she lay on was hard. Not bed.

Consciousness came and went a couple more times, her awareness fleeting, her thoughts chaotic. Once she surfaced to an awful smell, then to the realization that her cheek was resting in something sticky. Her own vomit. With a cry she hurled herself back and whacked something behind her.

Panic rose in her chest. *Why can't I see?*

In her peripheral vision, there was a flash of red. She tried to turn her head to see what it was and flinched. Only one eye would open. She groped for her face and found her eyelid crusted shut. With something. The smell was bad, but it didn't matter, not when she hurt so much. She closed her other eye and gave up.

Finally she awakened and remembered the other times. *Not a coffin.* Her questing fingers found cold metal, with strange dips and curves and even a few holes. She succeeded in rolling all the way over and almost passed out again. Her head wanted to explode. *Blood,* she thought. It was blood crusting her eye. *I hit my head.*

She'd become used to the vibration and the sounds that might have been occasional gusts of wind. Not wind, she finally recognized: cars passing on a highway. Her mind fumbled for understanding. She was in a car. Locked in the trunk of a car that was moving. Bewildered, she turned the notion over and over. Not knowing why this was so wrong, but also confused about where she should be. She couldn't think. It was because of the headache.

Suddenly she slid sideways and barely managed to get an arm up to keep her head from hitting the side wall. She was being pitched backward despite herself. *Oh, gross, into the vomit.* The car was braking, that was it. Fear rose like the contents of her stomach had earlier, clogging her throat. Once the car stopped, she wouldn't be safe at all.

But it *had* stopped. The engine turned off. She heard a door open, then slam. She squeezed her eyes shut. If she pretended she was still unconscious...

Footsteps came close and she flinched, but then they began to diminish. The driver must be walking away. She strained until she didn't hear the footsteps at all, until the silence was absolute.

Then, frantically, mindlessly, she shoved upward with all her strength, despite knowing the trunk lid wouldn't give way. *Stupid, stupid. Think.* Just like that, she had a picture of herself—it must be her—leaning into an open car trunk. She could smell fresh lumber, hear a man's impatient voice.

"What are you waiting for? Push down the back-seat." Because she wasn't very big, she'd had to all but crawl into the trunk before she could reach the latch to yank, then push the back of the seat until it flopped forward.

Panting now, she groped above her for a latch. *Please, please, please let this car have seats that fold down.* Her fingers closed around a familiar, plastic T-shaped piece dangling at the back of the trunk and she pulled. If there were other people in the car... If the driver hadn't been alone...

There was a clunk and a sliver of light. She pushed, and half the seat folded down—not the whole one. It wasn't what she expected. This wasn't the car she remembered, then.

Through the opening and the windshield, she saw that it was night outside, and that there were bright lights. No one was in the car with her. Whimpering, she crawled right through the vomit and then the hole into the passenger compartment. Opened the back door and almost fell out onto pavement. She stumbled into a curb and lifted her head to see a gas pump. She wanted to run, run, run, but an inner voice told her to push the seat back in place, shut the car door. Maybe the driver wouldn't know he'd lost her. While she carefully closed the door, the sound was so loud she cringed and crouched behind the fender, holding her breath to listen. But she heard no footsteps, no roar of anger. The car sat alone at the pumps.

She crept around the trunk and saw the minimart with a brightly lit ARCO sign. He must have gone inside to use the bathroom or buy something.

Run, run, run.

This time she did, her footsteps slapping on the pavement. Weaving like a drunk on numb legs, she fell once to her knees and skinned her palms but was barely slowed. Still no shout of alarm. She reached the windowless side of the gas station and kept going. Darkness lay beyond. If there was a moon, it must be low or behind clouds. The pavement gave way to dirt. She slammed into something rough, something that scratched at her face and had arms with clawlike hands.

Scrambling backward, she saw enough of an outline to understand. A tree. Her eyes were starting to adjust and she saw more trees, rows of them. Small, sculptural ones. An orchard maybe. She ran down the aisle between rows. Ran and ran, then cut between rows and ran some more, until the lights at the gas station were far away. Then, her stomach heaving again, she dropped to the ground and tried to shrink herself to nothingness so that she would fit behind the narrow bole of a tree. There she cowered, listening. Shivering. Shuddering as cold crept into her bones. Eventually hearing a car start up and take off. Others passed on the highway. Trucks with their heavier rumble. Vehicles came and went at the gas station. Night became the gray, pale light of dawn that left her feeling terrifyingly exposed. But no one came.

The sun rose until it was high in the sky, but gave little heat. The trees were bare of leaves, which meant it was winter.

Why don't I know *what season it is?*

She didn't know anything. Was afraid to let herself examine why she didn't. She was nothing but an animal caught far from its burrow, horribly exposed. She was cold. So cold, despite the strange, too-large shirt she wore. At last it wasn't so much courage as desperation that had her creeping slowly back toward the gas station and the highway. The worst was crossing the last open stretch onto pavement. The restroom doors were on this side. Hiding behind a big, white propane tank, peeking around it every time she heard footsteps, she had to wait almost forever before a woman came out of one of the restrooms and walked away, key dangling from a hand, without looking back. The door was just swinging shut and she raced for it. It was slamming when she slipped her fingers into the crack just in time. This hurt barely registered.

Hurry, hurry.

She hardly even examined herself in the mirror, beyond recoiling from the blood and vomit matting her hair and dried on her face and wondering why she was wearing this man's shirt/jacket thing that was as long as a dress. With liquid soap, hot water and paper towels she scrubbed desperately at herself. She managed to get most of her head under the stream of water and used the hand soap to wash her hair, too. It hurt, hurt so bad, and the water kept running red no matter how many times she rinsed. She unbuttoned the olive-green shirt with an embroidered patch on the shoulder and scrubbed the blood and vomit off it, too. It had to be military, but it looked old, like somebody had worn it forever. Not her, she thought. Right now, it was all she had to wear, except for the thin cap-sleeved T-shirt beneath, so she wrung it out then put it back on wet. She'd be even colder, but that had to be better than being bloody and stinking with puke. Plus, wearing the shirt felt…necessary. Like it meant something.

The face she finally saw looked shell-shocked, but okay. Skin dead-white, her eyes dilated, but no bruises showed. The wound was on the right, near the back of her head. Touching it once had hurt, so she wouldn't again.

She cracked the bathroom door enough to see that there was no one in sight, then rushed back behind the building.

Now what?

A thought shaped itself. She could go inside and ask for help. The clerk would call the police. Somebody, somewhere, would know where she belonged.

A whimper slipped out and she looked down to see that she was hugging herself again, shaking. There were faces, the same man she'd remembered telling her to put down the seat. And a woman, too, whose stare was so icy that the girl had shriveled and crept away.

No, no, no. If they were her family, she couldn't go back to *them.*

Then…I must be running away. She calmed as she accepted a truth, something she did know. They had been cruel to her…or something. She rocked herself, trying to remember, and couldn't. But she knew they weren't to be trusted, not those people, whether they were her family or not.

For most of the day, she watched from behind the propane tank as cars and trucks arrived and left. Finally a U-Haul truck pulled in. She heard the metal scrape of the rear door being lifted and crept forward to watch as the driver checked the load. Leaving it open, he disappeared around the side of the truck. She ran again, faster than she'd ever run in her life, *slap, slap, slap* on the pavement, and slithered into the back of the truck, trying not to make it bounce with her weight. There wasn't much weight, though, because she was small and skinny. Heart pounding, she lifted a quilted pad and shinnied beneath it, finding herself wedged beside a wooden dresser. Another squirm and she made it behind the dresser. Something—a chair leg maybe—pressed into her back. Then she waited some more, trying not to breathe, until the footsteps came, and the metal door was released to drop, bounce once, then stay down. She heard the man snap closed the padlock, then get in behind the wheel.

Once more, lying on her side in the darkness, she felt the vibrations of an engine and movement. But this time, she tugged the heavy quilt closer, buried her chin inside the collar of the damp shirt, and let the terrible fear slip away. She was…not safe, but safer.

Tears trickled down her cheeks, wetting the hand she'd laid beneath her head. Her last fuzzy thought before sleep claimed her was, *I won't go back, no matter what,* even though she had no idea where she was going, and less of an idea where she'd been.

CHAPTER ONE

"SOME BONES HAVE turned up."

Police Captain Colin McAllister lifted his head. "Bones?"

He'd waved Duane into his office a minute before. Lieutenant Duane Brewer headed Criminal Investigations, which meant that when he wanted a word, it was more likely to be about a corpse than a shoplifter. Still, it had taken Colin a moment to tear his attention from his computer monitor. He'd been trying to figure out how to plug holes in manpower without leapfrogging academy grads, with their shiny new badges, to detective. The problem was becoming chronic, and he knew who to blame. He'd known for ten years where the cancer lurked that was sickening the Angel Butte Police Department. He was just too damned stubborn to jump ship the way the others had.

He saved the work on his computer and leaned back in his leather desk chair, studying the man who'd been his mentor and whom he now outranked.

Fifty-four years old and thickening around the

waist, Duane was the quintessential detective: patient, thorough and dogged. A loner, he liked what he did and hadn't been happy about the promotion to lieutenant. Colin had begged him to take it.

"What's the story?"

"You know those trees they've been taking out in the river park?"

Already feeling apprehension, Colin nodded. The infestation of pine beetles had become obvious when needles turned brown and fell. Some fungus had swept along in the wake of the beetles, taking advantage of the weakened trees. The city parks department had made the decision to cut out the infested ones before they fell in the next windstorm.

"They're digging out the stumps, where they can get a bulldozer in."

He knew that, too.

"Pulled one out today and some human bones came with it."

"Not an Indian burial?"

"No. The foreman's pretty shaken up. Hasn't found a skull yet, but there's a lower jaw. The teeth have fillings in them." Duane ran a hand through his thinning hair, looking shaken. "Colin, I haven't been out there yet, but it sounds like this isn't more than a couple hundred yards from where Maddie was grabbed."

Maddie Dubeau was Duane's niece. Frantic at her disappearance twelve years ago, Duane had insisted on taking over the investigation, and nobody had been able to deny him. He'd let Colin, then a young officer who had been first responder, stay involved, going door-to-door with questions and searching the grid. They hadn't talked about the case in years, but Colin knew that Duane had to be even more haunted by their failure to find her than Colin had been.

His own gaze shifted to a bulletin board where he kept a few photos. Victims whose killers had never been found. A two-year-old beaten to death by her father despite multiple calls to 911 from concerned neighbors, babysitters and medical personnel. Two kids who'd disappeared and never been found. Faces he wouldn't—couldn't—forget. Some were personal failures, some were department. He wanted their eyes watching him, even if he didn't often look back at them.

Madeline Noelle Dubeau's picture was one of them. It was her last school photo, taken her freshman year of high school. This was more flattering than the one on the learner's permit he'd found at the scene but had bothered Colin in the same way. In it, she was smiling politely, as though the photographer had insisted, but her wide, cautious eyes weren't happy. Looking at it, he thought that this was a girl who always stayed a step back, who didn't expect the best from anyone. Just shy, he'd told himself every time he tried to delve into her secrets, but he couldn't make himself believe it.

He'd never asked Duane, who didn't like talking about her.

Duane rose and went to the bulletin board, standing with his back to Colin's desk. His shoulders hunched under his jacket. "I don't keep a picture of her out. I can't stand to."

"Sometimes I'm convinced if I look long enough, I'll be able to tell what she was thinking." Impatient with himself, Colin grabbed his weapon from the top drawer and stood, then snagged his suit jacket from the back of the chair. "I'll drive myself, but I want to see the site."

"You won't have any trouble finding us." After taking one last, long look at the photo of Maddie, Duane flipped a hand and walked out. Colin followed, pausing only to let his assistant know where he was going.

Not until he was behind the wheel of his SUV did he think back to that night. He hadn't been two months on the job when he'd been sent to the park to investigate an elderly neighbor's report that she'd heard a woman's scream.

Teenagers liked the park at night; even in his short time patrolling, Colin had already broken up keggers half a dozen times there. The park, a sizable one, was within city limits, and a stretch along the bank of the Deschutes River was manicured and included a picnic area and playground. Ten or fifteen acres had been left in wilderness, only a couple of dirt paths showing that kids cut from one neighborhood to another through the swath of forest. That night, though, he hadn't been able to feel the presence of anyone at all. Kids weren't good at being absolutely quiet. They were prone to giggles or nervous rustling or shushing each other. And he hadn't known why, but the fine hairs at his nape stirred from the moment he stepped into the darkness, swinging his flashlight beam in an arc to pierce the darker shadows beneath madrona and snowberry.

Sitting here now, in the parking lot outside the police station, he let himself remember how it had been. The moment the yellow beam caught a glint of metal.

He'd been maybe twenty-five yards into the woods when he saw it. A good ten feet off the trail a bike lay on its side. He'd stepped close, squatted on his haunches to look closely and felt a chill. No, the mountain bike wasn't just lying there, as if temporarily flung aside. One handlebar dug deep in the rusty-red soil and left a track two feet long. Maybe his imagination was excited by the deep night here under the ponderosa and lodgepole pines, by the eerie quiet, by the dispatcher's description of the shrill scream cut off sharply. But Colin couldn't help picturing the bike rider hanging on tight, trying to use the bike as an anchor, while someone wrenched him—no, *her,* if the neighbor had been right—off of it. The front tire rim was bent, the spokes mangled. He thought someone might have stepped right there, the way you might plant a foot on a pet carrier to yank a reluctant animal out.

Rising to his feet, he swept the flashlight beam in a careful pattern. Footprints wouldn't show up well with the ground so dry, but he could make out scuffed vegetation. Closer to the path, furrows and imprints marked the soil. And a dark patch. He edged nearer, still trying to keep his distance. If this was a crime scene, he didn't want to taint it and be given hell by the detectives.

Something had been spilled there, and was still wet. Colin had stretched out to his full reach and touched the edge of the spill, then brought his finger to his nose and sniffed. The acrid scent was unmistakable. Blood. A fair pool of it had been lost here. Not enough to suggest someone had bled out, but too much for an innocent accident, even a head wound.

He had just made the decision to go back and call this in when he spotted something else, almost hidden beneath a ceanothus. A wallet...no, a coin purse. Leather, in the shape of a cat's face, whiskers, nose and eyes burned into the hide and colored. Cute. He tucked the flashlight beneath his arm, put on a pair of latex gloves and picked up the coin purse. Change rattled as he unzipped it and found folded bills in there, too, and a driver's license. No, he saw, his stomach clenching: a driver's permit, the kind issued to young teens.

He found himself staring at the photo. A girl's

face, young but somehow not hopeful. She was shy, probably, gazing warily at the camera. A few freckles scattered across a small nose. Instead of being youthfully soft, this face was thin, the wings of cheekbone too prominent, the chin too pointed, the forehead too high. Hair was scraped back into a ponytail. In this light he couldn't tell what color her eyes were.

Brown, said the description. Hair brown, too. Her name was Madeline Noelle Dubeau. He remembered feeling stunned. He knew that name. Marc Dubeau was a prominent local businessman, a friend of the police chief's. That last name wouldn't be common in central Oregon. This almost had to be his daughter.

Madeline, he noted, was fifteen years old, turning sixteen on November 26, when she would be eligible to take the driver's test for her license.

She was the same age as Colin's sister, Caitlin.

He turned the flashlight beam again on that dark patch where blood sank into the soil. Anger and a sick feeling squeezed his chest. Would Madeline Dubeau ever have a chance to get that driver's license?

Colin had tried to convince himself he was letting his imagination run away from him, that she'd had a friend with her who had already helped her make her way home. Or driven her to the emergency room.

But, however green behind the ears he'd been, he

knew better. The prickles on the back of his neck said otherwise. Something bad had happened to this girl.

Now in the SUV he grunted, still staring ahead unseeing through the windshield, and remembered the chill when he found out her maternal uncle was a cop, a detective. The department had thrown everything they had at the case, but in twelve years, they had never found a trace of Maddie Dubeau. Unless, today, it was her bones that were wrenched from the earth along with the tree roots.

Shaking his head, he finally backed out and turned onto the street heading north toward the far end of the park.

Traffic, pedestrian and vehicular, was nothing like what it would be in another few weeks once ski season opened. Angel Butte brimmed with tourists during the summer and again when winter arrived. Right now was a lull, when locals took advantage of the chance to dine out or stop by one of the brew pubs without long waits.

Ten minutes later, he left his 4Runner behind a line of other police vehicles on the street and strode along the bulldozed road carved between the stand of woods and the fenced backyards of the nearest homes.

This was early November, with a bite to the air as the thermometer hovered just above freezing. The snow level on the jagged peaks of the Three Sisters and the greater bulk of Mount Bachelor to the north had dropped, a harbinger of the months to come. Colin had substituted a parka he kept in his SUV for his suit jacket. The pungent scent of pine was more powerful than usual, after chain saws and dozers had downed a dozen tall, ancient ponderosas, scarring what had been untouched forest. His every step kicked up the red-dirt legacy of the area's volcanic past, coating his dress shoes.

He wasn't thinking about the dust or the smell or the yellow equipment or the voices he heard. He was still caught in his memories of that night, and turned his head to orient himself. Just before he'd parked, Colin had noticed where the trail emerged. He was passing near enough to where he'd found the bike to hit the place with a well-thrown stone.

A chill traveled up his spine. What if Madeline— Maddie to her friends and family—had lain here all these years, waiting? So damn close?

What he couldn't figure was why he was surprised that they might, at last, be finding her body. He'd expected that someday she'd turn up. After twelve years, dead was a lot likelier than alive.

"Damn," he said softly, and kept walking. By the time he reached the crowd, he had made sure his face was expressionless.

Heads turned his way, some wearing hard hats. Others he knew: Duane, of course, and two detectives, Jane Vahalik and Ronnie Orr. Vahalik was good. Experienced, despite being only in her early thirties. She'd spent time on the Drug Enforcement

Team and been a detective in Criminal Investigations for...he thought three years. Maybe four. Orr had moved over from patrol just a month ago and been assigned to her for training.

He nodded at all of them. Then, hiding his reluctance, he looked toward the vast root ball of the tree and the gaping hole left below it. Not a usual crime scene. The ground had been bulldozed and trampled beyond any hope of combing the top layers of soil for clothing or jewelry or, hell, a cigarette wrapper that might still hold fingerprints. The top feet of soil were heaped where the dozer had pushed them.

Some lucky folks were now going to be assigned the task of sifting through that pile of dirt and needles and branches.

Duane was already standing beside the bones that had been thus far uncovered. Colin joined him and crouched to see better. The pitiful collection was stained red by the soil. Flashes of ivory showed where some had been snapped apart by the violence of their unearthing. Most were unidentifiable to Colin, but he could make out a long bone in multiple pieces, a pelvis, half a dozen shattered ribs and the jaw with a couple of dental fillings.

"Those look too large to be Maddie's." He wanted to feel relief, to be sure, but couldn't.

Beside him, Duane grunted. "I think you're right. Assuming those pieces are part of a femur."

Colin was studying the jaw. "Only a couple of

small fillings. Molars are all in, but the wisdom teeth aren't completely." He glanced up. "Do you know about Maddie's?"

"No idea. I don't even know when they're supposed to come in."

"I think it varies. Sixteen? Seventeen?"

"A kid, then." Duane paused. "Maddie was almost sixteen."

Still feeling apprehension, Colin nodded.

He'd wanted a definitive answer. He had wanted to be told right here, right now, that this wasn't Maddie Dubeau. Why, he couldn't have said. Some kid, maybe a young adult, had died and been buried here. It wasn't as if any good news was in the offing—say that this skeleton would turn out to belong to a scumbag drug dealer who would be unmourned. If—no, when—they figured out whose bones these were, a mother and father, a girlfriend, sisters or brothers, *someone* was going to be hit with the worst of all possible news. The end of hope. If not the Dubeaus, someone else.

He wondered if Duane held out any real hope Maddie was still alive.

"Okay," he said with a sigh. "You know what to do. Keep me updated."

Both men stood.

Colin said slowly, "Wasn't it just last year that girl's bones were found out near Prineville?"

Those had been in Crook County's jurisdiction. "I wonder if they ever identified them?" Duane said thoughtfully. "There was that other girl three, four years ago, too. At the foot of Angel Butte. Wasn't she yours?"

"Yeah." Colin had been lead investigator. The small volcanic cinder cone rose right in the middle of Angel Butte and was another city park, where the marble statue of an angel had "miraculously" appeared in the late 19th century to overlook the town.

That girl had been identified. Turned out to be a runaway from Salem, a really sad case. She'd disappeared when she was only fourteen, turned up dead here just before her sixteenth birthday—Maddie's age. She had been pregnant, they could tell that much, but her body was so decayed no cause of death was ever determined. They hadn't gotten anywhere near to figuring out how she'd come to be buried beneath a foot of red cinders.

Duane was the one to shake his head. "No reason to look for connections yet. This may turn out to be male. Or older. Hell, he probably got knifed in a drunken fight."

"Maybe."

After a momentary silence, Duane said, "You have a hunch."

Colin moved uncomfortably. "Why don't I make a few calls? You have enough to do here, and you're right. Chances are it's a waste of time." But he had to satisfy this uneasy feeling, and Duane, like any other cop, would understand.

After a moment, his lieutenant nodded and

turned away. "All right," he called. "Folks, let's get pictures, and then we've got some work to do."

Colin was reluctant to leave, but he was, essentially, an administrator now. He had to demonstrate trust in not only Duane, but also his detectives. Let them do their job. If he stayed, all he'd do was make them nervous.

He knew from experience, too, that more bones would be uncovered slowly. Officers and evidence techs wouldn't be digging with shovels; they'd use trowels. From here on out, this would more nearly resemble an archaeological dig than a normal crime scene. It was going to take days, maybe weeks, given the scale of the damage wrought by the bulldozer.

But some answers should be forthcoming soon. With teeth, a femur—assuming that was one—and a pelvis, the medical examiner or a forensic pathologist ought to be able to nail down age and gender. A good guess at how long ago the victim had been buried would provide a starting point, too.

Walking away, he was surprised to feel a clutch of something like grief.

Don't let it be Maddie.

Damn it, he thought, her parents would probably be *relieved* if these bones proved to be hers, if they knew at last, once and for all, what had become of their daughter. Who was he to want to prolong the agonizing, fading wisp of hope that she was only gone, not dead?

No one. He had no right to wish that kind of suffering for them. And, Jesus, he didn't like to think about what Duane was feeling right now.

But it was his own memory, his own sense of failure, that caught at him now. Instead of going straight back to his SUV, he went to the trail and walked back into the park. Not far—just to the curve where he had found the bike that night. Voices and the sound of distant traffic were muffled here. He stopped, looking at the spot where her blood had soaked into the earth. He remembered the darkness, the thick silence. The crime scene tape that by morning had wrapped from tree to tree, the careful search for evidence never found. And the photos the newspaper had run, not only the one he had kept, but also candid shots of Maddie when she was younger.

Never smiling. Only in the school photo had her lips curved in an obligatory smile. Otherwise, her face was always solemn. Today, he felt the same unease he had then, the same sense that the common description of her as an introverted dreamer wasn't quite right.

He stood for a moment, as if at a grave site, then finally, shaking his head, turned away. Some old wrongs could be righted. Some couldn't.

COLIN SPOKE TO a Sergeant Fletcher in the Crook County sheriff's department about the bones that had been found by a rock hound out past Prineville the previous year. "Nah, we never identified that kid," Fletcher said. "Medical examiner's best guess was that she was maybe fifteen, sixteen years old. She thought female, but you know that was a big maybe."

Colin made a sound of agreement.

"Thing is, we never found the skull. Probably carried away by an animal. With no teeth to match to dental records, no fingerprints..." Probably he was shrugging. After a moment, he asked, "Have you thought about checking with other jurisdictions? I have this feeling Deschutes County had some bones, too."

Goddamn. *If I were a serial killer,* Colin thought, *I'd spread the bodies around, too.* Good way to avoid anybody getting too interested, in case a few of those bodies were found eventually.

If these were related, the few that had been found almost had to be the tip of an iceberg. Think of how much empty country there was out here, with the high desert stretching to the east, the wooded, rugged mountains of the Cascade Range to the west. How many places to dump a body.

He didn't like this line of thinking, but couldn't avoid it. He thanked the sergeant and asked him to call if he thought of any more details or heard of anything relevant.

His gaze strayed to the bulletin board and Maddie Dubeau's picture. Did this explain her disappearance? He didn't want to think so.

Duane called a couple of hours later. "It can't be Maddie," he said baldly. "We'll check dental records, too, but…Marge says this one is male."

Relief was sharp, a jab to the chest rather than a gentler flood. Colin cleared his throat. "Age?"

"Can't pin it down. Apparently some people get wisdom teeth real early, some not until their twenties, some never. Late teens, she thinks, but she wants more bones."

Colin grunted. "I don't have good news for you," he said, starting with what the Crook County sergeant had told him. "Deschutes County had a kid, too, found four or five years ago, buried in the cinders on Lava Butte. Some teenagers were out there at night, drank a few six-packs—climbing up and sliding down, you know how it is—and they uncovered bones. A boy smashed the skull with his foot."

"Bet that still gives him nightmares."

"No shit," Colin agreed. "That one was shot. There was an exit hole in the back of the head. Since, unlike Crook County, they had teeth, they were able to identify the victim. Another runaway, a girl from Vancouver last seen in Portland. Sixteen years old."

"The one here in town was about the same age, too, wasn't she?" Duane said thoughtfully.

"There are a hell of a lot of kids that age on the street."

This wasn't a problem they had much in Angel Butte. Winters were too cold in central Oregon for anyone to sleep in doorways or alleys year-round, and the town was too small for prostitution and panhandling to hide in shadows. But in larger cities, it was another matter.

"I called Bend, too," Colin continued. "They didn't have anything related. They think. A Detective—" he glanced at his notes "—Jacobs is going to do some research. He's only been with the department for four years. Klamath County's getting back to me."

"If this one is a guy and those were girls, there's likely no tie." A serial killer was wired to choose victims to meet a certain need, usually at least part sexual, which almost always meant they were of one gender or the other.

"Probably not," Colin agreed. Which didn't mean these bones weren't in some way connected to Maddie's disappearance.

Duane gave an update on the search, which so far had turned up only a few additional small bones from a hand or foot.

The two men left it at that.

Colin rocked back in his chair. Well, the latest bones weren't Maddie Dubeau's. That was something.

She'd be twenty-seven years old now, if she were alive. Twenty-eight in a few weeks. He didn't even have to think about it. His relationship with his sister wasn't close, but he'd sent her a birthday card just last month. Like Cait, Maddie wouldn't be a skinny kid anymore.

Some people didn't change much from their early teen years, others so much so their own parents wouldn't recognize them if they hadn't been there every day while the transformation happened. The plain became pretty, the beautiful, ugly...or just ordinary.

Which way, he wondered, would Madeline Dubeau have gone?

He shook his head at his own foolishness. She was dead. She had to be. It was past time he quit clinging to the stubborn belief that she had somehow survived. How could she have? She had been a kid. A girl, small, fine-boned, physically immature for her age. Injured, snatched late at night and never seen again.

The very fact that she haunted him suggested that she *was* dead, didn't it? The living left you alone in a way the dead didn't. Just look at him; he didn't give a damn about his mother, who was alive and well in San Francisco, but his father he still actively hated even though he'd been buried four years now.

Colin swung around in his chair to look out the window at a courtyard and the brick back of the jail. Despite the calls he'd made today, this investigation wasn't his. It was Duane Brewer's, Jane Vahalik's, Ronnie Orr's.

I'll call Cait tonight, he thought. *Arrange to get*

together with her when I'm in Seattle. He'd be there in two weeks, for a symposium Microsoft was holding on new technology for law enforcement personnel. Cait was his only real family. He could try harder. The fault was as much his as hers.

And right now, he had work to do. He swung back around to his desk and computer, and didn't let himself glance at the bulletin board again.

CHAPTER TWO

"HEY, THE BOOK lady is here!" Aliyah cried.

Girls jumped up from the sagging sofa and miscellaneous easy chairs and rushed to crowd around Nell Smith. The music video on the TV was forgotten.

Katya, after barely glancing away from the television, said, "Big freaking deal." Katya had appeared at SafeHold half a dozen times in the past two years. She never stayed for more than a week or two. She had to be nearly eighteen, and Nell worried she would soon be ineligible to stay at the shelter for homeless teens.

"Nell! Cool," said Savannah, a wispy, pasty-skinned fourteen-year-old boasting three eyebrow piercings, half a dozen in each ear, a lip labret and a belly button ring. If there were other piercings in unseen places, Nell didn't want to know.

"Did you bring me the new *Vampire Academy* book?" Kaylee asked eagerly.

More titles flew.

She grinned at their eager faces. "Yes, yes and yes." All they wanted to read were paranormal romances, but Nell's selections were written for teenagers, by talented authors.

She volunteered here on a regular basis, typically spending every Sunday afternoon and one weeknight evening just hanging out and talking to the girls. Girls were housed separately from guys, although the two buildings were linked by a courtyard and a shared kitchen and dining room.

Nell also came weekly to represent the Seattle Public Library, maintaining a shelf of books in each of the two buildings and filling special requests when she could. She'd packed other shelves with books that were weeded from the library collection, donated, or picked up at garage sales. Many of the kids who came in here weren't readers and never would be. Others thought they weren't but got seduced. Some laboriously studied for their high school equivalency exams, or to catch up with school—if they could be convinced to care.

What she loved most was encouraging reading for the pure joy of it. These were kids who hadn't had much joy in their lives. She, like many of the other adults who worked and volunteered here, knew the bewilderment and fear and anger they felt. When she'd been where they were, books were her salvation. They'd offered her the world, filled her emptiness. Now she had a mission, one she never tried to disguise. Josef gave guitar lessons, Dex organized soccer games, Chloe taught computer skills. They all had something different to offer.

A couple of girls poked heads out into the hall, saw who was here and retreated in disinterest. Nell had already noticed two newcomers in the living room, neither moving from their seats, both watching the excitement with confusion. One was a black girl with her head shaved. Long skinny arms wrapped herself in a hug that was painful to see. The other girl was white, overweight and suffering from acne. Nell caught a glimpse of needle tracks on the inside of one elbow.

She smiled at both of them. "I'm Nell Smith. Otherwise known as the book lady. I bring library books regularly."

"DVDs, too," one of the girls said, already delving into today's section. Her lip curled. "*Sense and Sensibility?* Really?"

"Try it. Guaranteed."

There were a lot of rolled eyes. She grinned.

"Nell," said a voice behind her. "Good. You're here."

She turned with a smile to greet Roberta Charles, the director, principal fund-raiser, cook and loving arms of SafeHold. Roberta had two other people with her today, though, one of whom sent a flash of dismay through Nell. He held a giant camera on one shoulder. A TV camera. He was already assessing the room, the shabby furniture, the excited clump of girls. Nell.

"Ah…I'll get out of your way," she said. "Just let me grab the books that have to go back."

"No, no!" Roberta said. "You're one of my best volunteers. Linda Capshaw is here from KING-5 to do a feature on us. She's hoping to talk to staff and volunteers as well as some of the kids."

Nell was okay with talking. The idea of chatting about what they accomplished here at Safe-Hold didn't bother her; she'd done it before. It was the camera that spooked her. She was being idiotic; what difference would it make anymore if her face should appear somewhere? Probably none. Which didn't keep her heart from pumping alarm through her bloodstream in quick spurts.

"Sure," she agreed. "Not on camera, though. I'm shy."

"I'm not." Aliyah struck a pose, one skinny hip cocked. Giggling, three or four of the other girls flung arms around each other and tried to look sexy.

These, Nell knew, were the ones who weren't hiding from anyone. The ones with no family to care that they'd gone missing. A few of the others were melting away or ducking heads to hide behind lank hair. Nell wished she didn't have her own hair bundled on the back of her head. She'd have hidden behind it, too.

The camera was rolling. She turned her back and quickly put out the new books and piled the ones ready to go back into her plastic crate.

"Requests?" she asked.

Clarity, a shy thirteen-year-old who had arrived

pregnant—too pregnant for abortion to be an option—and was awaiting foster care placement, leaned close and whispered, "Can you bring something about adoption?"

"Of course I will." For a moment, forgetting the visitors, Nell smiled at the girl. "A lot of what's written is for adopters, not birth mothers, but it would still give you some guidance. I'll see if I can find some stuff written by kids who were adopted, too." She took the chance of giving Clarity a quick hug. Thin arms encircled her in return. Nell's eyes stung for a moment as tenderness and pity flooded her. God. What if she'd gotten pregnant back then?

Some flicker of movement pulled her back to the moment, and she took a suspicious look at the cameraman. He was currently half-turned away from her, sweeping the room, not seeming to pay attention. Respecting her wishes? How likely was that? But she could hope. Her fault for having left herself vulnerable for a minute.

The KING-5 woman looked vaguely familiar to Nell. Or maybe she was just a type: blond, exquisitely groomed, wearing a royal blue suit. "Do you have time to talk right now?" she asked.

"Just for a minute. I do have to get back to the library." Under Roberta's approving eye, she joined the women. It was fantastic that SafeHold was getting some publicity. Desperately needed donations always followed. But, while there were many things she'd do for these kids, appearing on air wasn't one of them. The only picture she allowed to be snapped of her was for her driver's license. Unavoidable, and barely resembling her anyway.

"SafeHold," she told Linda Capshaw, who'd asked for permission to record her voice, "offers these kids hope in so many forms. Many practical, of course." She elaborated, concluding with, "Sometimes, all we offer is sanctuary. We have at least one girl here right now who won't accept anything else." She carefully avoided glancing toward Katya. "But every so often, she shows up and has a couple of weeks here, where she knows she's safe, where she gets enough to eat, where people are kind and nonjudgmental to her. Some of these kids have been abused and simple kindness means everything to them. Others need windows opened to give them glimpses of chances they never dreamed were there for them."

"How did you become involved?" the blonde asked, sounding genuinely interested, although it was hard to tell for sure. Getting people to open up was, after all, her most essential job skill.

Nell took a deep breath. This was always hard to say. "I was a teenage runaway. Not in Seattle, somewhere else. I'd rather not say where. But I lived on the streets for over two years. A local shelter was my salvation. When I moved to Seattle and read about SafeHold in the *Times,* I called immediately. What's that been?" She glanced at Roberta, even though she knew to the day when she'd first walked in the door. "Five years ago?"

The director nodded. "Just about, I think."

"I work for Seattle Public Library, too. As a technician, not a librarian. I don't have a master's degree. But because of my involvement here, I'm the one who brings books, DVDs, whatever, weekly."

They chatted for another ten or fifteen minutes, Nell keeping a wary eye out for the cameraman. Then she made her excuses and left, sooner than she would have liked to go. Usually she'd have made the effort to sit down and talk to the new residents, find out who, if anyone, was missing since Sunday. But she'd be back Thursday evening—soon enough.

Yes, she told herself while she loaded the crate of books and DVDs into the back of her old Ford, she was a coward. What else was new? It was smart not to take chances, that was all. She hadn't grown up in Seattle, she knew that much, but she had no idea how widely local stations were broadcast. And her face…well, it hadn't changed that much since she had first found herself alone and scared, on the streets, knowing that worse than starving, worse than having to sell her body, worse than *anything,* was the possibility of being seen by someone who knew her.

She was someone entirely different now. She'd created a life out of whole cloth, starting with nothing. But unless she someday had the money for plastic surgery, she couldn't do anything about her face, and *that* hadn't changed.

Nell almost laughed as she got behind the wheel and started the windshield wipers to combat the autumn drizzle. As if she'd want to be on camera anyway! There was a lot she didn't know about who she'd been, but she had no doubt at all that she'd always been shy. Whatever dreams she'd had, being on television wouldn't have been one of them. No one changed that much.

COLIN SPRAWLED ON the king-size hotel bed and reached for the remote control. He'd like to find something mindless. His brain was on overload after a day of listening to speakers talk about new technology undergoing trials in various police departments around the world. He was glad he'd come; knowing what was out there was worthwhile, but most of this was beyond the scope of his relatively small department.

He was to have dinner with Cait and a boyfriend who was apparently serious. Either that, or she was bringing the guy as a sort of screen, because she didn't want to have to make conversation with her brother for two hours. Because of her work schedule they weren't meeting until seven-thirty. Yawning as he flipped through channels, Colin realized he'd have to be careful not to nod off. He'd made the drive late last night and gotten up early to have breakfast with a group of other police chiefs and captains from agencies the size of Angel Butte, which had just over a hundred officers.

The news caught his eye. Some damn idiot had driven the wrong way onto I-5 in the middle of the night—blood-alcohol level sky-high. Killed a forty-two-year-old woman driving home from her job at Sea-Tac Airport.

"Son of a bitch," he muttered.

There was a news flash: "Coming up, join Linda Capshaw for a visit to a shelter for runaway teens." Then commercials. Colin left the station on, given that he'd been thinking about runaways a hell of a lot the past few weeks. Every major city and many minor ones had similar shelters, but he was interested in seeing what this one offered. Did they keep kids on their radar in any meaningful way? Did they see to it that the teens got dental care, which might mean X-rays?

Duane and the two detectives had gotten nowhere in their attempts to identify the latest bones that had appeared when the tree roots were pulled up. It had turned out that Klamath County also had an unidentified teenage girl, found two years ago; the body had been too decomposed for them to lift fingerprints, and they hadn't turned up a dental match. Given that the bodies found at Angel Butte and Deschutes County had both turned out to be teenage runaways that had likely passed through Portland, Colin wanted to check with shelters there. Just a couple of days ago, Duane's team had found a fragment of the upper jaw, with yet another dental filling, which meant that they could identify this kid for sure, and maybe the Crook County one, if they could find dental records. It was a long shot, but worth pursuing.

He had to wait through another report before his patience was rewarded when a perky blonde smiled and said, "Welcome to SafeHold. Yes, there are a number of shelters for teenagers in the Puget Sound area, but word on the street is that SafeHold is the place to go for real help."

The camera panned a room in which teenage boys lounged on shabby furniture, ignoring the fact that they were being filmed. Then came a talking head, Roberta Charles, who was the director. The brief snippet was mostly the inspiring stuff, about how kids went there for sanctuary. Then, as the camera moved on to showing a group of girls in what appeared to be a modern dance class, followed by boys playing one-on-one basketball in what looked like an old school yard, another woman's voice said, "SafeHold offers these kids hope in so many forms. Many practical, of course. Some kids go from here to group homes, drug treatment or foster care." A man wearing a stethoscope was seen talking to a boy whose face was turned from the camera. "They get desperately needed medical care." An earnest older woman sat at a table with a girl, the two poring over an open textbook as the voice continued. "They're encouraged to resume schooling and get tutoring to help them succeed. Legal aid is available for those in trouble with the law." A handcuffed kid was being placed in the back of a patrol car. Then back to the shelter: some girls hammed for the camera in another shabby rec room, a flickering TV in the background. The blonde journalist said, "Dedicated volunteers like Nell Smith, popularly known here as 'the book lady,' mean everything to these lost children." Her back to the camera, a young woman was piling books into a bright red plastic crate. The next moment, she was talking to a girl who looked too damn young to be in a runaway shelter, too slight even to have begun to menstruate. And, sweet Jesus, she was pregnant. Colin should have been past being shockable, but he wasn't. Linda Capshaw was speaking again, as the camera lingered on a touching moment, the young woman hugging the pregnant girl. There was only a glimpse of their faces, one he'd have missed if he'd yawned at the wrong moment, but he felt as if he'd been jolted by a Taser.

Cursing, he lunged upright and stared at the TV, which had gone back to the studio, where trite bantering led to a weather report. His heart slammed in his chest and his nerve endings buzzed.

Was he was going completely nuts? God knew he'd been thinking about Maddie Dubeau more than was healthy these past weeks. But damn, damn, *damn,* that woman looked like her. Still thin, cheekbones still high and sharp, chin pointy. He wasn't sure about the freckles, it had gone so fast, but her eyes were brown, her hair was the same color as when she was a kid.

He let an expletive escape. He *couldn't* be mistaken. He couldn't.

But this woman's name wasn't Maddie or anything like it. Nell Smith. He closed his eyes and saw her, smile warming as she wrapped her arms around the girl, eyes momentarily closing and her expression softening into something achingly gentle.

How *could* this Nell Smith be his Maddie Dubeau? It made no sense; this hadn't been a case of a parent abducting a child and raising her under a different identity. Maddie had been fifteen, not five. You couldn't persuade a fifteen-year-old that all her memories of who she'd been were false. And Maddie hadn't been a runaway. If she was alive, why wouldn't she have gotten help, called her parents? Found her way home?

The local news had segued into national, making him remember that he had to leave—*now*—or he'd be late getting together with his sister. Who hadn't sounded that excited about seeing him.

He didn't know why he kept trying, and was no longer in the mood. It had been two years since he'd seen her, and that time they'd had lunch. She'd been rushed, claiming she had to get back to work. His brilliant, pretty sister. Maybe he should let Cait go, along with his mother.

But he considered her his only family, and he was a stubborn man. He turned off the television reluctantly, wishing he had a way to replay that short clip. He reminded himself there wasn't anything he could do about locating Nell Smith tonight, and he'd been looking forward to seeing Cait. One thing at a time, he told himself. He already knew that he wouldn't be attending day two of the technology symposium tomorrow. He'd be visiting a runaway shelter.

Taking the elevator down to the parking garage below the hotel, Colin thought about coming right out and asking why Cait was so uninterested in having any meaningful relationship with him, her only sibling. But he knew he wouldn't do it. Her answer might be too honest. Too final.

NELL CAST AN uneasy glance around the library. Nothing seemed to be out of order. A mother and several children were straggling from the children's area, all carrying their selections. A couple of teenagers whispered at the end of an aisle of shelves, a group studied at a long table, and a number of adults sat throughout the library reading. Nobody seemed to be paying any attention to her.

So why did she keep having the creepy feeling that someone was watching her?

Well, duh. Despite her request not to be filmed,

she had appeared on TV. She'd worked last night but had known the spot was being aired and had set her TiVo. Watching it, all she could think was, *No, no, no.* She'd grabbed the remote and rewound, praying her face hadn't been visible enough to be recognizable. But there she was. Two patrons had already commented today on how excited they were to see her on KING-5. She kept *expecting* to find people staring at her.

The definition of paranoia.

She smiled at a mother, then the stair-step array of children as they checked out their books. Perhaps she'd shelve some of the materials she'd just checked in, since things were so quiet.

Once again, she felt that peculiar prickling on the back of her neck, and she swung around quickly. This time, a man was looking at her. He'd been hidden previously by a newspaper held open before him. Now he was closing and folding it, his gaze resting on her.

Because she happened to be in his sight line? Her pulse was jumping despite her determination not to let herself become alarmed about nothing. So what if a guy was looking at her? Maybe he was thinking about asking a question. Maybe he'd seen her on TV. Maybe he would come on to her. That did occasionally happen, although she was good at squelching men.

She sent a vague smile his way and pushed a rolling cart of books out from behind the counter. She could reshelve new books while keeping an eye on the front desk.

He was still watching her. As if his gaze had a weight, she felt it even when her back was turned. Nell couldn't decide why it bothered her so much. He certainly wasn't one of the mentally ill homeless people who wandered in here; she'd only peripherally noticed what he wore, but thought he could be a businessman.

Maneuvering the cart, she sneaked another glance. Yes, slacks and a white shirt, open at the neck, but it was after five, which probably meant he was off work and had left his suit jacket and tie in the car. Dark hair cut rather short. Not exactly handsome, his face was still compelling. Hard. And though his posture was relaxed, with his legs stretched out and his ankles crossed, she doubted, although she couldn't have said why, that he was relaxed at all.

Ignore him.

It wasn't as if she was alone in the library. If he was still watching her an hour from now when she got off work, she'd have someone walk her to her car, which she'd driven today because it was her night to go to SafeHold.

She shelved in reasonable peace, pausing only a couple of times to talk to patrons and answer questions. A lively discussion with a regular about Alice Hoffman's latest distracted her enough that she almost forgot the man. At some point, he picked up another section of the newspaper and read it, although he never lifted it high enough to disappear the way he had earlier. He might not be paying any attention to her at all, or he might still be keeping an eye on her. She couldn't tell.

He hadn't moved from his chair when her replacement arrived and she slipped away to get her coat and a couple of books she'd plucked off the new-title shelf for herself. But he was nowhere to be seen when she headed for the front doors.

She was almost to her car, keys in hand, wishing it didn't get dark so early at this time of year, when a man said quietly, "Ms. Smith?"

With a sharp gasp, Nell spun around.

It was him, of course. She couldn't imagine where he'd come from, how he'd gotten so near without making a sound. The lighting was good in the parking lot, but still cast odd shadows. He loomed over her.

The books fell from her hand, thudding to the pavement, and she backed up until she pressed against the fender of her Ford.

Seeing her fear, he lifted both hands and retreated a step. "Hey! It's okay. I'm sorry if I frightened you. I won't hurt you. I meant to catch you inside before you left."

She didn't take her eyes off him or bend to pick up the books she'd dropped. "What do you want?"

"I recognized you," he said simply.

"I don't know you." Nell was certain of that.

"No. No, you wouldn't. I'm a police officer, Ms. Smith. I recognize you from pictures taken before you disappeared."

She had to swallow before she could get a word out. "I don't know what you're talking about."

His eyes were colorless in this stark, artificial light. Not brown, she thought; something pale gray or blue. They were keen on her face, as if he were drinking in the sight of her. No one had ever looked at her so intensely.

"I saw the news clip last night. I knew you right away."

She prayed he couldn't tell that she was trembling all over. Thank God the car was at her back, supporting her. She summoned a cool voice that sounded barely interested. "Just who is it that you think I am?"

"Madeline Dubeau." He paused. "Madeline Noelle Dubeau. Maddie."

Maddie. Oh, God, oh, God. She had called herself Mary in Portland. And she'd liked the name Eleanor, when she found it, because Nell sounded right to her. Like somebody she could be.

"My name is Eleanor Smith. I don't know a Maddie...what did you say the last name is? Dew...?"

"Dubeau."

Nell shook her head. "I've heard we all have twins."

"I don't believe it. I've searched for you for what seems half my life. *I know you.*"

Her heart was pounding so hard it hurt. She should say, *I'm not this person you want me to be. Please leave me alone.* She would say it, but first... she had to know.

"Why?" she whispered. "Why have you been hunting for her?"

He lifted a hand, and she flinched, but he was only reaching to squeeze the back of his own neck. "I was the responding officer when somebody heard your—her—scream. I found the mountain bike, the blood. Your wallet with a driver's permit. I was new on the job then, and maybe that's why I let myself care so much." His hand lowered to his side, slowly, and she thought he was being careful not to alarm her again. "Last night when I saw you on the news—" he cleared his throat as if to give himself a second "—I thought it was a miracle."

She had to get rid of him. Had to convince him he was wrong.

"I'm not your miracle," Nell heard herself say so harshly, she didn't know her own voice. "I'm sorry to have to disappoint you, but I'm not this Madeline person. You truly are mistaken, Mr....?"

He only looked at her, but she knew, *knew,* he saw her terror. "I'm Colin McAllister. Captain."

"I'm not even from this area," she said.

"Neither am I. Neither is Maddie." He waited a moment, then asked softly, "Where are you from, Ms. Smith?"

"Where are *you* from, Captain McAllister?"

"Central Oregon."

"I'm from the Midwest," she said. Eleanor Theodora Smith had been born in Eugene, Oregon, but she couldn't tell him that. He was a cop. If he looked hard enough, he'd find that same Eleanor Theodora Smith was also buried in Eugene, beneath a bronze plaque expressing her parents' grief.

"I've upset you," he observed. "That wasn't my intention."

"What was your intention?" She could combat this fear only with aggression. "Did you imagine that I don't know who I am and would be thrilled when you told me?"

"No." He was frowning now. "No. I thought…"

"What?"

"I thought perhaps Smith was a married name. And that Nell is a shortened version of your middle name."

"It's not. I'm Eleanor."

"Or," he continued, as though she hadn't spoken, "that you were using a false name to hide."

She flung her hands up, as though at the ridiculousness of that notion. "I won't even ask," she said. "Now, if you'll excuse me, Officer…no, Captain. I really need to be going."

He didn't move. "Ms. Smith. May I give you a business card? Just in case there's ever anything you want to tell me?"

She should refuse. Eleanor Smith wouldn't have any reason to accept, would she? But Nell couldn't seem to think. And his card would tell her where he came from. Where Maddie Dubeau was from. No, that was silly—she could find articles online, if he were telling the truth. But what if she couldn't find anything? Couldn't figure out how the name was spelled? The card would give her a way to reach him, if she dared. If she chose. Nell was appalled to discover how tempted she was to learn about the part of her life she hadn't wanted to remember.

The keys were biting into her palm, imprinting themselves. She managed a shrug. "I can't imagine why I'd have any reason to call you, but if it will make you feel better I can take your card."

"It would make me feel better." He took one from the pocket of his slacks and held it out without actually moving closer. *She* was the one who had to take a step, feeling like a small animal hungry enough to creep up and steal a scrap of meat from a mountain lion's meal, even though he crouched over it. She snatched it from his hand and retreated immediately, poking the card deep into her purse.

"I'd like to hear from you," he said quietly. "I swear to you that I'll keep anything you tell me confidential. We can just talk. I won't tell anyone who you are or where. I swear," he said again, his voice deep and serious.

Nell scrutinized that hard, unrevealing face for a long moment, trying to see whether he was telling the truth, but how could she ever know? The risk was too great. And he was probably wrong anyway, about who he thought she was. Her shock of recognition might be false. He hadn't even said how long ago this Maddie had disappeared. She wasn't going to ask.

She only nodded. After a moment he backed up a couple of steps, his eyes still holding hers, and then he turned and strode away.

With a whimper Nell crouched, scooped up her books and hurried around her car. Even once she was inside with the engine running and the doors locked, she didn't feel safe. She had to get away from here.

She'd intended to get a deli sandwich somewhere and then go to the shelter. As shaken as she was, she couldn't. She just couldn't. All she wanted was to go home, to lock herself in the sanctuary of her apartment.

But what if he followed her?

She drove, taking a circuitous route, gradually calming herself as she took one random turn after another and no other car stayed behind her.

Of course, he could have stuck some kind of locator on her car. She'd read about things like that.

If he were really a cop, though, he wouldn't have to. He'd be able to find her.

Finally she made it back to her own street and the parking slot that she was lucky enough to have beneath the building. She scurried into the elevator, grateful to have it to herself, relieved it didn't stop at the lobby level. Inside her apartment, she turned the dead bolt and put on the chain, shocked to see that her hand was still shaking.

Then she simply stood there, waiting for the sense of security to wrap around her. It never came.

She wasn't safe. Somebody had recognized her. If this Captain McAllister were determined enough, he could find a way, legally or not, to get her fingerprints. The life she'd built so carefully could collapse, like a house carried down the crumbling bluff by a mudslide.

A terrible sound escaped her, a shuddering cry.

I have to run. I can't be here when he comes looking for me again. I can't.

She sank down, right there inside the door, her back to it, and let her purse and the books fall. Her breathing was loud in the silent apartment.

What if he meant it? What if she could trust him? What if she couldn't?

Nell drew her knees up, hugged herself tight and rocked.

The most insistent voice in her head was the one that whispered, *Am I Maddie?*

CHAPTER THREE

COLIN DIDN'T SLEEP well, and made his morning start early enough to be home in Angel Butte by mid-afternoon. I-5 south to Salem, then east through the Willamette National Forest to Santiam Pass. Not the easiest or quickest route home, but the most scenic. He didn't know why he'd bothered, since he wasn't in the mood for scenery. Every so often, though, he couldn't help being pulled from his brooding by a glimpse of one or another of the ancient or newer volcanoes, the forests of lush Douglas fir and cedar, the clear waters of the North Santiam River. This pass would have been even more spectacular earlier in the fall. Somewhere he'd read that right here was the highest concentration of snow-capped volcanoes in the lower forty-eight states, and it was easy to believe.

Once he crossed over the pass to the drier eastern side, lodgepole and ponderosa pines replaced the fir and cedar. The six-thousand-foot-plus cone of Black Butte rose on the left, and he was swinging south. Through Bend, and he'd reached the home stretch.

Not once had his cell phone rang, although he'd laid it on the seat next to him and kept glancing at it. Once he even checked to be sure he hadn't somehow reset it to vibrate without noticing.

It was too soon. He knew it was, but doubt about how he'd handled her and hope were both eating at him. The iPhone had changed from being an irritant to a beacon. He grunted with rueful amusement—there were cops who wouldn't go to the john without their weapon; he wouldn't go without his phone.

Even though he was starved when he reached Angel Butte, he still decided to stop by River Park before going home.

The scene wasn't quite a replay from a few weeks ago. The heavy yellow equipment had been moved. The contractor had been relieved, Colin knew, for permission to go ahead with the job before weather made it impossible. He could see the bulldozer through the trees and hear the roar. Black smoke rose from a burn pile near the river.

Where the bones had been found, four officers were still combing through the heap of dirt. They were all bundled up against the below-freezing temperature. The pile of mixed dirt and brush was in the process of being shifted inch by inch. At least they were getting somewhere, he saw; he hadn't come down here in over a week.

Jane Vahalik had a paintbrush in her hand and was gently whisking dirt from an object.

He strolled over. "How's it going?"

She gave him a nasty look. "I'm freezing my ass off, that's how it's going."

Her trainee radiated alarm at the disrespect his FTO was showing their captain. Colin only grinned, then studied the knob of bone Vahalik had unearthed. "Still finding bones, I see."

"This is the biggest one in days." She sighed. "Did you have a good trip?"

"In a way," he said. "Glad to get over the mountains ahead of the storm they say is moving in."

Sinking back on her heels, she mumbled something highly profane. Colin sympathized. It was early season yet, but if the forecasts were to be believed this crime scene could well disappear under a foot of snow by tomorrow. The ground was already crunchy; if it froze hard enough, the search would be over for who knew how long. Although recovering the bones was important, at this point they were all more interested in finding something, anything, that might have been buried with the kid. Even scraps of clothing could help with identification.

"Brewer come by today?" he asked.

"Yeah, I saw him not half an hour ago." Vahalik turned her head and then nodded. "Right over there."

Duane was coming toward them from where the heavy equipment was working. When he stepped over the sagging yellow crime scene tape, his mood looked as piss-poor as his detective's. Colin walked to meet him.

"You know what?" Duane took off his gloves and shoved them into the pockets of his parka. He must have had a hat on earlier; his graying hair was spiking every which way. "I'd like to dig up the whole goddamn park! You know there are other bodies buried here. There have to be."

Colin couldn't argue. He'd also wondered if the red cinder of Angel Butte didn't cover more bones.

Feeling the cold, he shoved his hands into the pockets of his slacks. Damn, the change in temperature from rainy Seattle to the eastern side of the mountains was dramatic.

"You know we can't log and tear up this section of woods just because."

His lieutenant glared at him. "What do you want to bet Maddie's here, if we just knew where to look?"

Emotion swelled in Colin's chest until his ribs ached. The force of his desire to tell Duane that she was alive was like a punch. To say that he'd *seen* her, with his own eyes. Talked to her. Somehow, sad-eyed Maddie had survived whatever happened that night. Done more than survive, had found a way to touch the lives of other kids whose eyes were sad, too.

But he couldn't. He'd promised her. He'd known, watching her press herself back against her car while fighting abject terror, that the only way he could ever learn her story, ever bring her home, was to walk away and let her make the choice herself. If he'd tried to compel her, she would flee. She would hate him, and he didn't want Maddie Dubeau to hate him.

And also...seeing how afraid she was, Colin had to ask himself why. Twelve years later, and she was petrified because someone from her past had recognized her? Did she have a good reason? Would he be endangering her if he brought her into the open?

A part of him was thinking he should do just that. His conscience was scraped raw. What if he came face-to-face with her father? It was bad enough not telling Duane. Colin didn't think he could look Marc Dubeau in the eye, knowing what he did.

No, he thought. He had to keep his promise. He'd leave Maddie's photo where it hung in his office and hope that someday his cell phone rang and he would hear her voice.

"I've always believed she's alive," he said abruptly. "Don't ask me why, but I still do."

The older man stared hard at him. "You've never said that before."

"Are you going to tell me I'm dreaming?"

Duane gave a short bark of laughter, then rubbed a hand over his face. "No. You've got good instincts. You always did. I hope you're right, Colin. I hope you're right."

Colin waved at the scene around them. "Bring me up-to-date."

NELL GAVE SERIOUS thought to disappearing again. She went so far as to pack a couple of her suitcases so they were ready for her to grab at a minute's notice.

A voice of reason tried to quiet her panic. What had been dangerous to her teenage self might not be a threat to the adult she was now. It might even be that she'd spent all these years afraid of the wrong thing. This Captain McAllister said there was blood, a bike lying on its side. Someone had heard a scream. Maybe she'd had a perfectly good life before she was attacked. A family she loved.

But—reasonably or unreasonably—she didn't think so.

Which still didn't mean she had any reason to be afraid of the man and woman and boy she distantly remembered, now that she was grown up. It might only be that she'd thought they wouldn't understand whatever trouble she'd been in. And she had, after all, been a teenager skewed to believe parents *wouldn't* understand.

Irrational or not, panic made her stomach jittery. She hardly slept.

The next morning, she went straight to the bank and withdrew a couple thousand dollars.

Just in case. Better safe than sorry.

During the next two days, Nell made tentative, if probably ludicrous, plans. She spent the lunch hour of the first day wandering a cemetery in search of a grave marker for a child who would have been

the right age if she'd lived. Whose name she could
steal. She stood staring down at one such marker,
an infant who had died at three days old, when she
thought, *Oh, that would be brilliant.* Jeez. If she
picked someone who'd been born and died here in
King County, right where Eleanor Smith would
have to disappear, she might as well draw a big
red arrow for anyone searching for her. This way.

Walking back to her car across the springy, wet
grass, she gusted a sigh. Assuming an identity
wasn't easy these days. The internet and shared
databases made both hiding and appearing anew
harder than it used to be. Harder, even, than twelve
years ago. Plus, she'd have to start all over again,
maybe give up her dream of graduate school, and
she didn't know if she had that in her.

What she didn't do, not right away, was look up
Madeline Dubeau on the internet. A part of her
knew she didn't have to, had known the moment
he'd said the name that she was Maddie. Whatever
was wrong with her wasn't complete amnesia, the
kind that made a man stumble into the emergency
room at the hospital and say, "I don't know who I
am." She did have memories, some clear as if they
happened yesterday, tactile and real, while others
were misty, barely seen.

She simply knew, had always known, that she
didn't want those memories to clear. The terrified,
unthinking creature she'd been had held one cer-

tainty: her only hope was not to go back. Not to be who she was.

She wished now she had kept running, not stopped so soon. This policeman wouldn't have stumbled on her if she lived in Maine or Florida. Back then, though, she hadn't known where was safest because she didn't know where she was from. How could she guess, when she had no idea how long she'd been in that car trunk before she became lucid?

She had come to think of her escape that night as her birthing story. The car trunk was her womb. Except a womb was supposed to be a safe place, nestled beneath a mother's heart. Babies were forced out of the womb when the time came, crying their reluctance, only to be met with welcoming arms. They didn't flee in terror into the night, grateful for the lash of tree branches, the scrape of bark.

If she had to start over again now, it wouldn't be quite the same, of course; at least this time she'd retain her history and sense of self. But it would be a rebirth, nonetheless. Too close to what she'd already had to do once. And…impractical. She'd been reacting like a terrified kid, not the adult she was now.

She could call up newspaper clippings and read about Maddie Dubeau. If seeing her own face in them, the faces of her parents or friends, brought back her memories, would that be so bad?

Alone in her apartment, Nell hugged herself with intense anxiety, trying to reason with a bone-deep terror that felt as primal as mankind's instinctive fear of fire or snakes or the dark.

I like my life. Why would I want to know where I came from?

Because, she admitted. Because she was lonely, and as things stood she didn't dare let anyone close enough to have the right to expect answers. Because she felt hollow when she was with a group of friends, like her readers' club, and they shared stories of their childhoods and families until she could see whole tapestries spread out, with rich colors and details so fine they made her heart hurt. Because she would like children of her own, if only she knew why the kind of trust a marriage took was impossible for her.

Because she hated being afraid of something she couldn't even remember.

The next day, Nell went online and, first, did a search for the policeman who had confronted her in the parking lot. Captain Colin McAllister. It was reassuring when his name popped up immediately with dozens of references. Mostly in central Oregon newspapers, but a few times in the *Oregonian,* Portland's daily. She randomly clicked on sites and read about testimonies in court, press conferences, promotions. The article in the *Angel Butte Reporter* about his promotion to captain of the Investigation and Support Services Division had a photo of him in uniform, gazing gravely at the camera. His eyes were hooded, watchful. They were gray, she decided, peering so closely her nose was almost pressed to the monitor. He wasn't smiling, and his brows were knit together a little, adding a couple of creases to his forehead. And yes, he definitely had that remote look she was used to seeing in cops who came by SafeHold.

Not sure why she did, Nell printed the picture. Maybe if she kept studying his face she could decide if he was trustworthy.

Finally, pulse racing, she typed *Madeline Noelle Dubeau* into the search engine and, after a shaky moment, hit Enter. There were bunches of articles, not just in the Angel Butte paper but also in the *Oregonian* and even the *Seattle Times*. She chose one in the Portland *Oregonian,* and was unexpectedly stunned to see her face. She saw the date, and realized how lucky she'd been not to be recognized. She'd been in Portland by then, as naive and, in truth, almost as helpless as a newborn, trying to figure out how to survive while also staying invisible.

Now, she thought in bemusement, *I know how old I really am.* She'd been close, but was a year older than she'd thought.

The article summed up the history. *Her* history. It was assumed that fifteen-year-old Maddie had been abducted, leaving behind her mountain bike, her wallet and blood that DNA testing confirmed was hers. Her parents had thought she was upstairs in her bedroom when she had instead been riding her bike through a wooded section of park. The best guess was that she was on her way to a friend's house in a neighborhood beyond the park. The friend, Emily Henson, hadn't expected Maddie. Investigators had declined to share any leads police might be pursuing.

Nell read hungrily, article after article. There were her parents. Her father, Marc Dubeau, owned a major resort and had, at the time, sat on the city council. A lean, dark-haired and dark-eyed man, he looked like he might be as French as the name. He was handsome, and she couldn't see herself in him at all. Her mother was always in the background in photos, either grief or personality making her retreat inside herself so that her face was expressionless, her wide eyes seeing something that wasn't in front of her. She was blonde and blue-eyed, but aside from coloring Nell looked strikingly like her. The triangular, almost catlike face with a broad sweep of cheekbones and sharp chin, the eyes that were almost too big for the rest of the face. The look came together more elegantly for Helen Dubeau than it did for Nell, whose hair was plain brown and who had somehow acquired freckles across her nose. But they were recognizably mother and daughter, a fact that left her staring and winded.

Yes, these were the people in her fragmentary

memories. This was the woman she pictured waiting for her in the hall outside her classroom with other mothers. There were no photos of her brother, who'd been kept out of the public eye, but he was mentioned. Felix was three years younger than she was, a seventh grader that year.

She printed articles, photos, until there was a stack a quarter of an inch thick on her desk. When she was done and closed the browser, she put Captain McAllister's photo on top, so that it was the one she was looking at.

Exhaustion swept over her. She ached, as if she'd been hauling heavy boxes all day, climbing endless flights of stairs. She barely summoned the energy to stumble to the bathroom and brush her teeth before she tumbled into bed. She fell into sleep as if it were the darkest depths of her forgotten past.

"WHAT KIND OF fiasco is this?" Bystrom snapped, stabbing the front page article in the *Reporter* with his finger. The Bend *Bulletin* lay beside it with a similar headline. "How the hell am I supposed to make us sound like anything but idiots when the mayor asks me about it?"

Colin and his counterpart, Brian Cooper, who headed Patrol Services, exchanged a fleeting, expressionless glance. Colin wished—man, he wished—he could dismiss Angel Butte Police Chief Gary Bystrom as the dumb shit he often sounded, but the SOB was more complex than that. Unfortunately.

He looked like the Hollywood version of a sheriff or police chief, the kind who'd risen through the ranks and now used hard-won wisdom and sometimes bitter experience to lead and inspire his officers. Blond hair had gracefully turned white; he wore a tan as if he'd spent a lifetime out in the field squinting against the sun. What creases and wrinkles his lean face bore made him more handsome. His tall, athletic body was still spare and showed the uniform to advantage. He liked to wear his uniform.

The tan, they all knew, came from the sun reflecting off snow and water. Bystrom was an ardent skier and fly fisherman both. Everyone in the department was grateful that he pursued his hobbies so passionately, because it kept him out of their hair more often than not.

What Bystrom was really good at was politicking. He and the former mayor, Pete Linarelli, had been best friends. Members of the city council strongly supported their police chief. He socialized with most of them, and with most of the important business people in Butte County, too. When Maddie Dubeau disappeared, he had frequently been pictured with her parents, his face reflecting his deep concern, a comforting hand on Helen's arm.

Colin had checked out his background and knew he'd skated through ten years as a patrol officer, back when Angel Butte was a third the size it was now, a backwater not yet transformed into a tourist town with the resulting increase in crime. He'd served briefly as a community liaison, become an administrative sergeant and then, with stunning speed, lieutenant. He made captain by forty, chief by forty-five. He hadn't served a day in Criminal Investigations, on the Drug Enforcement Team or the SWAT team.

Temper tantrums were his answer to screwups caused by inadequate manpower, training or weaponry. And yeah, Colin couldn't argue; this was a big one. Also the kind Colin and Brian both had been expecting, had considered inevitable, given the budget cutbacks.

What happened, so far as Colin understood it, was that a detective on his way home from work had stopped at a Quik-Stop store for some diapers for his eighteen-month-old kid. He'd interrupted a holdup in progress and, though undoubtedly irritated because he'd now have to do paperwork rather than go home, had the perp facedown on the counter within seconds. Unfortunately, a rookie officer answering the original alarm then burst through the door and managed to shoot the detective despite the store clerk's attempt to explain and the fact that the detective had yelled repeatedly, "I'm police! I'm police!" The wounded detective had to bring down the rookie and take his gun away, a wrestling bout that the robber had taken advantage of to escape.

The good part was that Andy Palmer, the detective, had taken the round in the fleshy part of his left arm and he was right-handed. The excusable part was a kid only five weeks out of the academy getting overexcited. Inexcusable? The fact that officers were spread so damn thin he'd been out on his own way too soon, with backup more than ten minutes away.

The chief didn't want to hear any of that. He wanted to know what a detective had been doing pulling his gun without having his badge in his other hand. The diapers he'd been clutching were no excuse.

Colin ground his teeth.

And the kid. Where the hell was his field training officer?

Brian Cooper explained that he had ridden around for a month with an FTO, but they'd needed him on patrol.

"You know how after that annexation we're underfunded and shorthanded...."

Wasted breath. They weren't allocating their resources adequately. They needed to teach their men to do the job and do it right. What Bystrom was going to tell the press, the council and the mayor was that the kid's sergeant hadn't been authorized to send him out on patrol alone. There had been a failure of communication, which he was going to right. Bystrom wanted that sergeant, and maybe the watch commander, slapped hard for embarrassing this department.

Colin suggested that this might be a great opportunity to go to the council for increased funding to plug some of the gaps that had left them so vulnerable. Use this as a lesson in what could go wrong.

Bystrom stared coldly at him and said, "I'm supposed to tell them we can't do the goddamn job, but they should throw more money at us?"

The two police captains left the chief's office and walked together in complete silence downstairs and straight out the station's front door. They still hadn't spoken a word when they reached the playground and picnic area half a block away, blanketed with eighteen inches of snow on the ground from this pre-Christmas winter blast. Neither of them was wearing a parka. Neither cared.

They paused and stood side by side, gazing toward the river running between puffy white banks. Their breath emerged in clouds.

"That asshole," Brian said at last.

Colin made a sound that on a better day would have been a laugh. "No news there."

"We could have lost an officer yesterday, and to friendly fire. Bystrom doesn't give a goddamn about Palmer." He let loose with another expletive. "But if Palmer had ended up dead, our fair leader would have looked damn fine telling the world how Angel Butte police officers take care of their own, and how he'd be there for the young wife and two preschool children. After which, hell, he'd have probably hit the slopes. Didn't I hear the summit lift on Bachelor is open?"

"Yep."

After another silence, he asked reflectively, "Do you think he has the new mayor in his pocket yet?"

To the consternation of the old guard, Linarelli had lost the election earlier this month to a Democrat who'd served only one term on the city council. Nobody yet knew what to make of Noah Chandler, whom everyone remembered had worn his hair in a ponytail when he moved to Angel Butte ten years ago and opened the town's first brew pub. Still only thirty-five, he now owned three, the one here in Angel Butte, one in Sisters and a third in Bend. He was an entrepreneur who was going places. The ponytail was long gone; nobody could argue he didn't have finely honed political instincts. Colin had voted for him and celebrated when he won. He hadn't yet gone out on a limb and taken the problem that was his boss to the new mayor.

"I doubt it," he said. "Did you see the press conference they did together? They didn't look real friendly."

"No, they didn't," Brian agreed thoughtfully.

A phone rang, and they both glanced down at their belts. "Mine," Colin said, lifting it to see the number. He didn't recognize it, but the area code was 206. Seattle. He heard the way his voice roughened when he said, "I've got to take this," and turned away.

"Later," Brian said with a nod, and started back toward the station.

Colin answered the phone. "McAllister."

A woman said hesitantly, "This is Nell Smith. You gave me your card. I'm, uh..."

Triumph roared through him. "Maddie Dubeau." He'd expected to wait a lot longer than four days for her to decide, however tentatively, to trust him.

There was a pause. "That's what you called me."

He waited.

"You said we could talk." There was restraint in her voice. Maybe more. Fear, at a guess.

"I meant it. I've waited a long time to talk to you," he told her.

"I don't understand," she said, so softly she was nearly whispering.

A group came out of the station and turned his way. They were all under him, a mix of people from Records and his own support staff. He nodded and started toward the parking lot.

"Listen," he said, "are you somewhere I can call you back in ten minutes? I don't want to be overheard."

"Oh! No! I mean, yes, that's fine. I'm home."

"Okay. Ten minutes," he promised, and hit End. He called his administrative assistant and said, "Something has come up. You can reach me at home."

He made it there in eight minutes and let himself in. He took just long enough to crank up the thermostat and ditch the tie, then pulled her number up on his cell phone and looked at it with wonder that made him feel almost boyish. Maddie Dubeau. Who would believe this?

She answered on the first ring. "Hello?"

"This is Colin McAllister."

"Oh." Pause. "Thank you for returning my call."

He'd have given anything to be able to see her face. "I'm sorry I scared you that night," he said.

"It wasn't so much because we were alone in the parking lot." She took a breath he could hear. "It was just because..."

"I recognized you."

"Yes. You're the first person, in all these years."

"Are you going to tell me what happened?"

"The thing is...I don't remember." In a rush, she said, "The first thing I knew, I was in a car trunk. I was unconscious some of the time. Finally the car stopped, and I found a latch that folded the back-seat down and got out. It was...it was an ARCO station, you know, with a mini-mart, at a freeway exit in the middle of nowhere. I hid for a long time, and eventually managed to get in the back of a U-Haul truck."

Hearing the stress in her voice, he made sure his was soothing. "You ended up in Seattle?"

"Portland. I stayed there for the first couple of years."

"Why didn't you get help? Come home?"

The silence this time was so long he almost broke

it. Finally, she said softly, "I didn't remember my name. I didn't know where home was."

"Damn," he whispered. He sank down on a bar stool in his kitchen. "Maddie…"

"Nell." She sounded upset, maybe even angry. "I'm Nell."

"Nell." He cleared his throat. "When did you remember?"

"I didn't." Now her voice was small and tremulous. Oh, yeah, she was all over the emotional map. "I still don't. Exactly. That's why you scared me."

Stunned, he said, "But when I said your name, you knew."

These pools of silence had such emotional density, he had trouble surfacing to draw a breath. Her distress was nearly unbearable when he couldn't read her expressions, couldn't touch her.

"Yes," she said. "But not until I heard you say it. It was like…something I already knew slipped into place. See, I do have memories. Jumbled ones. When I went online and saw pictures of my parents, I knew their faces."

"You were scared because I could identify you."

"I've always been scared. I never wanted to remember. I know I was abducted, but…I think I was running, too. I think I *knew* someone was after me. Maybe even that…whoever it was might kill me."

A chill crawled up his spine, one that reminded him of that night, when he'd stood in the dark staring at that bike and the blood that had pooled in the red dirt.

"You don't think your parents could protect you."

"No. Or else…"

The chill spread, lifting the small hairs on his forearms. "You're afraid of them, too."

"Maybe," she whispered. "I don't know."

Now he was the one to let the silence grow while he tried to think.

"Why did you call?" he asked at last. "Why are you admitting this to me?"

"I thought maybe I could trust you. It's been hard, never telling anyone. And not knowing if I'm really crazy."

"I don't know a lot about amnesia," he admitted. "I'll tell you this. I encourage my officers to listen to their instincts. When we feel unease, or fear, there's a reason. We notice things our conscious minds don't acknowledge. That doesn't mean they aren't real."

Nell was quiet for a minute. When she said, "Thank you for saying that," she sounded calmer.

"What is it you thought you could trust me to do?"

A hitch of her breath told him her anxiety had kicked up again. "I don't know! I don't know what I want!"

"Maybe," he said, "it's time you came home."

Silence again. "Do you know them? My parents?"

"I've seen your mother. Never talked to her. Your

father I have occasional dealings with. They seem like decent people, Nell. I'm pretty sure not a day goes by that you're not on their minds."

She was panting now. "I need to think about it."

"Okay," he said, making his voice gentle. "That's good, Nell. There's no hurry. I won't pressure you. I promised." He couldn't have even said where he was; he had never been focused so intently on the tiniest whisper of sound coming through a phone receiver. All he could see was her face. Not the one in the photo, but the woman in the parking lot. His chest felt bruised. "Maybe I can call you tomorrow. We can talk. Not about this. Just to get to know each other. If you have to trust me, you should know me."

The small sound she made might have been a laugh, or a sob. "Yes. Thank you. I'd like that. I work until five...."

"In the evening, then. I'll call."

"You've been...very kind. Thank you, Captain."

"Colin."

"Colin. Goodbye."

He said goodbye, too, then sat where he was, trying to understand why he felt so much.

Damn it, he had to think like the cop he was. He wasn't twenty-two anymore with a hero complex.

On the face of it, her story was unlikely. He'd never believed in the kind of amnesia that gave someone an excuse for having walked away from a failed life. Short-term memory loss, sure. After trauma, people often lost the previous day, say, although usually only temporarily.

In her case, if she were telling the truth, she sounded as if she'd *wanted* to forget. The head injury had helped her along. Given her subconscious justification to ditch memories that were too painful to hang on to.

He didn't know if that made sense, but it was the best he could do. He was confident she wasn't a con artist who'd learned that the Dubeaus were well-to-do and thought she'd get something out of them. Nell Smith was Maddie, no question. It wasn't just her features that made him so sure; it was what was in her eyes. Big and brown and beautiful, those eyes had been hiding so much. They still were.

There in the quiet of his own kitchen, Colin made a harsh sound. The only explanation for his own credulity was that there was simply something about her. There always had been.

And that would have to do until he figured out the rest.

CHAPTER FOUR

"I'm not sure you'd recognize big parts of town even if you hadn't lost your memory," Colin said. "Twelve years is a long time."

Transfixed by the quiet rumble of his voice, Nell clung to her phone. She'd silenced it earlier when she went to her book club, but hated the idea of missing a call from him. She had become so hungry for his calls, she felt pathetic. How embarrassing if he ever knew she had put his photo on her refrigerator door where she could see it when she paced through her small apartment talking to him. This call had started with him wishing her happy birthday—Maddie's birthday. She was still reeling from knowing when she was really born. The fact that he'd remembered and wanted to call today of all days had brought her close to tears.

"I checked the town out online," she told him. "To see if anything looked familiar."

"Did it?"

"Maybe the river. And…and a park." She had started breathing hard when she looked at those pictures.

"There are only two large parks within city limits." A new thread in his voice was hard to single out and identify. Compassion? Pity? "Angel Butte and River Park, which combines a couple of picnic areas, a playground, a boat landing for canoes and kayaks, and maybe fifteen acres of old ponderosa forest."

The always-hovering panic clutched at her throat. "That's where you found my bike."

"Yes."

She didn't know why her hands were shaking. Whatever happened was a long time ago. Of course she knew it was that park. And didn't she want answers?

I don't know. No. Maybe.

She focused on his face in the newspaper photo she could have seen clearly even with her eyes closed. Those watchful, penetrating eyes made her feel safe.

Which didn't mean she wanted to talk about this anymore.

"You've never said where you grew up." He had promised—hadn't he?—to let her get to know him so that she could trust him. He'd been keeping that promise, although in their four previous conversations he had mostly told her about his job and some of his frustrations. Otherwise, they'd talked about unimportant things. Their plans for Thanksgiving, the way they celebrated holidays in general, national politics, music, movie and book tastes. It had occurred to her they'd had the kind of conversations that newly dating couples had.

"I grew up right here," he said simply. "If I didn't think of Angel Butte as home, I'd have looked for another job a long time ago."

"But you said your sister is here in Seattle."

He was silent for a moment, making her wonder if this were more personal than he wanted to get.

He promised, she told herself stubbornly.

"My parents divorced when I was sixteen and Cait was only ten. My mother has moved around some. Cait ended up going to Whitman College, and she's now in grad school at the UW."

Nell nodded; she'd finished her B.A. at the University of Washington, which also had one of the nation's top graduate programs in library and information science. She had been saving, but the idea of not being able to work more than part-time for the two years it would take her to earn her master's degree made her cautious.

"The divorce was bitter," he said, before she could ask an innocuous question, like what his sister was studying. "I didn't see much of them after that."

He'd closed up, as if he were reluctant to betray emotion.

"Why?" she asked, then flushed with shame. "I'm sorry. That's really nosy of me. I can tell you don't want to talk about it, and it really isn't any of my business."

"That's not true, Nell. I want us to be friends. The fact that I know so much about you has got to make you uneasy. I've been hoping we can find a better balance."

Uneasy? What a weak word to describe this complex brew. It bubbled in her chest, sometimes barely simmering, sometimes reaching a furious boil that splattered her painfully and threatened to overflow.

He didn't wait for her to respond. Instead, he went on.

"I haven't spoken to my mother in, oh, seven or eight years and not often before that. I hated my father, and she chose to take my sister but not me when she left."

"You hated your father?" And he had lost his mother, too.

"He abused my mother and beat me. I...tried to protect her, and most of all Cait, but it wasn't always possible. I was as big as he was by the time I was fourteen or fifteen, and I quit taking it. We fought, sometimes physically. Punched holes in the walls, threw furniture. I suspect that, by the time my mother worked up the nerve to leave him, she associated me with the violence as much as she did Dad."

"So she saved herself and not you."

"That's what she did," he said flatly. "I forgave her in one way, because she did save Cait, too."

"I can't imagine abandoning my own child."

She could hear him breathing. Somehow she

wasn't surprised when he managed a wry chuckle. "By that age I was hairy, six feet tall, uncommunicative and angry all the time. Probably didn't bear much resemblance to her little boy."

"Still." Nell pictured boys she'd gotten to know at SafeHold. Rebellious, obscene, angry and, yes, violent, but also bewildered—the vulnerable boys still visible beneath the troubled teenagers.

"Still," Colin echoed, and she heard that same bewilderment in his voice, although she doubted he was aware of it.

"I'm surprised you didn't run away."

"Crossed my mind, but I was too proud. I vowed never to back down. If he beat me bloody every day, I wasn't going to surrender one iota of defiance and hate." Colin was all man now, sardonic and almost amused at the idiot boy who had set himself up for such brutality. "Kept my vow, too."

"What happened?" she asked.

"Finally left for college—none too soon—at Portland State University. Started out thinking I was pre-law, but after a few courses in criminal justice, I was sucked in. The couple of times cops came to our house, I saw that Dad was intimidated by them. I guess there's nothing subtle about my choice."

Nell found herself smiling. "No."

"Fortunately, I got over the swaggering 'I am armed and more powerful than you' phase quickly. I hadn't been home in four years. I'm sure I took the job in Angel Butte because I wanted to face down the monster from my childhood, but..."

Nell didn't say anything, only waited for him to think through how much he wanted to share, or perhaps choose the right words to describe how he had felt.

"While I was gone I'd grown, or he'd shrunk, I was never sure which. No surprise, he was a heavy drinker and was showing the effects by that time. He owned a tavern when I was growing up, but he'd lost it. Angel Butte was changing, brew pubs were already hot and his place was dimly lit, unwelcoming to women, homey only to intolerant sons of bitches like him. Business declined and he had to give up. Ended up bartending for someone else—finally lost that job, too. He was a heavy smoker and died of lung cancer four years ago."

"I'm sorry," Nell said simply.

"Don't be. I'm sorriest that Cait and I are strangers. She's the one part of my family I'd have liked to keep."

Nell had an unsettling thought. "She must have been close in age to me."

Was she wrong in hearing an undertone to this silence?

"She is," he agreed at last.

"I wonder if we knew each other. If we were ever in a class together."

"That...never occurred to me. I suppose you

might have been." He sounded a little disturbed at the idea.

Nell's pulse quickened. "She might have recognized me, if we'd happened to run into each other."

"From when you were ten years old? I doubt it."

"I'd have been safer if I'd moved farther away. I told myself I didn't know where I was from, but…" She tried to reach for calm, even though this touched on the fear that had always lived inside her: *What if someone recognizes me?* "I suppose I wasn't very brave. I was running away but clinging to the familiar at the same time."

"Most kids who run away get hauled home. The ones who don't often stay on the streets. They don't go to college, build a solid life for themselves. If they manage to find that kind of security, they don't reach out to help kids as lost as they were. Don't tell me you weren't brave, Nell." His voice roughened at the end, making it hard for her to form a rebuttal.

"Don't make me out to be more than I am," she said at last. "I did things…"

"Yeah." Now she heard a tenderness she had no defense against. "I know you must have. Fifteen years old and afraid to turn to any adult? How much choice did you have?"

Did he really understand what she'd been trying to tell him? Nell couldn't tell, and lost the courage to elaborate. She didn't even know if it mattered. Maybe it didn't matter what *she* had done. Maddie Dubeau was the one he longed to bring home, not Nell Smith. She couldn't afford to let herself forget that.

"I should go," she said. "I'm working in the morning."

"I suppose I should get to bed, too. I've probably dumped enough on you for one night anyway."

"You didn't dump. I asked." She hesitated, then closed her eyes. "Thank you. For telling me all that. It helps, knowing your life hasn't been trouble-free, either. Which means I'm not nearly as good a person as you're trying to make me out to be. I should wish you had a perfect childhood with a loving family, and you made all that up to convince me we were, I don't know, fellow travelers."

He laughed. Really laughed, rich and deep. "I'm not trying to fit you for a halo, Nell."

"I'm not an angel. Don't call me that."

She was as shocked at her sharpness as he must have been.

"I won't," he said after a discernible pause. "It didn't occur to me." He was soothing her again, much as he had that night he frightened her in the parking lot. Using his voice to convince her he was harmless, that he would never hurt her.

She wondered if his mother had been afraid of him.

Breathing fast again, she said, "I really have to go."

"Would it help if I came back to Seattle, so we could talk face-to-face?"

Yes. Oh, yes. Please. As her lips formed the words, her eyes stung. She was torn between a desperate desire to see him again and terror that was just as strong. His willingness to let her take their conversations at her own pace had been the reassurance she'd needed. If he had pushed too hard, insisted on trying to delve into her memories, or had shown up unexpectedly, she would have known she couldn't trust him.

"No," she made herself say. "I like talking to you, but…"

"All right, Nell. I promised. No pressure. I just find…" He hesitated. "I'd like to see your face, that's all."

Her shakiness wasn't only about panic now. She wanted to see his face, too.

"You've been really patient." He had been. "Given me a huge amount of time. There must be a million things you'd rather be doing."

"No." The certainty in his voice was rock-solid. "There is nothing I want more than to help you feel ready to come home."

Would she ever feel ready?

A sound slipped out that might have been a laugh.

No. Facing her past would be harder than anything she'd done since she escaped from the trunk of the car and shivered her way through that cold night, not knowing who or where she was, only that she didn't dare go back.

But Nell knew again that if she didn't reclaim the part of her that was Maddie she would be continuing to live only half a life. Now that she knew she was also Maddie, now that she'd seen pictures of her parents and even the house where she'd grown up, she couldn't block out the past the way she had.

"I think," she heard herself say in a voice that shook, "I might come to Angel Butte."

"Home."

"I don't know if it's home. Nothing I do remember makes me think it is. But maybe…maybe whatever or whoever I was running away from will have shrunk like your dad did. I want to find out there's nothing to be afraid of anymore."

He said some things—how glad he was she had made the decision, how gutsy he thought she was—but most important he renewed his promise not to tell anyone about her, not to warn a soul that she was coming.

One of the things he said shook her a little because he delivered it so thoughtfully. "It might be interesting to see how people react to your reappearance."

"I have to get time off from work," she said. "I'll let you know."

After they'd said good-night and ended the call, Nell discovered she was sitting on the kitchen floor, very close to the corner, her back to the cupboard, her knees drawn up tight.

"Gutsy," she said aloud, and laughed until she cried.

Too ANTSY TO sit behind his desk, Colin killed an hour watching the SWAT team train, went by a house where an ugly domestic scene had occurred the night before and finally simply drove the streets of his town.

He wasn't fit company right now. Knowing Nell was on her way worked like the most powerful shot of caffeine he'd ever had. His heart kept racing and occasionally thudding out of sequence. It felt like Christmas morning when he was young, before his father's drinking and temper tainted every family occasion. A couple of times he caught a glimpse of himself in the rearview mirror and discovered he was grinning like a fool.

Not something he wanted anyone to catch him doing. If he'd hung around the station, he might have come face-to-face with Duane. Usually Colin prided himself on his ability to hide what he was thinking. He doubted he'd succeed today, especially with a man who knew him well.

Yesterday he'd been okay, even though he'd known Nell was planning to leave after she got off work. He'd made it home before he started envisioning her car like an electronic blip on his mental screen. Leaving heavy downtown Seattle traffic.

Hitting Tacoma. An empty stretch, then Olympia. Had she reached Chehalis yet? He wondered if she'd made reservations at a Portland hotel, or had waited to spot one at a freeway exit and gambled on vacancies.

"I know I could make the drive in one day," she had told him, "but I'd rather it be daylight when I get there."

He didn't blame her. Given that she would be arriving on the first of December, she was nervous about driving on snowy roads and would rather cross the Cascades in the morning when she was fresh. Colin had checked weather reports last night and again first thing this morning. It sounded as if Highway 26 had been plowed where it climbed high by Mount Hood. He hoped she'd stop for coffee and even lunch rather than pressing on.

At lunchtime, he finally called his assistant and told her he was taking half a day. As useless as he was, he might as well make his absence official.

Just after one, Nell called.

"I'm on the outskirts." She sounded tense. "You're right, I wouldn't have recognized a thing. There's a Walmart here."

"Walmart is everywhere. And yes, we have a half mile stretch filled with chain stores and restaurants, pretty much like every other city in America."

"Did you make a reservation for me?"

"Why don't you meet me at my house?" he suggested. "I'm there now."

Her hesitation was brief. He gave her directions and paced while waiting, one ear cocked for the sound of a car in his driveway.

He had the front door open before she came to a stop. She drove a peanut of a car—a Ford Focus, the one she'd backed right up to in the parking lot at the library.

As if he gave a damn. Part of him couldn't believe she was here. But the driver's side door opened, and there she was, just as he remembered her from the library, unmistakably Maddie Dubeau. Her warm brown eyes were wary, but the young Maddie hadn't looked on the world with much faith, either.

Seeing her this time was different, though. He'd felt a punch that evening at the library because, damn, he'd found Maddie. But getting to know her during their long phone conversations had complicated his thinking. The woman he was looking at now wasn't Maddie grown up. She was a woman named Nell, who had amazing cheekbones, legs a mile long and a build he thought was a little short-waisted to make up for those legs. He was surprised by her lush mouth, something that either had changed since she was a teenager, or hadn't shown in those photos because she kept her lips pressed together so tightly.

He was attracted to her. Nonplussed, Colin did his best to shut it down. *She's Maddie Dubeau. This isn't personal.*

It was all he could do not to wince at the inner jeering. Still, the lecture had worked to an extent. Maddie. She was Maddie.

"You made it." Despite the evidence before his eyes, he still fought a disbelief that mixed with his newly confused feelings.

She made a face at him. "I swear my knuckles were white driving over the pass by Mount Hood."

"Wasn't it plowed?"

"Yes, but it was still icy and there were snow-banks to each side so I couldn't even pull over and let drivers by who wanted to go faster."

"I'm sorry," he said. "You could have flown in."

"No, I'll need my car." She turned to look around her. "This is really nice. I pictured you in town."

"I wanted privacy." He only had an acre, but that was enough. His chalet-style house was built on a ridge of exposed lava and shielded by ponderosa pines younger and smaller than those in the park. He'd encouraged native growth, too. One of his jobs growing up had been mowing the lawn. He could live without ever mowing again.

"Come on in," he said. "Coffee is ready."

When she stepped inside his house, her eyes widened. "It's beautiful."

Outside, he had thought she'd been pretending to be interested. Now she didn't look as if she were faking it anymore. Nell's scrutiny made him self-conscious and Colin glanced around. "I haven't done much decorating."

"With that fireplace and those windows, it doesn't need much."

The river-rock fireplace had sold him on the house, though the vast expanses of glass hadn't hurt even though he had known they would raise his heating bill substantially. The view from here looked northwest, toward a spine of mountains. It even caught a snippet of Mount Bachelor.

The floors were broad planks of chestnut. Low built-in bookcases formed a long seat beneath one wall of windows. The ceiling-high river rock took up most of another wall, with an ancient slab of wood inset as a mantel. He'd hung a Navajo rug above it instead of a painting.

Nell disappeared to use the bathroom while he poured the coffee in the kitchen that opened to the huge living room. When she reappeared, he saw the stress on her face that she'd been trying to hide.

She added both cream and sugar to her mug, then perched on a stool at the breakfast bar. Colin sipped his own coffee and watched her.

"My parents have a house right on the river."

"I know. You remember it?"

"Not exactly." She stirred, gazing into her coffee as if seeking patterns in tea leaves instead. "I looked them up online, then used Google Earth to see the house. I guess I've retained enough fragments that the house didn't surprise me."

"It's not far from the park."

"So it makes sense that I was cutting through on my way to wherever I was going."

"Yes. Except that it was dark and you hadn't told your parents you were going anywhere."

Her eyes, strangely blind-looking, met his. "Are you sure about that?"

"No. But if they were lying, they're good at it."

"You saw them? That night?"

"Yeah, I did. The detective who was initially taking the lead asked me to accompany him when he went to talk to them. Of course we hoped it would turn out you'd made it home on your own. That you'd bumped your head, your mom or dad had taken you to the E.R." He paused, remembering. "Instead, they were both home. They didn't believe you'd gone anywhere. Your father went out to the garage to see if your bike was there, your mother went upstairs to your bedroom. I remember when she rushed back down, I saw your brother standing at the top of the stairs looking scared."

"Did you talk to him?" She was focused intently on him.

Colin shook his head. "Later, I'm sure detectives did. That night we were finding out whether you were home or if they'd heard from you. Letting them know about the bike and the blood."

She touched the side of her head. "My hair was matted with blood. It was all over my shirt. I'd puked, too, in the trunk. I was a mess."

"I don't suppose you saw a doctor."

"I didn't dare." Her brief smile didn't fool him into thinking she was happy thinking about this. "I have a scar. Sort of a ridge. Probably because I didn't get stitches or maybe my skull was fractured and it knit funny. Not that it matters, since it's hidden by my hair."

"Let me see it."

She looked startled; it had come out sounding more implacable than he'd intended. "Um..." She reached up and sifted through her hair. "It's right here."

Colin circled the end of the counter, standing close enough to her he could slide his own fingers into her shiny brown hair until he felt the thickened ridge of a lengthy scar. He traced it end to end, feeling rage rising in his chest, but other emotions, too. Her head was tipped to one side to give him the best access, but she watched his face sidelong. He could see how fine-pored her skin was. The curve of eyelashes was something he'd never noticed on a woman before. Her hair was fine, almost childlike in texture, and having it slip through his fingers as he gently withdrew his hand was a more sensual experience than he'd intended. A scent he suspected was uniquely hers made his nostrils flare, too. He couldn't easily identify the herbs, but thought there was a hint of mint. And beneath it, woman.

He smoothed her hair behind her ear, saw that his fingers had a faint tremor and withdrew his hand sharply. He retreated around the breakfast bar again, leaning a hip against it so that she couldn't see the way his body had responded to the closeness.

Maddie, he told himself desperately.

"I don't suppose you saw the gas station where you made the great escape." He said that as much to refocus himself as because he wanted to know.

So much emotion swirled in her eyes, he knew the answer even before she spoke. He almost regretted asking.

"Yes. I...watched for it. It wasn't that far north, between Redmond and Madras. It's awfully dry out there, but there is an orchard and a vineyard somebody is irrigating. I can show you where it is, if you care."

He nodded. "Eventually. Not right now. I'm sorry, Nell. That must have been rough."

Her smile was wry. "I told myself it was like visiting the hospital where you were born. I'm different from most people, though, because I remember."

"You cut your own umbilical cord."

"Exactly." Cradling her mug in both hands, she inhaled, then sipped. Hiding behind it, he thought. When she reemerged, her expression was merely inquiring. "Did you find a place for me to stay?"

He tensed. She might hate this idea, but his instincts told him to keep her close. Having taken a leave of absence from the library, she was free to stay for a couple of weeks to a month, at least. "I made a reservation in case you insist," he said. "But I have a better idea."

Her wariness became more pronounced.

"There's a small apartment above my garage. Bedroom, bath, tiny kitchenette. It's been empty since I bought the house. I'd feel better if you stayed here, at least until we're sure nobody is disturbed by your reappearance."

Her eyes searched his. "You really think somebody might be?"

"I have no idea," he said truthfully. "We don't even know if you were being kidnapped, say for ransom, or the driver of that car thought you were dead and was heading somewhere to dump your body. The fact that you were so convinced it wasn't safe to come home is the part that unsettles me. If you knew the person who attacked you…" He shrugged.

Nell bent her head, once again hiding, this time behind fine brown hair that fell forward. Colin waited, not taking his eyes off her.

"If only I remembered," she said in a small voice.

"The trouble is, even if memories start coming back, that particular one may not. After head trauma, people often forget the event that caused it and frequently the day leading up to it."

"I remembered something on the way here."

His gaze sharpened.

"Nothing important. It was going through Bend and seeing the signs for the turnoff to Mount Bachelor. I knew suddenly that my family skied. I didn't really enjoy it because I was always cold and I wasn't very good. I think my brother raced."

Colin nodded. "He did. I searched old newspapers after I saw you in Seattle. I wanted to get more of a sense of your family."

"Felix." With the tentative way she said the name, Colin could tell she was trying it on her tongue. As if she hadn't said it aloud before.

"Have you met him?" she asked.

Colin shook his head. "Your parents kept him out of the public eye. He never appeared at press conferences. After that first night, I never saw him again."

She nodded.

"Would you like to see the apartment?"

On her nod, he took the key from the hook in a cupboard and led her across the frozen, crunchy ground to the detached garage with a peaked roof that echoed the roofline of the main house. The locked door opened to the foot of a staircase that was enclosed and a little claustrophobic. Better than an exterior staircase that would have been treacherous in winter.

Being optimistic, he'd turned the heat on a couple of hours ago to take the chill out of the air. The apartment was pretty bare-bones—he winced at that description. Livable, though, with a double bed, dresser, small table and pair of chairs. He had gone so far as to stock the kitchenette with extra dishes and pans and even a minimum of silverware from the house.

"It was unfinished up here when I bought the house," he said, looking around.

"Have you ever rented it out?"

Colin shook his head. "No. I guess, in the back of my mind, I thought…"

Understanding softened Nell's face. "That Cait might want to come home."

Startled, he turned his head to meet her eyes. There wasn't another person alive who could have guessed why creating this apartment had mattered to him. He'd revealed one hell of a lot of himself to her, and she'd done some reading between the lines, too.

"Yeah," he admitted. "At least I thought I should have someplace for her, if she ever needed me."

That sounded asinine even to him. By the time he had bought this house and had the dormer added and the apartment finished, his sister had been twenty-four years old. An adult. Long past thinking of her big brother as a refuge, assuming she ever had. He'd held on to his delusion too long, he thought now—and not for the first time. But today, his chest had lightened at the idea of Nell staying here. At being able to look out his bedroom window at night and see a light up here.

At being able to provide *her* with a refuge.

"If you really mean your offer…" Nell's brown eyes shimmered as if tears threatened.

"I do. I'd be happiest if you would."

She took a big breath and swallowed. "Then I'd love to. I'll try not to…to lean on you too much, but knowing you're there makes me feel a lot less scared."

"I'm the one who talked you into taking a chance and coming home." He let the leash he'd been keeping on his intensity slide, hoping it wouldn't scare her. "I'm asking you to let me support you. Having you here…" He shook his head, unable to find adequate words. "It's amazing." He sounded a little hoarse. "The fact that you trust me, that means a lot to me, Nell." *Enough already. Ease up,* he told himself. He tried for a friendly smile. "I'd like it if you'd have dinner with me. I already have some chicken marinating—I didn't figure a restaurant would appeal much."

"No." While tremulous, her smile was real. "I don't want to be recognized until I've seen my parents, at least. And since you recognized me so easily, other people probably will, too."

"You'd be likeliest to catch your parents home in the evening," he pointed out.

She nodded. "I thought…tonight. I'm here. It would be silly to hide out for the next twenty-four hours."

Colin smiled at her. "Will you let me come with you?"

"A truly gutsy woman would say no." Even her eyes smiled this time. "Me, I'd be grateful if you would."

"Good." He backed onto the landing. "Let me haul your bags up."

"Oh, I can…"

"Settle in," he told her. "You'll need to look around and tell me what I forgot. Maybe take a nap."

"I can plan my strategy."

"You can do that, too."

A minute later, when she popped the rear door to her hatchback, he reached for the larger of the two suitcases.

Elation rose from the incredulity.

Maddie Dubeau was home.

CHAPTER FIVE

NELL KNEW THE house, as she'd known the faces of her parents when she saw them online. This was one of the gracious, older homes right on the river, lawn sweeping down to the rocky bank. Even shrouded by darkness, she knew it was painted white with dignified black trim, and that a huge old weeping willow hung over the murmuring water of the Deschutes. Her father had already strung the Christmas lights, sparkling white. Their Christmas tree, she suddenly remembered, had always been silver-themed. Mom didn't like garish colors.

Colin pulled into the driveway, set the brake and turned off the engine. Neither said a word. They gazed at the house in silence for a minute, and then he got out and started around to her side. Nell quickly unbuckled and joined him.

Windows were warm golden squares, but the porch light was off. A streetlamp half a block away cast a circle of yellowish light. The temperature had dropped with nightfall. Nell told herself that was why she shivered, but she wasn't convinced.

I don't remember that night. I don't.

But prickles tiptoed up her spine anyway.

Colin took her arm, looking down at her, his face shadowed. She remembered the night he had confronted her at the library and how much he'd scared her. Tonight, he was all that gave her the courage to walk toward the deep front porch.

She knew without looking where the doorbell was.

They stood side by side, listening to the bell toll. Footsteps came faintly, loud enough to allow her time to brace herself for the moment when the porch light came on and then the door opened.

Marc Dubeau stood in the opening, expression impatient. In that first, fleeting glimpse, Nell saw that he hadn't changed much from the man in her memories. Hair at his temples had turned silver and new lines aged his face, but he was still thin, handsome and fit.

He looked first at Colin, his eyebrows climbing in surprise, and then his gaze flicked to Nell. Shaking only inside where nobody could see, she thought, *That's just like him. Courteous to women, but always assuming men are more important.*

Then shock transformed that lean, dark face. His grip tightened in a spasm on the door. "Maddie?" he whispered.

"Yes." That sounded inadequate. "It's me."

"What...?" He closed his eyes and gave his head a bewildered shake. "My God. Come in." Standing back, he held the door wide-open. "Maddie."

That same note infused his voice. "Captain," he said to Colin.

Colin had released her arm when they reached the porch, but now he gripped it again, just above her elbow as if to steady her. They both stepped inside, and she knew the entryway, too, with a wide staircase rising from it and arched openings to each side, one leading to the living room, the other a formal dining room. She heard canned voices from a television.

"Let me take your coats." Her father sounded shaken and his eyes never left her. As they unzipped, he raised his voice. "Helen?"

Nell let Colin take her parka, grateful for his warmth at her back. *Let me support you,* he'd said, and meant. Not something she was used to.

Her gaze stayed trained on the doorway to the living room. A moment later, a woman appeared in it. She wore wool slacks and a sweater that had to be cashmere. Her blond, chin-length hair was elegantly styled. She'd aged more than her husband had, but oh…that face was so familiar. From memories, and from Nell's own mirror.

"Mom?" Nell managed to say, past the lump in her throat.

Helen's shock was even greater than her husband's, or only more visible. Her hand flew to her throat and she stared for the longest time before tears flooded her blue eyes. "Maddie?"

"Yes," she said again.

"Oh, dear God." She sagged and her husband
went to her side and put an arm around her. "We
thought…"

"I know."

Nell had braced herself for her mother, at least, to
want to hug her. Instead, Helen visibly pulled herself together and reached her hand out, but the gesture was tentative. Nell took her hand and waited
for some deep sense of connection, but nothing
came. There was an emptiness as she realized she
could be clasping a complete stranger's hand.

It was a relief when her mother let her go.

"This is…such a surprise. Marc? Did you know?"

"No. Please," he said again, gesturing toward
the living room. Looking at Colin, he said, "You
found her."

"By chance," Colin agreed. He rested a casual
hand on Nell's back and took the seat right beside
her on the sofa.

*Yes, I know this room, too, although the sofa is
new. Or only reupholstered?*

Taking a wing chair, her father stared at her.
"This is… I don't even know what to say. I've always believed… You can't know what it means to
us to have you home again."

She felt like a long-lost daughter, home again,
and yet she also had a peculiar sense of distance, almost as if she were hovering over the scene. Thinking, *He's saying the right things, but I can't tell
what he really feels.*

"Thank you," she said politely. Out of the corner of her eye, she stayed aware of Colin, so large and solid. His hand lay casually on the cushion only inches from hers. She wanted to grab it and hold on.

"I don't understand this," her mother blurted. "Where have you *been?* How could you disappear and not so much as call? Do you have any idea what you did to us?"

Colin studied her mother with a sort of clinical interest. Even with his dysfunctional family background, he'd clearly expected her parents to throw themselves at her, weeping. Instead... Well, even Nell didn't quite know whether they were in shock, were only mildly pleased to see her, or were angry because she'd been so inconsiderate as to shame them in front of the world for losing their daughter. Perhaps they were simply very reserved people. That felt right when she thought about it. She couldn't summon a memory of being hugged.

"I suffered a head injury," she said, her own reserve as bottomless. *Nature or nurture?* she asked herself, in one of those fleeting, totally irrelevant diversions. "When I woke up, I had no idea what my name was. I eventually created a new identity and a new life. My name is Nell."

"You've lived all these years without knowing you're Maddie?"

"Yes."

Colin must have moved his hand, slightly, but enough so that it brushed hers.

Marc's dark eyes fastened on him. "How did you find her?"

"I happened to see her interviewed on a local television show in Seattle. I tracked her down, and we talked."

"In Seattle? You were up there for some kind of conference, weren't you? But that was a couple of weeks or more ago!"

"That's right." He wasn't bothering to sound apologetic.

"You didn't think we'd want to know our daughter was alive?"

"The decision to come home or not was Nell's. I gave her my word I'd let her make it."

Her father's gaze swung back to her. "Maddie. Goddamn it, your name is Maddie," he said fiercely.

"I haven't been Maddie in a very long time. My memory of her is still shaky. Incomplete. I've asked Colin—Captain McAllister—to call me Nell."

"In this house you're Maddie."

She nodded, because what else could she do?

Her mother's shock seemed to have been renewed. "You don't remember us at all?"

"My memories are scattered. Once Colin told me who I was, I went on the internet and looked at pictures of you. I recognized you then, from those memories. I think I was very frightened the night I left home, maybe even before I was attacked. Even after all these years, I was afraid to come back, to reveal myself. My silence may seem cruel to you, but…" She couldn't go on.

Colin chose that moment to enclose her hand in his, the clasp warm and strong, the comfort and support she so desperately needed. This was the first time they'd touched, bare skin to bare skin. It felt so right that relief and something more powerful flooded her.

Both her parents looked at their clasped hands. Her mother's eyes widened and her father's disapproval was obvious.

"I assume you have your bags in the car."

Colin's grip tightened.

"No." She tried very hard to sound regretful. "I don't mean to hurt you, but… This is a big step for me. I'm hoping to spend time with you, but I'm not ready to come home as if I am Maddie unchanged. I've taken a leave from my job, long enough that I thought it best to find an apartment." She was careful not to look at Colin.

"That's ridiculous!" Marc exclaimed. "This is your home! You have a bedroom upstairs." His voice softened. "We haven't changed a thing."

For the first time, she had to blink hard to hold back tears. "I'd really like to see it. Another time, though. I just arrived today, and I guess I'm feeling a little overwhelmed."

This silence was not a comfortable one. She was beginning to wonder if her parents' odd reaction to her was only the result of shock.

"Can you tell me about Felix?" she asked tentatively. "He's not home, is he?"

"Do you remember him?" her father asked.

She gave a flicker of a smile. "The same way. Fleeting memories. But they're all good ones." Suddenly afraid of how that sounded, she hurried on. "May I see a picture of him?"

"Certainly." Her mother rose, the movement seeming stiff, and turned to the fireplace. Several framed photos held pride of place on the mantel. "This is the most recent." She brought one in a silver frame to Nell. "We keep yours there, too. We've never lost hope."

Nell's vision blurred and she bent her head. Yes, she had hurt her mother, at least, and yet she couldn't seem to take her at face value. This scene still felt wrong, the undercurrents tugging at her.

She accepted the framed photo and gazed down at it. A handsome young man looked back at her, although she could see in him the skinny boy she remembered. He resembled their father and not Helen at all, with his dark hair and brown eyes. Wearing graduation robes, he was laughing, the hat with tassel in one hand.

"Where did he go to school?" she asked.

"Willamette." Marc said it with pride. "He's still there, in law school."

They talked more about him, their voices gradually relaxing as if Felix were a comfortable subject for them. He was halfway through law school.

His—*her*—parents hoped he would come home to central Oregon to practice. To Bend, if not to Angel Butte.

"I don't think he has entirely decided what kind of law to pursue," Helen said. "Of course, your father had hoped he would be interested in taking over the resort, but it seems that won't come to be."

Nell handed the picture to Colin, who released her hand to take it. He studied it as carefully as she had, then set it on the coffee table.

"I don't suppose you made it to college," Marc observed.

Nell's chin rose at what she interpreted as a dismissive tone. "Actually, I did. I have a degree in psychology with a minor in English from the University of Washington."

"Really."

Another drawn-out pause was more than she could take. She shot to her feet without any forethought. "I'm really tired from the drive. Can we get together tomorrow? Mom—" Why was it so hard to say a word that should come naturally? "Maybe we can have lunch tomorrow."

Shock seemed to have frozen both their faces, but they stood, too.

"Yes, of course," her mother said. "Perhaps we could go to the Newberry Inn. You always loved it."

She smiled, unwilling to admit she didn't re-

JANICE KAY JOHNSON   111

member the inn. "Twelve-thirty? Why don't we meet there?"

Colin moved even faster than she did. He was holding out her parka by the time she reached the front door, and helped her into it before putting on his own.

Marc held out his hand to Colin. "Thank you for bringing Maddie to us."

"I'm glad I was able to."

The two men shook. He nodded at Nell's mother. "Mrs. Dubeau."

"My husband has mentioned you. You were one of the police officers who came to talk to us the night Maddie disappeared, weren't you?"

"Yes, I was. Brand-new on the force."

"Maddie?" Her father touched her arm, his expression softer. "We've dreamed about this. You walking in the door. We're more grateful than you can know to have you here."

She nodded and offered a smile that wobbled. Tears burned her eyes again. "Yes. It's been…" She didn't know what it had been and gave up the attempt to put her complicated feelings into words. "Um…good night."

Again, Colin guided her down the porch steps and the walkway, this time with a hand on her back. He unlocked his big SUV and came around to the passenger side with her, as if unsure she could get in without help.

A moment later, they were backing out, Nell

very aware of her parents still standing on the porch, watching them go.

COLIN KEPT AN anxious eye on Nell during the drive home. She stared straight ahead, her hands locked together on her lap.

A block or so from the Dubeau home, he observed, "Not quite what I expected."

"No" was all she said, in a small, almost stricken voice.

He stayed silent after that, thinking she needed time to absorb the reunion with her parents.

But when they got home and she immediately headed for the staircase to the apartment, he said brusquely, "You don't need to be alone yet, Nell. Come and have a cup of coffee with me. We can talk as much or as little as you want."

She stopped, her back to him. It was a long time before she turned and nodded. Even given that the outdoor lighting leached color from the scene, her face was ghostly pale, her eyes huge and dark.

Colin took her arm again, more to reassure himself that she was here and real than because he thought she needed the physical support.

He left her in the living area while he put coffee on to brew, but was able to watch as she wandered, studying the books on his shelves rather than sitting down. When he joined her, she glanced at him.

"You're a reader."

"I am. I use the library plenty, but I like owning books, too."

"You haven't graduated to an eReader yet?"

"I'm digging in my heels," he said, going for relaxed. If she needed to ground herself with the commonplace, that was what they'd do. "If I did a lot of traveling, I'd probably want one. As it is, I like the feel and look and smell of books. I've never been a fan of reading lengthy documents on my computer. You?"

"I love books, too." She gave a small, choked laugh. "I guess you know that."

He smiled. "You dropped some at my feet the first time we met."

"So I did." Her smile widened, then faded as she searched his face with huge, desperate eyes. "Thank you for coming with me. I might have chickened out if you hadn't been there."

"Dragging you up to the door?" He smiled again. "You marched right up there without any pressure from me. You'd have done it, Nell."

She jerked one shoulder. "Maybe. I don't know. I panicked at the end. You probably noticed—I practically ran out."

"The whole visit was awkward."

"Yes." She nibbled on her lower lip. "I was afraid they'd weep and want to clutch me, but...instead they were so stiff. I don't know which is worse."

He understood. She had to be wondering right

now how glad her parents were for her to come back from the dead.

"Maybe my being there inhibited them."

She looked away. "If you had spent years fearing your sister was dead, and she came knocking on your door, would you even notice another person was with her?"

A question he didn't want to answer. "What matters is how *you* felt, Nell. Did alarms go off? Memories stir? What do your instincts say about their reaction?"

He knew he'd taken the right tack when the most obvious of her distress eased and her eyes unfocused, as though she were replaying a movie in her head.

"Let me pour the coffee," he said.

Returning a minute later, he set both mugs on the coffee table, but chose to sit in a chair facing her rather than beside her on the sofa. Some distance might be healthy for him. He was feeling entirely too much for a woman he had seen briefly two weeks ago, then had dinner with tonight. Barely an acquaintance.

Except, he reminded himself, for those half-dozen phone conversations, some which had been an hour or more long. Except for the fact that he'd kept the photograph of fifteen-year-old Maddie hanging where he could see it daily for twelve long years.

Nell cautiously sipped her coffee, then offered

him a hesitant smile. "You remembered how I like it."

"Being observant is a requirement for my job," he said, too abruptly.

Her smile went away and after a moment she nodded.

"Yes, memories stirred, but nothing meaningful. When I saw the house, I knew it. I could have walked in, closed my eyes and gone right to my bedroom, or to the drawer where Mom keeps the silverware. If I'd opened the refrigerator, I wouldn't have had to think to know the milk would be on the door and which shelf the margarine would be on."

He nodded. Memories like that were as much physical as anything. Like riding a bike, something you could do without even thinking.

"I could see the ways they'd aged since then. And...okay, I never even thought of casting myself into their arms. Which would suggest they never were huggers."

"Probably." He hoped someone since then had loved her enough to give her plenty of hugs. The contained way she carried herself made him doubt that had ever happened, though.

"No alarms," she said. "I mean, it all felt scary. You know?"

Colin nodded. She had hidden her fear, but he'd known it was there.

"I think, if either of them had ever hit me or...or

anything like that, I would know." Those big cara-
mel eyes pleaded for his agreement.

"Is there anything like that in the memories you
do have?"

She shook her head. "But none of them are *important* memories. The kind of thing you expect to
hold on to, like birthdays or winning the big game
and Daddy grinning with pride, or…" She seemed
to run out of ideas. "They're random bits. A voice,
the way Mom turned her head to look at me. Dad
telling me what to do. Sometimes the memory is
more me in relation to them than actually seeing
them, if that makes sense. Like when I passed the
turnoff to Mount Bachelor. I felt myself slumped in
the backseat of the car, wishing I could have stayed
home because I *hated* my ski boots and knew I was
going to be cold and that I'd be stuck alone anyway
because I was scared of the steep runs. I knew Dad
especially was disappointed because I was timid
and not the kind of athlete Felix was, and Mom
would be irritated because I'd probably forgotten
something like my gloves or goggles or I'd have to
go to the bathroom even before we headed up the
hill and they'd all have to wait for me."

He had no trouble seeing skinny, almost-homely
Maddie sunk in misery. The unhappiness infusing
her voice rang painfully true. Her body language
had changed as she talked, too. She had curled into
herself, as if she'd gotten lost in the memory until

she couldn't separate who she was now from the young Maddie.

What she was describing wasn't abusive by anyone's standard, but it fit with the unhappiness and doubt he had seen in her eyes back then, in every photo published in the newspaper or on the ubiquitous flyers that said, *Have You Seen Our Daughter?*

"But surely I wouldn't have run away just because my parents weren't the warmest people on earth." Lines crinkled her forehead as she looked at him in perplexity. "And…wouldn't I remember if there was something really bad? Wouldn't it make more sense if that was what I *did* remember?"

"No." He knew he sounded harsh, but he was battling an inexplicable desire to blunder over to her and take her in his arms. "When memories get repressed, it's always the bad stuff, Nell. We can stand a lot of unhappiness. It's the unbearable that gets shoved deep."

She shuddered. "I've always known," she said after a minute, "that what I don't want to remember is bad."

Colin had never much liked touching other people or being touched. Too many years on his own, he guessed. He liked sex as well as the next man, but never let relationships become intimate in other ways. Sitting on the sofa at the Dubeau home tonight, holding Nell's hand, he'd been stunned by the realization that he hadn't held anyone's hand since Cait was a little girl. But Nell... He wanted to touch *her*.

Or was it Maddie?

Because she reminds me of Cait?

Being confused like this didn't sit well with him.

He didn't like seeing her scared and sad and not being able to do anything about it, either.

"I picked up a tourist brochure for you that has a map of town. Not every street is on it, but enough to get around."

She blinked and then nodded, and he realized that reverting to practicalities had been exactly what she needed.

"Thank you," she said meekly.

"Part of me wants to trail you everywhere you go," he admitted.

"Of course you can't do that."

"I want you to be careful. Have you ever taken a class in women's self-defense?" *That's right, scare her even worse.*

Her pointy chin rose stubbornly. "Actually, I have."

"Practice what you learned. Be self-aware. Don't head out to your car without looking around—make sure no one is watching you. Look inside before you get in. Lock your doors before you even drop your purse on the seat beside you. Don't meet any-one in an isolated spot."

She stared at him in bewilderment. "I don't un-derstand. You're the one who convinced me to come for a visit. I left twelve years ago. That's a long time, Colin. Why are you suddenly..." She seemed to be searching for a word.

"Getting nervous?" He managed an apologetic smile. "Because it's an occupational hazard?" Pleased to see that relaxed her, he continued with a greater truth, because, damn it, he did want her to take every precaution. "Because I keep thinking about the evening when I cornered you at the library. Your fear ran deep, Nell. It wasn't the kind of fear a teenager feels when she's running from an abusive parent. Whatever or whoever you were running from is likely long gone or no threat, but...a lot of people you would have known are still here in town." He finished with a shrug. "That's why I'm nervous."

So much swirled in her eyes, he felt a familiar ache in his chest, but she sounded sturdy when she said, "I'll be careful."

"Besides lunch with your mother, do you have any plans yet?"

"I thought I might go by the high school in the morning and find out who my teachers were that last year or two, and which of them are still around. If they remember me, they might be able to give me a better idea of what I was like. Who I hung out with. If I could track down some friends..."

"Back then, your parents said your best friend was a girl named Emily Henson. She might be married or have moved away, but it's worth checking to see if her parents still live in the same place. In fact, let me go grab the phone book."

He found their names for her, and Nell asked if she could take the phone book until she could pick one up. He told her to use his since he rarely did.

Finally she gave him a smile that was made pert with that freckled nose. "So, Captain McAllister, does my itinerary for tomorrow meet your approval?"

He clasped his hands behind his head and leaned back in his chair. "As long as you plan on dinner here so I can hear what you've learned."

"You truly want to know?"

"Yeah." He cleared the gruffness from his throat. "I truly want to know."

She studied him with a puzzlement and worry she couldn't hide, but nodded at length. "I could cook, if you want to tell me when to plan dinner for."

"You're sure?"

"I enjoy cooking. Plus..." Her shoulders jerked. "I owe you. And no," she said before he could argue, "don't bother saying it. Of course I do. Making dinner is the least I can do."

"Okay, but let me give you a key to the house. No, don't argue. You've got a microwave and two burners up in the apartment. No oven, and a minimum of cookware. I've got staples here, plus the pans and what have you that you'll need."

Although alarmed at the idea of entering his

house when he wasn't here, in the end she surrendered, took the key and added it to the ring that held her apartment and car keys. He helped her with her parka, although unlike at her parents' house he could tell the small courtesy flustered her. It was mutual, since touching her flustered him.

She said good-night, and he watched her cross the short distance to the garage. He waited until he saw a light come on before he went back inside and locked the front door.

And yeah, seeing that light kindled a warm spot in him that had never made itself known before.

He lay in bed for a long time before he slept, thinking about the tense reunion at the Dubeaus', about Nell's unease, about her plans and the sense he had that she didn't know what to make of him.

He grunted, there in the darkness, because he didn't know what to make of her, either. His fascination with Maddie he understood, but it wasn't Maddie he was thinking about when he worried about her, or savored the idea of coming home tomorrow night to a woman in his house and good smells coming from the kitchen—and especially not when he found himself eyeing Nell's subtle curves and wondering what she was hiding beneath too-loose clothes.

And then he thought about what she'd hinted at when she talked about her first months trying to survive on the streets of an unfamiliar city, and his gut clenched. He had a bad idea he knew how

Maddie had learned to suppress the memories of home, and when he put that together with some ugly experiences with men when she was on her own... There was a reason, he thought, for those damn sacky clothes. Despite her pleasant demeanor with library patrons, Nell Smith had an aloofness he doubted many people had ever challenged.

It occurred to him she might not have been flustered when he insisted on holding her parka for her. She might have been scared because he was standing too close.

He swore under his breath.

Had Nell Smith ever trusted *anyone?*

Had Maddie?

CHAPTER SIX

"MADDIE DUBEAU." MRS. Chisholm shook her head. "It's really you."

She'd said pretty much the same thing three or four times already, but Nell supposed her shock was understandable. Unfortunately, it made Nell feel like squirming. She hoped she got over it. Everyone who'd known Maddie was going to react pretty much the same way.

Of the teachers she had the fall semester when she disappeared, only three still taught at the high school. Two of those hadn't awakened even a flicker of memory in her.

But the moment she saw the name Eva Chisholm, she'd pictured a raw-boned woman with no sense of style at all pacing in front of the class. Nell felt as though, if she strained, she could hear what Mrs. Chisholm was expounding on that day. In Nell's memory, Mrs. Chisholm was just starting to gray, which made her old in Maddie's eyes. Now, Nell realized the teacher might not even have been fifty.

Nell had slipped into the classroom after a bell rang and the classroom emptied. At the sound of the door, Mrs. Chisholm had glanced over her shoulder from where she was wiping a whiteboard clean. She had taken a couple of stumbling steps, then all but fallen into her chair.

"Maddie?" she had whispered. "Maddie Dubeau?"

Nell was having trouble moving her past the shock.

"You must have a class," she said. "I was hoping I could arrange a time to talk to you."

"This is my planning period. My goodness." She pressed a hand that was large for a woman to her chest. "I can't believe this. We all thought—"

"I know." Nell smiled apologetically. She had already given an encapsulated explanation of the missing years. "I'm hoping…well, to learn more about myself by talking to people who knew me then. The minute I saw your name, I remembered you. That encourages me."

In one way it did. In another, it scared her. Uncovering her history sounded like a good idea. It did. The reality of actually remembering made panic take wing inside her.

"I'm flattered," Mrs. Chisholm said. She was almost homely, with the large bones and big feet and hands Nell remembered. But she also had kind eyes and a rich voice that belonged on public radio. The moment she'd said "Maddie," Nell remembered the way she had read aloud so her students could hear the music in great literature.

"I have a minor in English," she blurted. "I majored in psychology. I think I might have chosen English if I hadn't been trying to figure out my own problems."

Mrs. Chisholm beamed. "That certainly makes sense." She paused. "Out of all my students, you're memorable partly because of what happened, of course."

Nell nodded her understanding. Mrs. Chisholm gestured to her to pull a chair up to the desk. It was, of course, a hard wooden chair with a straight back, the kind you hardly ever saw anymore except in a school. She found herself sitting primly, knees together and hands clasped on her lap. Like a slightly intimidated parent at an after-school conference? Or a student called in to explain her transgressions?

"I would have remembered you anyway," the teacher continued slowly, as if reaching into the past. "You were very bright, of course, and you actually paid attention." She chuckled suddenly. "You were one of the very few students I've ever heard read a part in *Romeo and Juliet* with passion and understanding. Only the once, and after that you were careful to plod along like all the other students did."

"I was teased." Oh, God, she remembered. Emotions came with the memory—embarrassment, but also pride, because Maddie knew she'd been good. Four or five kids had actually applauded when she finished, and they were some of the cool kids. Her cheeks had been hot when she finished, and she had ducked her head both then and as she was leaving the classroom, when someone had muttered, "Suck-up."

Someone else—she could almost see his face—had laughed, not nicely at all. "She's dreaming of being Juliet. There's a joke. What guy would kill himself over *her?*"

Her humiliation had been so acute that she had vowed never to draw attention to herself in class like that again.

She gave an involuntary shiver at how vivid that particular memory was. For a second, she'd been fourteen again. She even knew they had read *Romeo and Juliet* first semester freshman year, not the semester of her disappearance.

Mrs. Chisholm was still dredging up her own memories. "What sticks with me most is that I worried about you. I always have several students who make me anxious for one reason or another, and you were one of them. You had friends, but I wondered if you really opened up to them. You came alive when you read aloud, and sometimes when we had a good class discussion going, but otherwise you were so withdrawn. You always seemed surprised by praise." Her eyes soft, she sounded apologetic. "I'd met both your parents, and you didn't *seem* frightened of them, but…I did speculate. I even hinted a few times that you could tell me anything, and you only looked at me with those sorrowful eyes and said you didn't know what I was talking about."

Nell's throat clogged. "Unfortunately, I still don't know."

"As a teacher, it's terribly frustrating when I know something is wrong and can't do anything about it."

Nell smiled tremulously. "Now I know why I remember you and not most of my other teachers."

"I wish I could have helped then. I'm so very glad to see you here. I can't tell you how sad I was when I read in the newspaper about your bike being found in the park, and the blood, and you simply *gone*. It wasn't what I'd expected, but I felt as if I should have intervened somehow."

"The assault might not have had anything to do with why I was so shy," Nell felt obliged to point out.

Mrs. Chisholm raised her eyebrows. "Do you believe that?"

Nell hesitated. "I wish I knew," she said finally.

She asked if Mrs. Chisholm remembered who her friends were and learned that she had had two best friends, Emily and Hailey. "Allen!" the teacher said triumphantly. "Hailey Allen. My goodness. I'm surprised I remember that. I know Emily went off to college, but I don't recall ever hearing what became of Hailey. Emily recently got married, you know."

Why couldn't she remember her best friend?

"No, I haven't tried to track her down yet."

"Oh, she's still here in Angel Butte. In fact, she became a teacher. She's at one of the elementary schools, I'm afraid I don't remember which. Her husband is a newcomer, a pharmacist."

"Do you remember *his* name?"

She chuckled. "I'm afraid not. The notice of their wedding wouldn't have even caught my eye had it not been for Emily's name and the photo."

They chatted a little more, and Nell promised to come back for another visit before she returned to Seattle. When Mrs. Chisholm rose to her feet, Nell surprised herself by reaching for an impulsive hug.

"Thank you," she whispered, her voice choked.

Her former teacher gave an audible sniff. "You have turned into a fine young woman despite everything. I'm proud of you, Maddie."

Nell came very close to breaking into tears as she backed away, then hurried out of the room.

COLIN EXPECTED TO catch hell from Duane, and wasn't surprised when, midmorning, he burst into Colin's office without knocking.

Face stormy, he slapped his hands on the surface of Colin's desk and leaned forward, his face suffused with anger. "You've been feeding me a load of shit this past month."

Colin leaned back in his chair comfortably and grinned. "Not as long as a month."

Apparently, his good humor only pissed off

Duane. He snarled, "Helen says you've known for weeks."

Colin's smile faded. He could understand how betrayed Maddie's uncle felt. Duane had not only been his mentor, but Colin also considered them to be friends. He'd justified his decision to keep Nell Smith's existence a secret until she said otherwise, but he still suffered some guilt for it.

"I have," he agreed. "I wanted to tell you, but I made a promise to her."

He realized suddenly that Duane's eyes, currently slitted with temper, were nearly the same color as Maddie's. Not a comfortable moment to notice.

But Duane pushed himself upright in an abrupt movement. "Goddamn. Maddie's home."

Exhilaration rose in Colin, making him want to go back to grinning. "I told you I thought she was alive."

The lieutenant scrubbed his hand over the disheveled spikes of his gray hair. "You knew she was when you said that."

"I'd just found her the day before."

"Unbelievable." He sagged into a chair. "Helen said she has some memory problems." His voice expressed uncertainty.

"More than problems. She has amnesia. When she escaped, she didn't remember her own name. Where home was. Who her parents were. All she knew was that somebody had tried to kill her."

"Maybe it was a ransom deal."

They'd talked about this before, and Colin knew Duane didn't believe that explanation any more than he did.

"It was a pretty bad head injury. She's got a hell of a scar. There was a lot of blood, and a concussion severe enough to cause the memory loss. She could have been snatched without being harmed at all. No." He shook his head. "My best guess is, her abductor tossed her in the trunk of his car thinking she *was* dead, or would be by the time he got wherever he was going with her."

Duane's eyes met Colin's. "I got to tell you, I really thought she was dead. I figured you were deluded when you said that, about her being alive."

"I might have, too, if I hadn't talked to her the night before."

"Damn," he said again. After a moment of sitting there looking as if he had been poleaxed, Duane suddenly swiveled in his seat to stare at the bulletin board with the photos of faces Colin wouldn't let himself forget. "You already took her picture down."

"First thing this morning." Colin couldn't keep himself from smiling. He didn't know when anything had last given him more satisfaction than the one small act—pulling the pin from that picture, leaving a blank space where it had been, carrying the photograph to his desk and putting it in a drawer. One victory. He wouldn't have admitted to anyone that he intended to keep the photo close.

"I didn't hear Helen's message until this morning. I didn't believe it until I called her back. That's when I found out my good buddy Captain McAllister had brought Maddie home without letting a soul know what he was up to."

"We're doing this her way." His voice had hardened. Duane needed to know that they were going to keep doing this Maddie's way.

Nell's way.

"She's having lunch today with your sister."

"I know." Duane looked baffled. "Helen says Maddie claims not to remember me."

"She doesn't remember much at all, Duane. When she saw photos of her parents online, they looked familiar, that's all. I don't remember there being a picture of you in the news." No surprise there—their not-so-esteemed leader Bystrom seized every opportunity to speak for the department. In that case, he'd played up his friendship with the Dubeaus, although Colin had never known how real that friendship was.

Duane grunted. "I don't pay attention to crap like that."

"No," Colin said in amusement. "Not your style."

Shaking his head, the older man stood. "Who knew? I guess miracles do happen. I don't have to dig up the goddamn park after all."

Colin laughed. "No." He sobered quick enough, though. "Anything new on those bones?"

"With the ground frozen solid? Hell, no."

"I saw Palmer this morning." Andy Palmer was the unfortunate detective who had been shot by a fellow officer when all he was trying to do was buy diapers on his way home.

"Yeah, he got the go-ahead to come back to work. He's not a happy camper."

Colin raised an eyebrow. "I'm not real happy about him being shot, either."

"Stupid kid should've been fired."

"The kid was still baby-pea green. He shouldn't have been out on his own at all. The incident wasn't his fault."

Duane grunted again. "Just don't stick me with him until I've forgotten his name."

The glass in the door rattled when he left.

Smiling again, Colin glanced at the time on his computer monitor. Was Nell still at the high school? He wondered what she'd learned. At least she should be safe enough there.

Word of her reappearance would spread rapidly, though, and that reawakened his unease. He might suggest she emphasize the amnesia when she talked to people, instead of hinting at the memories that did float through her head. They needed to keep in mind that there was somebody out there who wouldn't like the idea of Maddie Dubeau remembering what happened that night in the park.

Brooding, Colin wished she knew why she'd slipped out of her house and was riding her bike through the dark park. He'd like to feel more confident that she was safe with her parents.

Groaning, he looked at the fat, open personnel file on his desk. He had too much to do to be mentally tracking Nell's every movement.

Nothing to worry about today anyway, he told himself. Certainly not at the high school or at the historic inn where she was to meet her mother for lunch.

Tomorrow, though... Tomorrow, he would really start worrying.

NELL USED THE hour before she was to meet her mother to drive around town. She drove the circular route to the top of Angel Butte and got out at the viewpoint to look at Angel Butte and the volcanic landscape stretching to the horizon in one direction, the Cascade Mountains in the other. There were glimpses of lakes here and there, and when she looked at one she knew suddenly that her father's resort was on the shore.

The angel that gave the town and butte the name gazed serenely out over the same landscape. Eight feet tall, carved of marble. According to local history she had been put in place in 1884. There wasn't much here then but a trading post and stagecoach stop. But farther northeast, in the ranching country around Prineville, a Wild West culture had arisen.

Vigilantes strung supposed wrong-doers up without
the bother of a trial. They came to suspect the man
who ran the trading post of some kind of skulldug-
gery and attempted to hang him. His story was that
an angel appeared to protect him, glowing white
and fierce in her holiness. The vigilantes retreated
in disarray, and the saved man kept a promise and
ordered the marble statue to be shipped all the way
from Italy. Getting it here unbroken was miracle
enough; carrying it up to the crater rim when there
was no road must have taken a dozen men and a
lot of unholy language.

How he could have afforded the gesture was left
unstated. Nobody wanted to challenge a man with
an angel straight from heaven on his side.

The previous name had been Carlson's Butte—
for the first owner of the post and stagecoach inn.
But that quickly disappeared from the records. Everyone knew it as Angel Butte. There she was,
watching over them.

She'd weathered over the years, and, according to the sign telling her history, she had been
hoisted onto her current granite-and-concrete pedestal the year Maddie had turned ten. Trees clinging to the cinder sides of the butte had grown to
the point where the angel could no longer be seen
from below. A little selective logging, plus the pedestal that boosted her up five feet or so, and once
more she commanded a wide swath of Oregon. Nell
thought she remembered a political debate about

whether spending the money for a fancy pedestal was justified. Her father, she thought, had been for it—probably because the angel was good for business.

Turning away, she breathed in the sharp, cold air with its distinct scent that seemed to light up every receptor in her brain. Was it the tang of ponderosa pines? The gritty, volcanic soil? She could stand here inhaling forever, but didn't let herself.

There had been flashes of the familiar in town. A red brick elementary school. Old West–style false-fronted buildings along the main street, decorated with Christmas lights and swags of pine with red bows. There were mostly boutiques and brew pubs and coffee shops instead of the more mundane businesses she could almost remember—a dry cleaner, she thought, old-fashioned cafés, a dime store. The town boasted some distinctive buildings she had read were turn-of-the-last-century, like the original stone-and-brick county courthouse complete with cupola, and the sprawling timber inn where she was to have lunch.

The big Nordic ski development outside town was probably responsible for much of the growth that sprawled even outside the city limits. Someday she would drive out to see it, but not today. She wouldn't find any memories there.

She had to hunt to locate grocery and hardware stores and the like, and suspected most had been downtown but had been displaced because of tourism. Only once did she brake sharply, her heart jolting when she set eyes on a small hardware store with attached lumberyard.

That's where I crawled into the trunk to unlatch the backseat and fold it down.

That memory that had saved her life when she regained consciousness in the trunk.

But she wasn't in the mood to dwell. With glimpses of snow-peaked mountains and the volcanic landscape of lava beds and tree-clad cinder cones, the area was beautiful. No wonder tourists had found this pocket of central Oregon. Despite the cold, she left her window cracked so she could keep smelling the air that called to her.

A light turned red ahead of her and, even as she braked, she had one of those disconcertingly vivid recollections....

The turn signal was on. Click, click, click. Dad was tapping the steering wheel impatiently, too. She slouched in the front seat beside him, wishing Felix was coming, too. Hanging around the resort all day alone would be boring, but better than staying home. Mom had wanted to take her back-to-school shopping. Maddie hated shopping. Mom always picked out clothes she *liked. She didn't even* listen *when Maddie tried to tell her what she liked. Suddenly sulky, she thought,* I'll never be pretty anyway, never. So why does she bother?

Oh, well. Once they reached the resort, Dad wouldn't pay any attention to her. She could feed the chipmunks—she liked doing that. She'd dangle her feet in the lake and lie on her stomach on the slab of rock and watch the silver flash of the minnows as they darted in the clear water. She'd brought a couple of books, too. Sitting in the sun and reading made her happy....

A car horn startled her back to the present. The light had changed to green and she shook herself and started forward cautiously. This time she drove straight to the Newberry Inn and parked, although she made no immediate move to get out.

She was breathing hard. This was like being schizophrenic or having multiple personalities. No, worse, like having *someone else* crawl under her skin. She wanted to remember, but she didn't want to sink into memories so powerful she was there and not here. And they weren't even helpful! They all seemed to be these dumb, random moments when nothing important was happening. Along with this most recent memory came the knowledge that she'd often gone to work with her father during the summer. Mostly, she'd liked going, because otherwise her mother would organize her. Sign her up for activities at the park or the seasonal swim team or—one horrible summer—ballet. Her parents just wouldn't give up. They couldn't understand how she could be so klutzy instead of athletic like her brother.

Nell gripped the steering wheel and thought, *I'm*

just not. Disconcerted, she didn't even know if that thought was hers, or Maddie's.

And to think she'd been envious when the friends in her book club reminisced about playing the clarinet in fifth grade or having to wear the world's ugliest saddle shoes for two whole years to correct flat arches. Or a first kiss to cement a relationship started when his friends told her friends he liked her and she said he could be her boyfriend because he was the fourth cutest boy in the class so why not. Nell didn't have those kinds of memories. *I'm not a whole person,* she used to think. *I must have been normal once, before...whatever it was that happened. Maybe I played the clarinet, too, or the flute. There might have been a first kiss, in fifth or sixth grade.* Except adult Nell looked at her still slight body and plain brown hair and the sprinkle of freckles and doubted any of the boys in fifth or sixth grade had thought of her that way.

Although later, there had been men who wanted a girl who looked even younger than she really was.

She didn't let herself linger on those memories.

Talking and laughing, two women passed in front of her car on the way to the inn, and Nell looked at her watch. Twelve-thirty. Her mother was probably waiting for her.

This was what she was here for, she reminded herself.

So don't be a wuss. Get on with it.

Feeling unexpectedly shaky, she got out, locked the car and followed the women to the front entrance.

AS HE WAITED for the garage door to lift so he could drive in, Colin smiled at the sight of the lights already on in the house.

Crossing the yard a minute later, Colin realized ruefully how unfamiliar this sense of anticipation was. Maybe he'd been an idiot to let memories of his own screwed-up family keep him from ever seriously considering marriage or starting a family of his own. Life was damn lonely without.

Yeah, but how could he asked a woman to marry him when he didn't even want to hold hands with her?

The memory of Nell's small hand in his slid under his guard, disturbing him. As did the thought that he wouldn't have her here now, if he had a wife.

The frown slid away as soon as he turned the key in the lock. At least she'd been smart enough to lock the door after letting herself in.

"It's me," he called, and Nell appeared immediately.

"Dinner will be ready as soon as I cook the spaghetti. I didn't want it to get mushy if you were held up."

He smiled, taking in her appearance. She'd dressed up a little for her day, in slacks and a sort of modern-day version of a twinset. She'd shed her shoes now, though, and was padding around his house in stocking feet. Cute socks—striped purple and school-bus-yellow. Interesting that when her clothing choices were subdued, she'd choose something so loud for the garments she expected to remain unseen. That thought made Colin wonder what her bra and panties looked like.

A stirring of arousal had him trying to block that particular speculation.

"How was your day?" she asked, then wrinkled her nose. "That sounds Stepford-wife, doesn't it? Sorry."

"I like that you asked," he said, tugging at the knot on his tie. "And my day was routine. Let me change clothes."

Once he was more comfortable in jeans and a sweatshirt, he followed the sound of running water to the kitchen.

"Smells good."

"I'm best at Italian. I hope you like it."

"Love it. Is there anything I can do?"

She shook her head, then changed her mind. "I haven't looked for place mats yet, or whatever you use."

"I'll set the table." He didn't tell her he couldn't remember the last time he'd taken a place mat from the drawer in the buffet. He ate at the breakfast bar, rarely lingering. He did cook for himself, unlike when he was younger and more likely to grab a bite on the way home, but he didn't make a production out of the dining part. Why bother, when he was alone?

Steam rose from the stockpot on the stove, and Nell measured out spaghetti and let it slide into the boiling water. Then she stirred the sauce bubbling beside it, tasted a small sample and said, "Yum."

His stomach grumbled.

"I'm amazed at how much the town has grown," Nell commented, clearly feeling the need to make conversation. "My memory is good enough to know it didn't look like this when I left."

"No. I've been here while the growth happened, and still have moments of disbelief."

"Is it all because of the new Nordic Center?"

"That was a catalyst, but the tourist industry in this entire region of central Oregon is booming. We're getting a lot of retirees, too. Good medical care, clean air, plenty of recreational and cultural opportunities. Bend and Sun River have gotten so expensive, newcomers started looking to towns like La Pine and Angel Butte, up north to Redmond. The skiers still have reasonable access to Mount Bachelor, but they can live a little cheaper and with less crowding."

"If you say so." She wrinkled her nose. "I'll concede Angel Butte doesn't look like Seattle or the suburbs yet, although there's more resemblance than there used to be." She turned off one burner. "Do you want to dish up at the stove, or should I use serving bowls?"

"We can dish up here. Let's save on the washing up."

She grinned impishly at him. "Is that because I'm the cook and therefore you're the washer-upper?"

Wow. An emotion he hardly understood slammed him, leaving him unable to give her a light answer. This was the first time he'd seen her face relaxed, her eyes alight with humor. Was this what she'd been like before, with a few words, he'd threatened the life she so carefully built?

I know you.

He had been so damn happy to find her, he hadn't let her obvious fear and resistance stop him.

"What's wrong?" she whispered, and he realized her smile had vanished and she was staring at him with wide-eyed alarm.

"Nothing." Self-recrimination came a little late, didn't it? And he still didn't know whether she was better off recovering her past. "I'm sorry. It was, uh, the way you were smiling. I haven't seen you do a lot of that."

Her eyes searched his. "You haven't seen me at my best."

He remembered the snippet captured by the television camera, when she'd spoken so softly with that pathetically young and very pregnant teenager, then hugged her so gently.

"I wouldn't say that." He cleared his throat. "Just…not happy, I guess. That's what hit me.

Maybe you were before I blew your safe little world out of the water."

"The first day, that's what I thought... Oh!" she exclaimed, turning to the stove. She mumbled to herself in obvious exasperation as she snatched the heavy pan off the burner.

Once they'd dished up and sat down, he got her talking about her day. The nuances of her voice were familiar, but now he could watch the flickers of expression on her face, too. During their phone calls he'd craved the sight of her.

She told him about the two teachers she'd managed to talk to, one of whom she didn't remember at all and who she thought remembered her only because of the publicity surrounding her disappearance. Her face softened when she talked about the other teacher, though, a Mrs. Chisholm.

"She was the best. Even I hadn't managed to forget her," she said with a little laugh. "We hugged, and she had tears in her eyes."

"Hey..." Fork halfway to his mouth, he paused. "I had a Mrs. Chisholm for freshman English. Big, strong woman?"

"That's her."

"Oh, God. *Romeo and Juliet*."

She giggled. Solemn Nell Smith giggled. "Did she make you read Romeo?"

"Mercutio. Turns out he was a mumbler."

Her face was still bright with laughter. "That fulsome language scared you, did it?"

"I felt like an idiot. Unfortunately, everyone else did, too. Had to be the worst Shakespeare read-aloud ever."

"I know what you mean. But when *she* read Shakespeare or anything else…"

"Yeah, she had a voice, didn't she?" His asshole father had met her during a rare showing at a parent-teacher conference, and on his way home he'd suggested she could have made big bucks working for a sex hotline. Colin remembered cringing. Mrs. Chisholm and sex, in the same sentence? Of course, after that he couldn't get it out of his head and a couple of times had closed his eyes and tried to imagine while she read aloud. His conclusion was that he would never, no matter how desperate, call one of those numbers. The sexy voice on the other end could be from an eighty-year-old grandmother. Or—God—Mrs. Chisholm.

After a minute, he asked Nell how lunch with her mother had gone and saw her expression shut down.

"It was…fine." She scowled. "No, *weird* is a better word. I've had friendlier get-togethers with parents who were mad we'd taken their kid into SafeHold. She was so distant. And I kept thinking she must know other people having lunch at the inn. I was braced for her to introduce me around and what the reaction would be. But we sat by a window, out of the way, and she didn't say anything to anybody. I got to wondering whether she'd requested the table in advance so she didn't *have* to introduce me."

She was trying to hide the hurt, but not completely succeeding. As if fear and pain stripped her of some layers, she always looked younger at moments like this. More like the Maddie whose picture had been on his bulletin board for so many years, he couldn't help thinking. Maddie meant nothing good to Nell Smith. The understanding made him feel guiltier than ever.

Colin didn't blame her for hurting at her mother's coolness, either. His father was abusive, his mother walked out on him, but at least there'd been emotion in his house. Good, hideous, everything in between. Then, he'd thought anything would be better. Now, he wasn't so sure, not when he saw Nell's face so pale that the freckles stood out in sharp relief.

To think how much sympathy he'd wasted on the Dubeaus, terrified for their daughter, mourning her—or so he'd thought.

"Back then," he said slowly, "I noticed your mother always hung back at public appearances. I thought she was in shock and trying hard not to break down where she could be seen. I respected her dignity."

"And now you wonder if she was feeling anything at all."

"I guess that is what I'm wondering."

Nell twirled spaghetti with great concentration

but didn't lift it to her mouth. "I had this really vivid memory today," she said haltingly. "Nothing important, but I knew in it that I was a disappointment to my parents, and especially my mother. Not pretty enough, not athletic or graceful. I was relieved that I was going to the resort to hang out all day partly because it got me away from Mom."

"I'm sorry," he said gently.

She bent her head. "I am, too."

He made sure the conversation was more general until they finished eating, but when she stood and said she would put the coffee on, he shook his head.

"There's something we need to talk about first."

She sank back into her chair, her eyes locked on his. "That doesn't sound good."

"I don't suppose you'll like it," he admitted. "It occurred to me today that rumors are going to start spreading like wildfire. You'll run into people you've completely forgotten but who recognize you. Let's head off the necessity of you having to explain yourself over and over by holding a press conference."

She gaped.

"We'll bring your parents in on it. We have a daily newspaper, Bend does, of course, and La Pine has a weekly. A stringer for the *Oregonian* will show up. Local TV news. Let's get it over with in a controlled venue." Seeing her horror, he wished he could shield her from all of this. And by God he wished her parents had fallen on her with tears and joy. "You can't stay incognito anymore, Nell," he said, regret sounding in his voice.

"No, I know. It's just—" The huff of breath might have been meant to be a laugh. "The day the KING-5 news team was filming at SafeHold, I was trying to avoid the camera. On the way home, I was thinking about it. I've always worried about encountering someone who knew me." She grimaced. "You know that. Because I haven't changed all that much. But I also know that I wouldn't have wanted to appear on camera, no matter what. Public recognition wouldn't have been my thing. Then what did I do? I made myself famous."

"You didn't make yourself famous," he said through gritted teeth. "None of it was your doing."

She shrugged in acknowledgment. He knew what she was thinking. Yes, it was still possible that some action of hers had led to the assault and abduction. He couldn't imagine what action that could have been. She'd been a good girl, not a troublemaker. Even if she had been…she was fifteen years old. A kid.

"Word will get out no matter what," he repeated. "If we don't do it this way, you're going to have reporters waylaying you everywhere you go. That might be worse."

"I don't know." Expression closing down, she jumped to her feet and began clearing the table.

Colin didn't push it. He helped her clear, then

loaded the dishwasher while she put leftovers in the refrigerator.

Finally, as she was pouring the coffee, her back to him, Nell said abruptly, "Okay. You're right. How bad can it be?"

He hadn't forgotten the hysteria back then, but refrained from saying, *It won't be good.*

Once again, Maddie Dubeau would be a nine-day wonder.

CHAPTER SEVEN

NELL WOKE THE next morning to find the world outside cloaked in white. Colin had said something about expecting a trace of snow, but this was more than that. For a moment she felt a child's sense of wonder at the quiet beauty. An occasional tiny flake still floated down, adding to the powder snow that made Mount Bachelor a world-renowned destination ski resort. Standing at the window looking out, she could tell from the set of tracks cutting through the smooth sheet of snow that Colin had already departed for work.

That was all it took, the sight of those tracks, to make her think about him. The better she got to know him, the more of a puzzle he became for her. Part of it was him, the man with the hard face and intense eyes who could still be so gentle that all of her certainties were shaken. The coward in her wanted to believe that gentleness was a lie. She could hold more of herself back if she was sure he was intent on manipulating her.

But Nell didn't believe it. He'd been too honest with her. By asking her to stay here, opening his

home to her, he'd also opened his life. She'd seen
the yearning on his face when he talked about his
sister. Nell was still stunned that he had held her
hand at her parents'. He hadn't bothered to worry
about the way her parents would interpret it. Resting her forehead against the cold glass, she closed
her eyes and remembered how that hand had felt,
engulfing hers. She shivered at another memory, of
him standing close to her, his fingers delving into
her hair and stroking so gently over that old scar.
She'd been sorry when he stepped away.

In fact, she'd felt something so unfamiliar, it
wasn't until later, lying in bed, that she had identified it as sexual attraction.

A few times she had wondered if he were feeling something similar, but she wasn't sure. Maybe
it would be better if she never found out. She had
always known that, if she ever came to trust a man
enough to want the kind of relationship she saw
other people having, she would have to tell him
more about her past. The part that would repulse
most decent men.

But he had hinted that he knew and understood.
*He thinks of me as Maddie. He's been obsessed
with Maddie.*

No matter what, that wasn't who she was anymore.

It would be better not to think of Colin that
way, even if he were the only man who had ever

made her feel safe. Safe enough to feel…well, other things, too.

I'll wait and see, she decided practically, and turned from the window to get herself breakfast.

Nell had eaten and was sipping the tea she preferred to coffee when she thought to check her phone. He'd left her a message.

"I made some calls, including a talk with your father. We're set for two o'clock at the police station. It's no longer next to the old courthouse." He gave the address. "Why don't you aim to get here at least half an hour early? We can talk about the kind of questions you'll be asked, how you want to answer." There was a long enough pause for her to think he might be done, but then he added, his voice subtly different, "If you go out, be careful, Nell."

Sitting locked in this apartment was not an option, certainly not this morning. All she would do was freak out about the upcoming press conference or think about Colin, the man. She needed a distraction.

Last night she'd searched Facebook for Emily Henson and Hailey Allen. She now knew the name of Emily's husband—Jason Barr—and had even seen a picture of him, albeit one taken with her when they'd apparently been mountain biking and were tousled, sweaty and laughing. He looked nice: thin, with sandy-blond hair and wire-rimmed glasses. Emily's face produced nothing as concrete as a memory, but it looked familiar and Nell felt a funny stir of emotion. She had lingered a long time on Emily's Facebook page.

She'd also found Hailey Allen and learned that, unlike Emily, who had gone away for college, Hailey had never left the area. After finishing a two-year program in culinary arts at Central Oregon Community College, she'd gone to work in a restaurant in Bend. A year or two ago she had opened her own restaurant in Angel Butte. Nell must have gone right by it yesterday.

Hailey might not have much time to chat, but Nell intended to drop by this morning and at least say hello.

She'd peered for some time at the pictures of Hailey, too, trying to reconcile them with any of the faces swimming through her damaged memory, but failed. It might only be that she looked different than she had at fifteen years old. Her hair was currently short, spiky and dyed shocking pink, plus she seemed to be clowning around in all the pictures on her page. Nell hoped seeing her in person would trigger something. It would be awkward to have to say, *I'm told we were friends, but I don't remember you at all.*

Of course, if she stayed in town long, she was going to have to get used to admitting that to a lot of people. In fact, last night Colin had said he'd be happiest if she made her amnesia sound even deeper than it really was.

She'd snapped, "Thanks, way to make me feel

safe," and told him good-night, marching through the cold to the apartment in what she told herself was a temper, but knew was closer to a new and improved anxiety attack.

What he didn't realize was how completely vulnerable she already felt. The idea of other people knowing her on a level she didn't even know herself, while she had no memory at all of them, made her want to curl up into a little ball like a hedgehog with all her quills bristling. Except she didn't have anything as useful as quills to protect her.

I have Colin.

He had definitely appointed himself her guardian, although she wasn't entirely sure why. That was part of what worried her, of course. Perhaps he'd realized right away that he would never be able to lure her back to Angel Butte unless he could convince her that he could keep her safe. Nell didn't like to think he'd wanted to produce her like a rabbit from a hat only so he'd look like a wizard on the job. Was he hoping for some kind of promotion?

But she didn't believe that his satisfaction and amazement at finding her were that self-centered. She thought he'd believed there were people here who had grieved and needed to know she had survived. The fact that *he* seemed to be one of those people still puzzled her, even as it made her feel soft inside. She might not understand, but she was clinging to the knowledge that, for whatever reason, she really mattered to him.

And she was depending almost entirely on him. Nell Smith, who never let herself really depend on anyone. Until him, she had never told a single person that she didn't remember who she was or where she came from.

It wasn't smart to need anyone so much. Which was one of the reasons she had to continue exploring her history on her own. The more she learned, the less vulnerable she'd be.

A YOUNG WAITRESS with half a dozen studs climbing each ear plus a nose ring wanted to seat Nell the minute she walked into the Kingfisher Café.

"I do want lunch," Nell said, "but I'm actually hoping to see Hailey. I'm an old friend."

"Oh!" The girl's face brightened. "I'll go get her. Um…what did you say your name is?"

Nell hesitated. "I'd like to surprise her."

"Cool!"

Fingers biting into her palms, Nell waited until a woman emerged from the back. She was short, a little plump and big-breasted. The spiky hair was hot pink like in the pictures, her expression inquiring, her face quirky and interesting.

Nell would have thought her a complete stranger if she hadn't known better.

Hailey Allen's shock was becoming familiar although it still made Nell wince.

"Maddie?"

"Yes." She tried for a smile. "Back from the dead."

"Oh, my God. Emily didn't call me."

She registered that Hailey assumed she would contact Emily first. Because they'd been closer friends?

"I haven't gotten in touch with her yet. I figured she'd be in school today, and, well, once I saw on Facebook that you had a restaurant…"

Hailey began to cry and reached out to hug Nell, who after an instant squeezed back. Someone else who was genuinely glad to see her. *So why don't I know her?*

Once Hailey had wiped her tears away, she led Nell to a booth at the back. "Sit," she demanded. "Talk. What *happened* to you?"

Colin's caution ran through Nell's mind. In this case, saying she didn't remember wouldn't be a lie. "All I know is that I was assaulted," she said. She explained about having come to in the trunk of a car, her escape and the amnesia that had kept her from making her way home.

"I saw Mrs. Chisholm yesterday," she concluded. "She told me about you and Emily."

"Told you…" Hailey's expression changed. "You mean, you still don't remember?"

"I'm afraid not. I have some scattered, completely unhelpful memories. At least I sort of knew my parents. And I can see my brother's face. So far, not much else." Which wasn't entirely a lie. "I'm… hoping you and Emily can tell me about the Maddie you knew."

"Well…of course we will. But how bizarre."

Nell rolled her eyes. "Tell me about it."

"But you know your name."

"I didn't until a few weeks ago." She explained about how Colin had found her. "When he said my name…" Her heart still clenched every time she thought about that moment. "I knew."

"Your parents must be over the moon. Flyers with your picture were posted everywhere. Your dad offered a reward for any information."

"I'm supposed to do a press conference this afternoon. The police officer's idea. I'm dreading it," she admitted.

Hailey jumped to her feet and insisted Nell have lunch before the ordeal. "I can sit with you for a few minutes. Oh! And I'll give you Emily's cell phone number. This is going to blow her away. I know she'll want to see you tonight."

Nell had a chicken sandwich with a spicy chipotle sauce and a cup of lentil soup that was amazing.

"I always loved to cook," Hailey told her. "Do you remember…? Um, I guess not. Half the time we hung out at my house so I could bake. The café is best known for the pastries." She wrinkled her nose. "I guess you can tell I like to eat my pastries, too."

"Were we friends for a long time?"

Hailey shook her head. "No, only from freshman year on. My family moved here that summer. Starting high school where I didn't know anyone was awful. You and Emily adopted me right away, though. Emily and I are still friends. Not as close— you know how it is, she went away to college and I work long hours and now she has Jason—but we stay in touch and get together maybe once a month or so. Text and talk sometimes. We got even closer after you disappeared. Where there'd been three there were two," she said apologetically. "It was actually weird. For a while, we were like rock stars. Everyone was so awed because we were friends with you, and they thought we must know something nobody else did. The police talked to us a bunch of times."

Nell tensed but tried not to show it. "Did you know anything nobody else did?"

"None of our lives were that exciting. Except after, I thought…" She stopped, gave a funny shrug. "I don't know. Emily and I hardly ever came to your house, even though you had such a cool one. My parents didn't have nearly as much money. You'd say things about your mom, but not that much. We both knew things weren't good at home for you. So at first I wondered if you'd just run away. But then we never heard from you and the police didn't find you, so I was afraid the wrong person had offered to help you run away, if you know what I mean."

Everyone, it seemed, had known Maddie was unhappy. Everyone, that is, except her parents, who either hadn't noticed or didn't care. And who, most likely, were the cause of her unhappiness.

Hailey told her the three of them listened to music a lot. "Teenybopper stuff. Britney Spears, *NSYNC, Aaron Carter. You had such a crush on him! Do you remember…?" She made a horrible face. "Aagh! There I go again. Sorry, sorry! I keep forgetting." Her eyes widened even more. "My mouth always runs away from me," she wailed. "I need to delete the words *forget* and *remember* from my vocabulary."

Laughter burst from Nell. Hailey's expression made her laugh even harder. Finally, she dabbed at her cheeks with her napkin. "Thank you. That felt good. And don't be silly. I *want* you to remind me of stuff. Please don't feel like you have to watch what you say." She laughed again. "Aaron Carter, huh? Didn't he get arrested not long ago?"

Hailey grinned. "I read about that. Please tell me you're not still into the same kind of music."

"That's safe to say. I like a lot of alternative stuff. Seattle has some great bands."

"Yes! Ooh. We'll have to share tastes." Her gaze went past Nell. "But not now. You need to go if you're going to be there at one-thirty. And I'm getting signaled from the kitchen."

Hailey refused payment, and they hugged again. This time it felt less awkward to Nell. It wasn't only the warm greeting. *I like her,* she thought. *We'd be friends if we met now.*

Hailey was the first person to make Nell feel

better about who Maddie had been. At least she'd known how to pick friends.

NOT WANTING TOO much advance buzz, and especially not wanting to give his boss any warning, Colin had taken a businesslike approach when he set up the press conference. Cold case closed, he'd said, although that wasn't quite true, of course. He wouldn't be closing the file on Maddie Dubeau's abduction until he was satisfied he knew who had struck her in the head, dragged her off the bike and dumped her in the trunk of a car with the intention of ultimately raping her, ransoming her or burying her. Maybe *and* burying her.

Colin stood behind the table, watching the dozen or so people either sit down or position themselves with cameras. He had Nell and her parents stashed away until he summoned them. Basic theatrical technique. Scanning the faces looking at him, he tried to remember how many of these reporters were old-timers and would recognize Maddie immediately. Three or four, he thought. Ahh—Bystrom was hustling in at the back, looking pissed. Colin had been happy that morning to find the chief was taking the second "personal day" in a row. All the same, Colin had left a voice mail and sent an email to cover his ass. Apparently the rumor had wafted to whatever ski hill Bystrom had been on that morning. At the moment, the city's police chief was shaking his head at some reporters who'd rushed to cut him off. He wouldn't be denying any knowledge, not Bystrom. Hell, no. He'd want to convince them he knew all and was only being mysterious.

Even though Duane had to be itching to see Maddie, Colin hadn't expected him here. Duane wouldn't want to expose his emotions to the press.

Colin remained standing. He didn't need the microphone set on the table. His voice carried.

"Thank you for coming," he said, pausing only until he had complete silence. "As I believe you're all aware, I'm Captain McAllister, Investigation and Support Services. Some of you may remember the name Maddie—Madeline—Dubeau."

Not hard to see the stir of interest.

"For those of you who don't remember—" He recapped the basic facts. "This was one of the most disturbing crimes ever committed in a town we like to consider safe. Any law enforcement officer will tell you he or she most hates crimes involving children. Maddie Dubeau was only fifteen at the time of her disappearance. She was a sophomore in high school and excited because she had just gotten a driver's permit." He paused. "We have found Maddie Dubeau."

"Is the body found in the park the Dubeau girl's?" called a reporter, whose voice rose above other shouted questions.

In answer, Colin opened the door behind the curved row of seats for council members and nodded at the three people waiting. "We're ready for you."

Nell swallowed visibly. Her eyes flashed to his for reassurance, and he smiled, not knowing if that was what she needed but hoping it helped.

She looked good today. Really good. She'd worn drapey black pants and a T-shirt in a silky, rust-colored knit beneath a cropped black blazer. For the first time, he had a good idea of the size and shape of her breasts and was almost sorry, because he wouldn't be able to get that new knowledge out of his head. Gold studs in her ears, her hair bundled in some careless way on the back of her head. Having it pulled back emphasized the catlike triangle of her face and the sharpness of her cheekbones. Subtly applied makeup enhanced those extraordinary eyes. He'd felt pride and more—throat-closing more—when he saw her. He wondered if her parents had felt similarly, but saw immediately that they'd assumed their public faces. Oh, yeah, they would gush about the joy and relief at having their beloved daughter home again. He felt sure there'd be no mention of the fact that neither could be bothered to hug her yet.

The stir became something a lot more when the reporters set eyes on the Dubeau family. Even a dozen—no, fifteen—people could make a hell of a lot of noise when they got excited. Camera shutters clicked and the questions kept coming. Colin waited until Nell sat right beside him, her parents beyond her.

Then he held up a hand for silence. "Ms. Dubeau has a short statement. After she has given it, she and her parents will take a few questions. Please wait until she is done to ask them."

He touched her shoulder when he would have liked to squeeze it. Allowed his hand to drop to his side when he wanted to maintain contact. He knew how scared she was, but her head stayed high.

"Thank you, Captain McAllister." She surveyed the room, meeting eyes. "I mean that in more than one way. It is the captain who found me and encouraged me to come home to Angel Butte."

She explained, making the story simple, leaving out plenty. She did not say what name she had been living under or where she'd been living. "Unfortunately," she concluded, "much of my memory is still lost. I do not know what happened the night I was attacked. I don't know why I was riding my bike through the park. What scattered memories I have are trivial, much like what I suspect most people remember from their early childhoods. Only a flash—a scene, a feeling, sometimes only an impression. I'm hoping to spend a few weeks getting to know my family and friends again." She took a deep breath. "My parents and I will take questions now."

The questions flew. Did she intend to stay in Angel Butte? "Probably not," she said with brevity and dignity. Could she tell them about her life now? "I work in a library and hope to go back to graduate school for a master's degree in library and information science," she said, the constraint in her voice obvious. "I also volunteer actively at a shelter for teenage runaways." Why? Did she believe she'd been running away? "No, but I do have the experience of being homeless and struggling to survive." She declined to say where she lived or the name of that shelter. No, she preferred not to say what name she had been living under.

Marc Dubeau's voice got husky as he described the shock and joy of having his daughter returned to her family. "We held out hope for a long time, but had come to believe she must be dead. Near-complete amnesia is so unusual, it never crossed my mind as an explanation. What Captain McAllister did not tell you is that he was also first responder the night she disappeared. He is the officer who found Maddie's wallet with her driver's permit still in it. It seems…fitting that he is the one to bring her home. My wife and I…" His voice broke. He cleared it and wiped at damp eyes. "I can only tell you we are grateful to him beyond description."

Helen said little, but cast occasional, tremulous smiles at her daughter.

Colin got madder by the minute. He kept an eye on Nell, but couldn't bring himself to look at her parents.

By the time he finally brought the thing to a

close, he wasn't surprised to see that Bystrom had edged his way to the front, where he shook Marc's hand and kissed Helen's cheek before beaming at Nell. He made sure his good side was to the cameras. He circled the table and bent as if to kiss Nell's cheek, too, but she shrank back enough to give even him pause.

To hell with it. Colin put his hand back on her shoulder. The quivering tension he felt beneath his fingers eased a little. He kept his hand right where it was, not giving a damn what anyone else thought.

Bystrom placed his back to any cameras. His eyes glittered with fury. "Grandstanding?" he murmured only for Colin.

Colin's eyebrows rose. "I let you know as soon as we made the decision to hold a press conference."

"We'll talk about this later," he snapped and turned back to exude good-old-boy geniality for the benefit of Dubeau and the lingering reporters and cameras.

Doing his best to keep his dislike from his voice, Colin introduced the chief to Nell.

She politely shook his hand. "I gather you know my parents?"

His smile was Photoshop-perfect, expressing both delight and sadness because she didn't remember him. "I'd go so far as to say you considered me another uncle when you were a child." Of course he made damn sure his voice carried.

Even Marc, bullshit artist, gave Bystrom a sardonic glance.

"I'm so sorry I don't remember you," she murmured.

Her mother laid a hand on her arm. "Dear, perhaps we should slip out before one of these reporters tries to corner you."

"I'll walk you out," Colin said.

"I'll see you in my office in five minutes," his boss said.

"Chief." He nodded with a minimum of civility. "Maddie?"

She gave him a startled look. "Ma— Oh. I'm ready."

They all retrieved coats and gloves, then started out. Nell accepted his casual hand on her back as they walked. A couple of sharp looks came from Dubeau, but he said nothing until they reached his Lexus.

"McAllister." He held out a hand. "I meant what I said. You have our undying gratitude."

"That's not necessary." Colin shook anyway. "It was chance I saw Maddie on TV. Luck."

"Nonetheless."

"Yes, indeed. Maddie, would you have dinner with us tonight? It might be a good chance for you to see Duane, too." Helen Dubeau gazed at her daughter with a wisp of something that might have been yearning. Real or pretend? Colin asked himself cynically.

"I've planned to get together with Emily and Hailey tonight. Can we make it tomorrow instead?"

"Oh. Of course." Helen's smile was obviously forced. "I didn't realize Hailey was still in town."

The sky was a pale, pearly gray, but snow had quit falling. The little that had stuck after the parking lot was plowed in the early morning squeaked underfoot. After leaving the Dubeaus at their car, Colin kept a hand lightly resting on Nell's arm in case she slipped as they headed for her shabby little Ford.

"Glad that's over?" he asked.

She let out an explosive breath that formed an icy cloud. "I cannot tell you." She looked up anxiously at him. "Did I do okay?"

"You were fantastic," he told her sincerely. "You handled the questions just right." Her dignity, combined with a quality of emotional fragility, had had the impact he'd hoped for—those reporters had gotten quieter toward the end, more respectful. Now, if only they would give her space. But he didn't tell her any of that. She wouldn't like the word *fragile* applied to her, and he wasn't sure it was even accurate. The very fact she'd survived twelve years ago meant she had guts and the smarts to make good decisions. Her willingness to come home despite her fear reinforced his opinion of her.

"You called me Maddie," she said softly.

There was something in her voice he couldn't quite identify. "You went out of your way not to tell anyone about Nell. I thought we should keep it that way."

"Thank you." She unlocked and opened her car door, but didn't get in right away. "Are you in trouble?"

"With Chief Bystrom?" When she nodded, he gave a shrug. "Our dislike is mutual. There's nothing he'll be able to do."

"Because you're the hero who brought Maddie Dubeau home."

He smiled. "Exactly. What he doesn't like is not being the ringleader for this circus. I thought you needed me there instead of him."

She shuddered. "Yes. Is he really somebody I should remember?"

"Your parents were friends with him and his wife," he said slowly, but, damn it, he didn't like the expression on her face. Had seeing Gary Bystrom triggered an unpleasant subliminal memory? "How close, I don't know. I take it you don't remember him at all?" He kept his tone casual.

"Not even a whisper. I just didn't like him."

"Okay. And you read him right. He's a jackass. Not something I should say aloud."

Her quick flicker of a grin made his heartbeat stumble. Colin hesitated, then bent his head and kissed her cheek. Her skin was cold but soft. He didn't let himself linger or wish she'd turn her head so their mouths met. "I'll see you at home," he said, straightening, hoping she didn't notice that he sounded a little hoarse.

Her gaze was startled and shy. "If you'd like, I can make dinner again." Her forehead puckered. "But you might not want company tonight. If not, that's fine. I'll just have a snack before I go out."

"I would love to have company." He made sure she could tell he meant it. "We even have leftovers. But I thought you were getting together with your friends."

"Maybe after dinner. I haven't even talked to Emily yet."

"Okay." He smiled and stepped back. "Drive carefully."

He walked far enough so she wouldn't notice he'd stopped, then turned to watch Nell carefully maneuver out of the parking slot and into the street. Had she been more shaken by being put on display than she'd let him see? Damn it, he should be driving her home, but of course it was too late.

Not until her car was out of sight did he sigh and head back in to face his irate commander.

CHAPTER EIGHT

"I CAN'T BELIEVE you're here." Emily shook her head in obvious bemusement. "And the three of us together again."

Emily and her new husband had recently bought a house in town only a block from the river. It reminded Nell a little too much of the Dubeau home, although this one was more modest. She could tell, though, that it was as dignified and gracious as Emily herself. Nell couldn't help thinking this was the daughter her own parents had wanted her to be.

Emily sat now in a wing chair, a pretty, elegant woman with her masses of blond hair worn up in a simple twist. She'd kicked off her shoes, but beneath slacks she wore tights or knee socks with an elaborate pattern of climbing vines.

It hadn't been her face so much as her Princess Grace carriage that brought back Nell's first memory of her.

"I used to tease you and insist your mom must make you walk around with a heavy book on your head for an hour a day," she blurted.

Both women stared at her. "You remember," Hailey whispered.

After a moment, Emily burst into delighted laughter. "Yes! After the first time you said that, I tried it." She wrinkled her nose, reducing the air of dignity. "I was really good at it."

They all laughed now.

Hailey sat on the carpeted floor, her back to one end of the sofa and her knees drawn up. She wore ragged, faded jeans and was engulfed by what looked like a man's sweater that had reached midthigh before she'd sunk to the floor. If she'd started the day with any makeup, it was gone. Maybe the bright hair was statement enough.

Seeing the two of them, the contrast, did bring hazy memories.

"Why were we friends?" she asked, then blushed as she realized how untactful that sounded. "I mean, Emily, you're so chic and I'm not."

"And I'm *really* not," Hailey chimed in.

A smile curved Emily's mouth. "You should remember," she said to Hailey before looking at Nell. "I looked like…like the classic flagpole even in eighth grade. I'm five foot eleven, you know. I *towered* over everyone, boys included, from kindergarten on. And I had these big feet." She lifted one in demonstration. Yes, it was probably a size eleven. "My mother kept saying—with thinly veiled desperation—that everyone would envy me someday, because I'd have the face and figure of a high fash-

ion model." That merry laugh rang out again. "That
didn't quite happen, but at least I did, eventually,
acquire some figure."

Hailey grinned at her, their intimacy momentarily excluding Nell. "But not until you were sixteen."

Emily smiled at Nell, erasing her momentary
feeling of loneliness. "I thought I'd *never* get my
period. Or meet a guy who's taller than me and
doesn't love having a girl he can cuddle against
his chest." Her fond gaze wandered toward the
kitchen, where they all heard the sound of running water. Nell had met Jason when she arrived
and liked him immediately. He wasn't that much
taller than Emily—six foot one or two, maybe—
and lean to the point of being skinny. He was also
gentle, friendly and obviously in love with his wife.
The way he'd looked at her had made Nell feel a
pang of envy. He'd chatted for a minute and then
excused himself, leaving the women alone.

"It's true," Hailey said. "The three of us were
sort of misfits, in different ways. Emily got over
it. I never did." She didn't sound as if she minded.

"I felt like a misfit." Nell knew that much. "Always so awkward, so…"

When she hesitated, Emily finished her sentence.
"So unsure of yourself."

Nell blinked. She'd expected to hear "so sad."
This at least was different. It also fit with her recently recovered memories. "Yes" was all she said.

"My mother kept bucking me up," Emily continued, her expression compassionate. "I'm pretty sure yours tore you down instead."

"Yes," she said again. She had ducked her head in a way that was uncomfortably familiar. *I still do that,* she realized in dismay. *Hiding.* "I wish I knew why."

"Maybe you should ask her," Hailey suggested. She, too, was watching Nell with kindness and sympathy.

Nell managed a smile. "Maybe I will."

"You were the first one of us to have a boyfriend, you know," Emily said slowly. Her forehead was crinkled a little.

"What?" Nell's heartbeat picked up speed and everything in her clenched with intense anxiety.

"Wow," Hailey said. She and Emily both were looking at her in puzzlement. "I'd forgotten. You talked about him, but I never saw him."

"I did, once, but only because I ran into you two by accident." A tiny hint of old hurt sounded in Emily's voice. "You'd barely told us about him. I guess it was new, but…"

"Who?" She swallowed. "Who was it?"

Emily shook her head. "That's the thing. He didn't go to school with us. You said he was older, like sixteen or seventeen. You thought he really liked you."

"How could he not have gone to school with us?"

Nell asked, trying to understand. "Was there a private school or something?"

"You said he was on his own. Like a dropout? Truthfully, it freaked me out. This guy you were keeping secret, who didn't even go to school? Or—wow—was even older than he'd told you. Later, I told the police about him, but I don't know if they ever found him."

Oxygen seemed to be short in the room. It was a struggle to make herself sound collected and only mildly surprised. "Maybe I made him up."

But Emily was shaking her head again. "Uh-uh. 'Cuz I *did* see him. He was actually pretty cute. At least, I thought so then." She grimaced. "All I remember is that he had dark hair and brown eyes and he was dressed kind of scruffy and he seemed alarmed by me."

"I don't remember him at all." *I don't.*

Then why am I scared to death? As if...

She didn't know. Only that this boy meant something.

"Did I tell you his name?"

Emily's forehead crinkled as she thought. "It would be in the police report. Buck. No." Her face cleared. "Beck. That was it. You never said a last name, though. Maybe Beck *was* his last name."

"You're right." Nell made a face. "My mother would have had a cow."

They talked about other things for a few minutes, and when Hailey excused herself Nell said good-night, too. Although she liked both of these friends, tonight she felt agitated and overwhelmed.

Beck.

Snow was falling again by the time she and Hailey left, but this time in big wet globs. The walkway and street were already slushy-looking. Emily had apologized because she and Jason had to park in the driveway. The garage, apparently, was full of unpacked stuff; combining separate households meant they had duplicates of lots of household items, plus furniture they hadn't decided whether to keep or not. "I swear, by next winter," she had said when they first arrived, "I want an empty garage and a remote control opener."

Hailey had parked at the curb in front of the house, Nell across the street, having wedged her small car in between two hulking SUVs. Hardly anyone in town drove a car, she'd noticed, never mind one as modest and aging as hers. Four-wheel drive seemed to be a necessity, and she was beginning to see why. Even Hailey hopped into a Subaru Forester. She was already halfway down the block when Nell started across the street, stepping carefully. Even so, icy dampness penetrated to her toes. She really needed new boots.

She was midstreet when she heard the roar of an engine. Somebody was driving *way* too fast. For an instant, confused, she came to a stop. It was so dark, with the falling snow obscuring porch lights and streetlights. No headlights touched her.

Then she saw it, huge, black and bearing down on her. Fueled by a shot of adrenaline, she tried to run, but her traction wasn't great in these boots, either, and she slipped and almost went down. It was terror that kept her on her feet and had her running and then throwing herself into the narrow gap between her front bumper and the white SUV she'd parked behind. She hit her shoulder on the way down and ended up splayed on the pavement between vehicles. The monstrous black SUV or pickup or *something* passed so close she braced herself for the scrape of metal. It didn't come. What felt like an angry roar receded.

Wet and cold, bruised and probably scraped, she nonetheless scrambled to her knees and then her feet. Instinct drove her to get into her car, lock the doors, get away.

Run, run, run.

But oh, God— Where were her keys? She'd had them clutched in her gloved hand.

Frantic, Nell scrabbled in the wet snow on the pavement, praying they hadn't slithered beneath one vehicle or another.

She could run back to Emily's.

No. She wanted her own burrow. *Colin.*

Her hand closed over the keys and relief poured into her, making her sag. Her shoulder and one knee hurt, but she made it back to the driver's side of her small Ford, unlocked it and all but fell inside, locking the door immediately.

She drove on automatic pilot, half numb, half terrified. For the first time she realized how well she knew the streets of this town, at least until she reached the outskirts.

Nell was shaking by the time she turned into Colin's long driveway and finally braked in what had become *her* parking spot. Lights were still on in his house. Motion-activated lights above the garage came on, too.

Stiff and hurting, her teeth chattering, she got out and limped across the yard to his front porch. She had barely pressed the bell when the door swung open.

"Nell…?" His expression changed. He reached for her, pulling her inside and, after a quick, hard look past her, closed the door behind her. "What happened?" he demanded. "Did you fall down?"

She hugged herself to try to contain the shivers. It was hard to talk with her teeth chattering. "I almost got run over."

"You had an accident?"

She shook her head. Her teeth clacked like castanets. "I was…I was…crossing the street," she managed to answer.

"Oh, damn." He began peeling her outer garments from her, after which he touched her cheek with such gentle fingers, she didn't know why her face stung. "You're hurt." His voice was guttural. Taking her completely by surprise, he swung her into his arms and carried her to the sofa, close enough to the fire that she sighed in new relief.

"You're soaking wet." Now he mostly sounded angry. "I want to see where you're hurt, then we'll decide whether you need the E.R. or just a hot bath."

A hot bath sounded like heaven, but the apartment had only a small shower.

"Show me."

Self-conscious, she pulled her turtleneck over her head and then craned her neck to see her shoulder. It was flaming red and when he gently manipulated it, she winced.

"You're going to have a hell of a bruise," he growled.

The shakes were subsiding. "I think I whacked my knee instead of twisting it," she said. Under his peremptory stare, she half stood and eased her jeans down, too. Her knee was swelling, but not badly, and, oh, boy, but she was going to have a hell of a bruise there, too, to quote him.

"I'm okay," she muttered, pulling the jeans back up. When she reached for the turtleneck, Colin tossed it away.

"We'll see how you feel after a bath. Here, put your arms around my neck."

No one had ever carried her before like this. Or at least…no one in her memory. Stiff and self-conscious and excruciatingly aware of his strength, his scent, his body, she kept her gaze fixed on Colin's strong jaw, rough with a day's growth of beard. In an effort to distract herself, she tried to picture her father carrying her like this and couldn't.

Colin's bathroom was positively sybaritic, the tub huge and surrounded by a forest of deep green tiles, a few scattered ones textured with what looked like the imprint of pinecones. He started the water running, tested it with his hand, then rose to his feet and looked at her. "Can you get undressed by yourself?" His voice was a little gruff.

"Of course I can!" Nell couldn't quite bring herself to meet his compelling gray eyes but that didn't mean she had to sound like a languishing heroine of some 19th century Gothic romance.

Although…she hadn't known the meaning of the word *shy* until now. Here she was wearing nothing but her bra and unsnapped, wet jeans. For once in her life she wished she wore boring undergarments. This bra happened to be black with hot pink polka dots, the cups framed with hot pink lace. And oh, yes, she hurt and the fear still came and went like ocean waves, pounding and receding, but that didn't mean she couldn't also feel aware of him with every cell of her body.

His hand curled into a half fist, he stroked the cheek that *wasn't* scraped with his knuckles. "Okay," he murmured, the deep voice tender. "I'll run over to the apartment and bring you dry clothes."

"Thank you," she said huskily.

He still didn't move for a moment, and she knew his gaze rested on her face. But then with a nod he went.

She peered first into the mirror and saw that a long scrape decorated one side of her face. Her hair was plastered to her head and dripping, and her eyes looked wild. No wonder he'd reacted with alarm at first sight of her on his doorstep.

Her knee was stiffening. Swinging that leg over the side of the tub was a challenge, but sinking into the hot water was heavenly.

When the door opened partway, she crossed her arms over her breasts, but all he did was set a pile of clothes on the floor and quietly close the door again.

Nell stayed in the tub long enough to warm herself through, but not as long as she'd have liked. She imagined Colin pacing outside the bathroom. He would want to know what had happened, and she needed to tell him.

He'd brought underwear but not a bra, she saw. Despite the long soak, her arm was reluctant to lift, so she decided to skip putting the one she had back on. She squirmed and wriggled to get the T-shirt and fleece mock-neck over her head, then had to sit on the closed toilet seat to ease the jeans up and get on the heavy socks. Finally, she looked in his drawers until she found a comb and used it to restore order to her wet hair. For the moment, she decided to leave her pile of wet clothes on the floor. She could ask him for a plastic grocery bag to stuff them in so she didn't drip all over the floor.

He must have heard the door open, because he was pouring boiling water into a mug when she reached the kitchen.

"Cocoa," he said without looking at her. "I hope you like it."

"It sounds wonderful." She smiled tentatively as he turned. "You must have a sweet tooth."

"Yeah, I do." His gaze swept over her, head to toe. "You look a little better. You should take some ibuprofen, though." He lifted a bottle from the counter and when she held out a hand shook out two pills into her palm. He'd already poured a glass of water, too.

Colin sent her to the living room and carried two mugs of cocoa when he followed her. This time he sat down beside her on the sofa and put the mugs on the coffee table.

"All right." He was, momentarily, all cop. "Tell me what happened."

She told him the story and watched his expression harden.

"No headlights." It wasn't a question.

She shook her head anyway.

"You think he was trying to run you down."

Nell's whole body tightened. "It...felt like it. But, honestly, I guess it's possible the driver didn't see me at all. Visibility was really bad, and if he just hadn't turned his headlights on yet..."

"Where did he come from?"

Startled, she looked at him. "What do you mean?"

"Was there any other traffic? Would you have heard this vehicle coming down the street, turning the corner?"

Chilled, Nell gazed down into her cocoa, cradled to warm her hands. "I think so. Even if I wasn't thinking about it, I wouldn't have stepped out into the street without a glance and without being aware of a car engine. I mean, that's automatic." She frowned. "I think he must have been parked at the curb down the block."

"Watching for you."

"Oh, God," she whispered.

He set down his own mug with an abrupt motion and clasped her free hand in a reassuring grip. "Nell, it may have been a neighbor or some idiot teenager."

"But you don't think so."

His dark eyebrows rose. "Do you?"

Once again she hesitated, only reluctantly shaking her head. "It felt...malevolent." She studied his face. "This is what you were afraid of, isn't it?"

"I wouldn't have encouraged you to come home if I'd expected anything like this. Like I told you, some of my worry really was a product of occupational paranoia. I may still be overreacting, but having something like this happen is too suggestive to make me happy."

"Maybe I should leave."

His eyes had darkened. "I think it's too late for that, Nell. Now people know you're alive, that your memory isn't a complete blank. Whoever he is, he may be afraid that this visit home will have triggered your memory to return. He could follow you."

"I haven't told anyone where I came from or what name I live under." Her voice had risen.

Colin held her gaze, his own steady, if worried. "You did tell your parents. Anyone could have noted the license plate number on your car. People could find out I was in Seattle a few weeks ago. I mentioned seeing you on the local news. Anyone could find you, Nell. I can watch out for you here. I can't if you're in Seattle."

Her fingernails were probably digging into his flesh, but she held on to his hand anyway. "Yes." She steadied her voice. "Okay."

He grilled her on what she'd seen of the vehicle and she was embarrassed to admit that she couldn't even swear it was an SUV versus a pickup with a canopy, and no, she wasn't absolutely positive it was black, only that it was a dark color. And no, she hadn't caught even a glimpse of a license plate.

"I was just so scared," she explained. "And it was snowing and…"

"Getting out of the way was a lot more important than trying to see a license plate. Hey." He let go of her hand and wrapped his arm around her instead.

After a stiff moment, Nell let herself relax

against him, laying her head against his chest, broad and solid. A bubble of laughter arose, and when he cocked his head to look at her face, she had to explain what Emily said about men preferring to have a dainty woman instead of an Amazon.

He chuckled. "Can't say I ever thought one way or another about a woman's height."

Of course she now burned with self-consciousness, because she'd implied he was cuddling her for, well, romantic reasons rather than simple reassurance. But he seemed to be rubbing his cheek against her hair even though it was still damp, and his big hand was gently kneading her shoulder. And did police officers make a habit of cuddling citizens even if they had just had a close call?

He let out a sigh. "Damn," he murmured. "I'm sorry, Nell. I got you into this."

Like another slap of snow in the face, he'd managed to remind her of his oversize sense of responsibility and, yes, his need to win, or maybe only find answers. One or the other of which had kept him looking for her all these years.

She didn't look at him when she straightened. After a moment, his arm fell away from her. She knew he was watching her, but she made a production of picking up her mug and taking a sip. Nell tried to think of something to say, then remembered she did have one more thing to ask him about.

"Emily and Hailey told me something." Finally

she did turn her head and met his eyes. "They said I had a boyfriend, I guess right before I disappeared."

His gaze sharpened. "Did they say who?"

"Only that his name was Beck, Emily thinks. She says she told an officer who interviewed her back then, so it should be in the reports somewhere. He wasn't a student at the high school. I said he was on his own, like maybe a dropout. Or I guess he could have been older, like a community college student?" But Nell couldn't imagine herself at only fifteen hooking up with a guy in college. "For some reason, I didn't want to introduce him to my friends, but she did see him once when she ran into us by accident. She said he looked wary."

"I read your file not long ago. I'd swear there was nothing about a boyfriend."

She shrugged. "It may not mean anything. I might have only met him the week before or something, but... How?" she blurted. "I was shy! And I could never have told my mother. Can you imagine?"

"No." He was scrutinizing her the same way he had that night at the library, before he'd introduced himself. As if she were a...a victim, or a suspect. It was disconcerting. What was it police spokespersons always said? *A person of interest.* Not a woman he'd tugged into his arms a minute ago.

"You don't remember him."

"No." Why did that sound defiant? Maybe because she had one of those creepy feelings, as if a ghost had brushed her. If she pushed up her sleeves, would she have goose bumps? "I was shocked when they told me."

All he did was watch her.

"You don't believe me," Nell said indignantly.

"I believe you." But he said it slowly enough, *she* didn't believe him.

"I really don't remember him," she insisted. Only…it didn't come out as strongly as she'd intended.

One of Colin's eyebrows quirked.

Dismayed, Nell looked down to realize she'd wrapped her arms tightly against her torso and was squeezing. Hugging herself for comfort.

"I don't," she said again. Third time's the charm. Except the theory didn't work.

"What is it, Nell?" It was the deep, tender tone that got to her, as it did every time.

"When Emily said that," she told him in a low voice, "about me having a boyfriend, I was surprised but also really anxious."

"Thinking about him scared you."

She closed her eyes for a moment. "Yes."

"Then we'll have to find out why." He sounded practical and calm, exactly what she needed.

"How can we? What if he was really on his own, like a runaway?"

"I doubt he was, at least in the sense you mean. I gave this some thought not long ago. We don't have street people in Angel Butte, and there's good reason. Winters are too damn cold. Admittedly, there wasn't any snow on the ground when you disappeared. Even so, where would this guy have been sleeping? If he'd been homeless, he'd have been dirty, probably stunk. Would that have appealed to you?"

She was shaking her head before he finished. "No, I probably wouldn't have let him get near me."

"So this Beck had to be living somewhere he could take showers, wash his clothes. He might have been staying with a friend, who introduced you."

She'd never hated more the giant empty whiteboard in her head where there should be a colorful riot of memories, impressions, *life*. All she could do was shake her head. Was Beck one of those bad things her brain was determined to block out?

"Tomorrow, I'll look to find out what Emily said at the time, and what was done to locate this guy."

Nell nodded, hopefully maintaining her dignity. "Thank you."

He frowned at her. "You look beat."

"It's been an eventful day."

"Yeah, it has." Again he made one of those lightning assessments. "How do you feel?"

Nell had to think about it. "Better. The ibuprofen helped, I think. The hot bath, too."

"You do know you're going to hurt come morning, don't you?"

"Yes."

"Think you can sleep?"

"Probably." Which would bring dreams. If only she could remember them better. She suffered from chronic nightmares that she suspected had to do with whatever had happened here in Angel Butte, but she couldn't be sure because the images always faded no matter how hard she tried to hang on to them. Tonight's near disaster was bound to make a nightmare surface.

Lines gathered on his forehead again. "Did you tell your friends where you're staying?"

The question kicked up her pulse. "No. I only said I'd gotten an apartment and Hailey said cool, that meant I was staying for a while."

His face relaxed. "Good. Let's keep it that way."

"Someone could follow me."

"They could. Keep an eye out. Whenever you're on your way back here, take a few extra turns and make sure no other vehicle is making them with you."

Nell almost laughed, remembering her frantic efforts to shake any pursuit that night after he'd confronted her in the library parking lot and said, *I know you.*

"I can do that."

She could tell she had made him curious, but he chose not to ask, only nodded and repeated, "Good. I'll walk you over to the apartment."

He was probably desperate to get rid of her. There was no reason whatsoever to feel hurt at the thought.

"Here I've consumed another one of your evenings," she said in chagrin. "I'm sorry."

He lifted her chin, and Nell realized she'd been hiding behind the fall of hair. *I'm not like that,* she thought, and wondered if she were reverting to the more introverted teenager she must have been. Shy was okay, a coward wasn't.

A spark that might have been anger lit his eyes. "I'd have been upset if you *hadn't* come straight here."

She swallowed with difficulty. "Message received."

His eyes narrowed, but he let her go. Only, it felt as if he were caressing her as pulled his hand back. It was all she could do not to turn her head to maintain the contact. Even…nuzzle a tiny bit.

They stared at each other for a moment. Nell had no idea what he was thinking. Her heart was pounding hard, but not in fear. Something more unnerving yet was happening to her.

"You ready?" he asked roughly.

Ready? For an instant she didn't understand what he meant. Or maybe she *wanted* to think he meant… Oh, God. Her cheeks warmed. What was *wrong* with her?

"Yes." She shot to her feet. "Do you have a plastic grocery bag I can put all my soggy clothes in?"

For a beat, he didn't move. She could swear there was heat in his eyes—probably the reason for the glow she could feel on her cheeks.

Then he moved his shoulders as if to ease tension, and at the same time managed to erase from his face whatever he'd been feeling. "I'll get one."

He kept his distance on the walk to the apartment door, staying several feet away as she unlocked. "You didn't say what your plans are for tomorrow."

"I've gotten a couple more names of people who should remember me pretty well. I'll try to talk to them. I also thought…" She hesitated. "I want to go to the park. I need to see where it happened."

He closed the distance and gripped her arm. "Not alone, Nell."

"I actually was hoping you could take a few minutes," she admitted.

"Of course I can. Call me when you're ready."

Nell nodded, feeling shaky again. "Yes. All right."

He looked down at her, his eyes shadowed in the artificial light. Then he nodded and let her go. "Good night, Nell."

"Good night." She whisked inside, locked the door behind her, and started up the stairs to the small apartment that didn't feel nearly as safe as it had before somebody had tried to kill her.

CHAPTER NINE

COLIN REACHED INTO the box and realized it was empty. He'd removed and scrutinized every last scrap of paper. *Damn.* How could this be?

A good deal of information on the investigation into Maddie's disappearance was computerized, so he'd started there. When he didn't find what he was looking for, he retrieved from the basement the box that held, in theory, all police and lab reports as well as any notes taken by investigators as they conducted interviews. All standard. If this were being opened as a cold case, a detective ought to be able to go through this box and come out of it knowing everything investigators at the time had known.

Missing was any reference to Maddie having a boyfriend at all, never mind his name.

In fact, there was no indication anyone had talked to Emily Henson at all after that first, preliminary interview the day after Maddie vanished. Colin *had* found Duane's notes from a later talk with Hailey Allen. Was it Duane who'd screwed up? Or had he assigned someone else to hit up Emily again? Or,

JANICE KAY JOHNSON   191

hell, had some member of the clerical staff spilled her coffee on what appeared to be an unimportant piece of paper and chose to toss it?

He was brooding when Nell called to let him know she was free for the rest of the afternoon. He asked if they could have lunch, and she suggested her friend Hailey's place.

"Give me fifteen or twenty minutes," he said. "I have one call to make before I leave."

That call was to Duane, who reacted explosively to the news that a potentially crucial piece of information had gone missing from one of *his* investigations.

"A boyfriend," he muttered. "A guy older than her, someone nobody knew. Damn it, I know I had somebody go back and talk to the Henson girl! I just can't remember who." He grunted. "Please tell me Maddie remembers him."

"No." Colin didn't say, *but mention of his name scares the shit out of her.*

"Why are you poking around in this?" Duane asked. "She's home."

"Because I don't like leaving it hanging. The very fact that she's home could make somebody nervous." He hesitated. "She had a near miss last night, Duane. Could have been an accident, but it could as well have been deliberate. She was crossing the street and was almost hit."

Duane swore. "I hadn't thought. I should have. Hell. Did she see enough to give you a lead?"

"Unfortunately, no." In what might seem like a non sequitur, he commented on the rising temperature. "Sounds like we might get a week or two above freezing."

Duane knew what he was thinking. "The crew is back to work at the park this morning. The pile shouldn't be in too bad shape. We had tarps spread over it."

"Good," Colin said. "Keep me on top of it. Hey. You haven't seen Maddie yet, have you?"

"I didn't want to push it. The poor kid has a lot to take in."

"Not a kid anymore."

Silence. "No. Damn, I still think of her…" He cleared his throat. "Anyway, I'm going to try to make it to dinner at Helen's tonight."

Oh, right. Of course Duane had been invited. "Good enough," Colin said, and they signed off.

At least that investigation could move forward, he thought, leaving his office. He wished he thought they'd uncover something that would allow them to identify the victim.

He got lucky and found parking half a block from the café, where he'd eaten a number of times. He'd even seen the small plump woman who ran it. Guessing what color her hair would be in any given week amused him. He'd never heard her name, though, and had had no idea that she was connected to Maddie Dubeau.

Just the sight of Nell waiting for him gave him a

jolt of pleasure. She must have just walked in, because her cheeks and nose were pink and her hair was messy, making him guess she'd worn a hat. She was trying to finger-comb it when she felt the draft from the open door and saw him.

"Hi," she said, a little shyly, not at all as if he were the man who'd carried her to the bath last night.

Or maybe exactly *because* he had lifted her into his arms and seen her without her shirt. In a bra that had lived up to his expectations after he'd caught that glimpse of her socks. Picturing the saucy little bra and all that smooth, creamy skin made him wonder what she was wearing today beneath the too-sacky sweater.

He didn't know what he said, but was glad to be seated immediately. He was good at controlling his facial expressions, but apparently not as good at suppressing his physical reaction to the woman who was trying to hide inside those boring clothes.

Damn it, why her? he asked himself, disturbed.

He had no answer, but couldn't tear his gaze from her face.

Nell and he were halfway through lunch when her friend Hailey appeared to give him the once-over, which he withstood with good humor. He liked that she felt protective. He watched when she returned to the kitchen, then looked back at Nell.

"You're still planning to have dinner with your parents tonight?"

"Yes, Mom called." She sounded carefully neutral.

He only nodded, despite feeling a pang of regret. Sometimes he enjoyed having dinner with a woman, but a cancellation never bothered him, either. The time with Nell had been different. Sharing his house, having her seem at home in his kitchen. Talking as if they were old friends, if not more.

He wanted to be more, but was still convinced that would be a mistake. Nell *was* Maddie, which made any relationship between them complicated. Made *her* complicated. God knew this wasn't a good point in her life.

She'd progressed to pushing bits of a lemon pastry around her plate. He suspected at best Nell wasn't a big eater, but as little as he'd seen her actually put in her mouth and swallow, Colin worried she was going to start dropping weight she couldn't afford to lose. He'd seen the same worry in her friend Hailey's eyes as she brought them the flaky treats on plates and said, "No, don't argue, these are on me."

"You'd better eat that," he said, nodding at her plate. "You don't want to hurt Hailey's feelings."

She wrinkled her nose at him, then stole a look toward the kitchen. "Oh, fine," she muttered, and took a bite.

Colin hid his smile, sipping coffee while she ate the melt-in-your-mouth pastry with resignation.

Over lunch she'd told him about the two people she'd succeeded in talking to today. One had been a neighbor girl who had babysat Maddie and her brother when they were younger. She'd cried when she saw Nell. The other had been her fifth-grade teacher, who had been especially caring. When Nell talked, he could see how much it meant to her to have people welcome her with honest joy.

He could only ask himself again what in hell was wrong with her parents.

He left money on the table that included a generous tip when he and Nell left.

"Why don't I drive? I'll drop you back here to pick up your car when we're done."

"Yes, fine." She waited while he unlocked. "I think I'll go shopping this afternoon. I need some new boots. Maybe some more warm clothes. I didn't bring that much with me."

As he drove, he tried to keep her from dwelling on where they were going. Coming up with questions to ask was easy enough. He seemed to be unendingly curious about her.

She couldn't afford skiing, but admitted to having gone ice-skating with some friends once and discovered she knew the basics. "Is there a rink here?" she asked.

"A couple of the resorts have them. I don't know about your father's."

She gazed ahead, her forehead crinkling. "I don't think so, but...I'm not sure."

His sidelong look took in the clench she had on the seat belt where it crossed her chest. Clearly his diversionary tactics hadn't been a complete success.

With the rising temperature the slush on the road was more water than ice. The forecast was for more of the same. If Nell wasn't too upset, he might take a minute to walk over to the scene where the bones had been found.

The reminder filled him with fresh wonder. Damn, only a few weeks ago he'd feared those bones were Maddie's, and now here she was. He stole another glance at her to see that she was staring straight ahead, deep in thought. It was disconcerting to realize he didn't think of her as Maddie most of the time. He'd had lunch with Nell. Held Nell in his arms.

It was Nell Smith who wore sexy bras, not sad-eyed, teenage Maddie. He'd never thought of Maddie that way, and he was having trouble thinking of Nell in any other way.

But Nell Smith was often sad-eyed, too.

And, hell, if he were confused, what must she be feeling?

He parked close to the trail Maddie had been taking that night. Several familiar vehicles were parked not far ahead, belonging to the crime scene crew and detectives who had resumed work a few hundred yards away.

So damn close to where Maddie had been snatched, he thought again. So close, he had trouble believing it to be coincidental. Unless, of course, Duane was right when he wondered if there weren't other bodies buried here beneath these old pines.

He turned off the engine and in the silence, Nell didn't move. All she did was stare at the forest that incongruously survived between a housing development and the road. Colin stayed where he was, waiting. They were doing this her way. He wasn't in such a hurry that there was reason to push.

At last she sighed and reached for the handle. "I'm glad it's daylight."

"You wouldn't be able to see much in the dark." Better than telling her the damn place was haunted at night.

By the time he got out, locked and reached her, she had tucked her hands in the pockets of a fleece vest and was eyeing the bulldozed road that led to the clearing where the trees had been taken out.

"Some of the trees were infested with pine beetles," he explained. "The park department is having the sick ones removed in hopes of saving the rest. Bulldozers have made a real mess."

She only nodded.

"This way," he said quietly, and led her to the narrow path used by kids. Easy to miss if you didn't know it was there. The ground was soggy and the undergrowth wet until they got under the trees. The peeling red bark of madrona added color against the brown boles of the ancient pines. White berries clung to some arching branches of snowberry bushes. That night twelve years ago had been dry, but otherwise he was looking at nearly an identical scene.

Nell kept up with him, her head turning as she took it all in. He couldn't tell whether she didn't remember a thing, or was keeping whatever she felt tucked deep.

He'd seen a lot of crime scenes in the intervening years. He shouldn't remember this one as well as he did. He should have had to work to orient himself instead of being able to stop in the exact same spot he'd been that night when his flashlight glanced off metal.

"Here," he said, stopping. "Your bike was about there." He pointed, remembering how deep the handlebar was dug into the soil and the chill that gave him. "There was some scuffing, but not clear footprints." He crouched. "I think the blood was about here. Your wallet had fallen a ways in that direction." He nodded toward the clump of low green ceanothus.

Nell was a statue. Staring. It was a long time before she even blinked. Alarmed, he slowly rose to his feet. Maybe this wasn't such a good idea.

"It's creepy here," she whispered, as if someone might be listening.

He glanced around, wondering if kids who still used this path had ever even heard about the girl who was abducted. If their parents had told them, warned them away from the park, did they feel a little thrill when they pedaled furiously through, defying those warnings? Maybe stories of Maddie had added some horror-movie excitement to teenage keggers.

The thought sickened him.

"It sure as hell was that night. Teenagers party here in the park sometimes. That's what I expected to find. But I knew as soon as I got here that I was alone. It was too quiet."

Not today, he realized. He could hear chain saws off in the distance. No heavy equipment; the ground might be too wet. There was noise from traffic out on the street, voices muted by distance.

She shivered. "I don't remember. I thought I would, but I don't."

Maybe not, but something was stirring uneasily in her head. She could be spooked only because she knew this was where it had happened, but the way her gaze darted around seemed extreme. He wondered if she'd stopped that night and heard a noise. That was what she looked like right now—as if she wanted to run but didn't know which direction.

His gloved hand closed over hers. "It was a long shot."

"You said I was unlikely to remember."

"I couldn't be sure, but whatever happened here caused the memory loss. You know, it was bad. There was enough blood to scare the crap out of me."

He had purposely tried to sound rueful. Her big brown eyes fastened on his face, and after a moment she almost smiled. The tension in her body eased. She made no effort to retrieve her hand from his.

"How old were you?"

"Twenty-two, only two months on the job. The car accidents I'd dealt with to that point were fender benders—I'd broken up keggers, arrested shoplifters." He didn't mention the domestic violence. Those calls had gotten to him, but not surprised him. "I hadn't seen anything really ugly yet. Later…" He stopped. Two or three years later, would he have reacted the same to the scene of Maddie's abduction, the face looking up at him from the driver's permit?

"You were a kid yourself," she murmured.

Colin huffed out a brief laugh. "Yeah, I guess I was. Although I wouldn't have appreciated you saying so then."

Her lips definitely curved, but failed to soften the stark lines of her face. She shivered again.

"You're cold," he said, but she shook her head.

"No. Oh, I guess a little. Mostly…" She pulled in a deep breath. "It's that same feeling I had last night, when Emily told me about Beck. As if a ghost brushed by me." She tried for a smile. "Predictable, I guess. I *expected* to feel something. You know?"

"I do know." Although it meant letting go of her

hand, he pulled her to him. Not a good idea, but she looked so damn vulnerable, she got to him.

For a moment, Nell was stiff, but then with a sigh she let herself lean, even wrapping her arms around his waist. The scent of her shampoo, of *her,* filled his nostrils, overriding the smell of pine and snow. Even with their bulky winter garments, she felt good against him. He laid his cheek against her head and closed his eyes. Some of his own frustration and tension eased. Hating the thought of letting her go, it was a long time before he spoke.

"You had enough?" he murmured at last.

She tensed, gathering herself. "I think so." Her arms dropped to her sides and she stepped back. That shyness was in her eyes again, but only until she turned her head, shivered again, then turned resolutely to start back.

Following her, he had no trouble deciding to skip a visit to the scene where bones were being retrieved. He didn't have any good excuse to visit anyway. He'd be told if anything important was found.

He and Nell had emerged from the trees and he'd just hit the remote to unlock doors when he heard someone call, "Captain?"

Jane Vahalik hurried toward him. Seeing her suppressed excitement, he went to meet her.

"Were you stopping by?" she asked.

"No." They'd met halfway between vehicles. "Should I be?"

She flashed a triumphant grin. "We found something good." Her gaze went past him and narrowed in interest. "Is that Maddie Dubeau?"

He turned to see that Nell had followed, but hung back a good fifteen feet, as if being careful not to intrude. "Yeah, this is Maddie. I was showing her…" He jerked his head toward the woods.

Vahalik's eyes widened and a soft "oh" emerged.

"Maddie," he said, "come meet one of my detectives."

Searching his face and then Jane's, she approached. Her "hi" was soft.

"It's a pleasure to meet you," Vahalik said. "You've made us all believe in happy endings."

Nell smiled more genuinely than she had back in the woods. "I'm glad if my miraculous return inspired you. Um, you must have business. I'll wait for you…."

He took her arm. "No, it's okay. What's up, Jane?"

"We found a backpack." Her voice was electrified.

"You're sure it's his?"

"Can't be a hundred percent, but yeah. We found, er…" She apparently remembered Nell's presence. "Some more remains with it."

"Bones," he clarified, not wanting Nell to imagine anything more gruesome. He couldn't remember if he'd told her during one of those phone conversations about the discovery here in the park.

"Ribs and clavicle. I wish it wasn't so slow,"

Vahalik said in exasperation. "We don't dare work faster, though."

Speed shouldn't matter. This victim had died a long time ago. He knew this edgy feeling in his gut was there only because of the location of this grave site.

Nell was listening—wide-eyed, he saw—and he knew he'd have to explain. For now, he focused his attention on Vahalik.

"Nothing to identify him yet?"

She shook her head. "It's a day pack, and in better shape than you'd expect." She shrugged. "Synthetic fabric. The kind of stuff that plugs up our landfills, but lucky for us. Canvas would have rotted into nothing but rusted metal buckles. This—" her grin broke free again "—protected the contents. It's all congealed into a giant glob right now, but Linda says she has her ways." Linda Nishimura was a gifted crime scene tech Colin had so far persuaded to stay in Angel Butte. "I could tell there was a wad of papers. If she can dry it enough to peel layers back…"

"Hail Mary." Damn, he couldn't help grinning, too. "She's taking it back to the lab?"

"Yes, leaving the rest of us to our labors."

"Excellent."

"I was just going to grab a thermos of coffee," she said, waving toward the GMC Yukon he knew she drove.

He nodded. "Good job." Nell was still watching Jane when he turned back to her.

"She's a detective? She seems young."

"Not so young. Close to my age, I think." He grunted. "We're so shorthanded, we're promoting guys who barely shave to detective. You should see her current trainee."

"You told me how worried you are about not being able to boost hiring after the annexation." She frowned as they started back to his 4Runner. "Which part was annexed?"

He'd forgotten how much he'd talked about during those lengthy phone conversations. "We doubled the size of Angel Butte. The business strip with the Walmart and the Staples and the Home Depot and all the rest of it was county. Now it's ours. There'd been a lot of residential construction beyond the city limits, too. I told you how the area has boomed. All that's our responsibility now, too."

"Did the city council not realize how much the extra services would cost?"

The throbbing in his right temple was becoming an unavoidable response to a subject that infuriated him.

"No, I don't think they did do the planning they should have. They were relieved when Chief Bystrom assured them the department could handle the additional patrols. The city council loves their police chief." By the end, he sounded as if he were chewing on a porous pierce of cinder. His mouth tasted as if he had, too.

His movements were jerky when he opened the passenger-side door for Nell.

"So he implied you were overstaffed before," she said thoughtfully. "That must make him pretty unpopular with the rank and file in the department."

"That's safe to say." And even more unpopular with the two captains who spent more time with their fingers stuck in holes in the dike than they did doing the job they'd been hired for.

She waited until he got in and started the engine. "Do you have a plan?" she asked.

Startled, he turned his head, meeting her level gaze. Yeah, she knew what she was asking.

"You mean, how I'm going to get rid of him?" Dangerous words. Even he and Brian Cooper, his counterpart who headed Patrol, left their hopes unspoken. The decision to trust Nell didn't take a split second. "I'm working on it," he said.

Nell stayed quiet for most of the drive. He was glad; it was better to put off talking about the partial skeleton found in the park.

A few minutes later, he left her at her car. She promised to be careful. Colin refrained from ordering her to report to him tonight when she got home from her parents'. If Duane were to be there, would he offer to follow her home? That could be good—but Colin was still reluctant to tell anyone where she was staying, including her family.

He hoped she knew he was available if she needed him. But giving himself a little space to figure out what he felt seemed smart right now.

Smart maybe, but he had a bad feeling that tonight, as soon as he heard her coming home, he'd be standing at his front window willing her to head for his front door.

NELL STARED IN shock at the man who descended her parents' porch steps in one bound and loped to meet her. "Felix?"

A huge smile dominated his thin face. "Maddie. It's really you." He snatched her into his arms and swung her in a circle. When he set her back down, she saw that his dark eyes were wet.

She tried to smile through her own tears. "You couldn't have done that the last time I saw you."

He swiped at his eyes, but laughed, too. "I was twelve. And—what?—five feet tall?"

"Skinny, too." Such joy rose in her, she felt as if she might levitate. "I remember you. Oh, my God. I do."

"I hope it's the good brother you remember and not the brat."

She laughed. "Of course it is!" She sobered. "Felix. You came."

He mock-scowled. "What, you didn't think I would?"

"No, I just...I didn't think," she admitted meekly.

"I was going to call you, but, oh, these past few days have been really overwhelming."

He wrapped an arm around her shoulders. "I can't really imagine." His eyebrows twitched. "Mom's at the door."

Nell found his tone more than interesting. He sounded uncomfortable. As though...well, she didn't know.

"Did Uncle Duane come?" she asked.

He looked surprised. "No. Was he supposed to?"

Her mother did kiss her cheek. Her father actually hugged her, once they reached the living room. Were they putting on a pretense for Felix's sake, or actually relaxing into acceptance that she was home? But she lacked the context memories would have given her. Felix had turned out handsome. He was lean, dark and, she suspected, could look wickedly sexy when he tried. All the pictures that filled her head were of a funny, mischievous, affectionate boy. What she couldn't understand was how he could be so open and good-humored while even as a child she had apparently been withdrawn and lacking in confidence.

Over dinner, her father was expansive, talking about the resort and the economic growth of the city and even touching on politics.

"You don't like the new mayor?" Felix asked.

Marc waggled one hand. "Can't tell yet. At least he cut the damn ponytail off."

Nell blinked. "A ponytail? The mayor?"

Helen gave her husband a repressive look. "He had that when he first moved to Angel Butte and opened a brew pub. He was always very neat."

"Yeah, his hair wasn't that long. Just kind of a stubby ponytail." Felix grinned. "I remember him. It looked good. I thought of growing my hair."

Helen gave him a fond look. "Don't tease your father."

The expression made Nell want to shrivel inside herself. *That's what I did then,* she thought. The good little girl, always trying to please her parents. If she'd stuck around, would she have decided to flout them by becoming a wild teenager? She couldn't quite picture it—but then there was Beck, the boyfriend who might have been a school dropout and who she certainly hadn't introduced to her parents. Her opening act of defiance?

After dinner, she asked if she could see her bedroom. Felix walked her up. He stood in the doorway, hands shoved in his pockets, one shoulder propped against the frame, as she stepped through a time portal.

It was a young girl's room, not a teenager's. There were no posters of rock stars or actors on the walls. In fact, there were no posters at all. The twin bed had a white eyelet canopy as crisp as if it had been washed and starched yesterday. The desk and dresser were painted white with gilt trim and elaborate handles. A few stuffed animals and dolls reposed atop the dresser. The only thing that

made her think this really could have been her bedroom was a bookcase painted to match the rest of
the furniture but stuffed with books. She crouched
in front of it and ran her fingers over the spines. It
was a hodgepodge: children's books, young adult
and some adult. Dickens. She smiled shakily. Mrs.
Chisholm was responsible for her Dickens phase.

Finally standing again, she faced her brother. "Is
this really what my room looked like then?"

"Messier," he said. "Not bad, because Mom was
so anal." He grimaced. "Is so anal. You had a computer. I guess they got rid of that."

"It would have been a little dated by now."

He laughed. "No kidding. Um. There was a bulletin board. We weren't allowed to ruin the walls
by sticking thumbtacks in or using tape."

She rotated until she was looking at the desk.
"There, right over the desk."

"Yeah." He sounded a little gruff.

"This room looks like something out of a model
home. Designed for a ten-year-old."

"Mom didn't pay much attention to what you
wanted."

She met his dark eyes. "What about you? Did
you get what you wanted?"

He shifted, and she recognized his level of dis-
comfort. "You really don't remember, do you?"

"Not much."

Felix glanced over his shoulder, and she realized
he was checking to be sure neither parent had fol-

lowed them up the stairs. Then he looked at her, and pain was apparent in his eyes.

"Yeah, I mostly got what I wanted. Especially from Mom. She was always harder on you. I never understood."

No, she didn't remember, but Nell wasn't surprised, either.

"Even when I was little, it was obvious. Her voice changed when she talked to you."

"What about Dad?" Her voice was low.

He twitched a little. "He might have been more invested in me because I was a boy. I'm not sure. Mostly it wasn't him, but he also didn't notice or pay attention to stuff that should have been obvious."

"I wondered if…" The words caught in her throat, but she felt as if they needed to be said. "If they'd have preferred I stayed tragically missing or dead."

"God, Maddie!"

She could tell she'd shocked him, but she was determined to follow her thoughts to the logical conclusion. "They didn't act the way most parents would when I showed up. Mom almost seemed mad because, wow, I put them through all that for nothing?" She drew a shaky breath. "It's been weird."

She suspected he wanted to deny it but couldn't. "Things were strained at dinner," he admitted after a minute.

"You should have been there when Mom and I

had lunch the other day. We had the kind of conversation you make when a stranger politely lets you share her table because the café is jammed and there's no other place to sit."

That pained look was back in his eyes. "Mom tried to make you in her image."

"I sort of looked like her, but I wasn't pretty."

He did some more squirming. Nell realized how far out of his comfort zone this conversation must be for a twenty-five-year-old guy. His "I don't think it was that" sounded weak.

"What then?" she asked in a hard voice.

"You just weren't…"

Waiting through his hesitation, she held herself stiffly. *I will not let this hurt.* But she knew better. Of course it would. Or at least it had, when she lived at home and wanted to be pretty enough, poised enough, graceful and athletic enough, to please her parents. What she felt now was more like an echo.

"She couldn't understand why you weren't more popular. She said it was your own fault. You hung back, you didn't *try.*"

"We fought."

Felix shook his head. "I wished sometimes you would. She'd be icy, and you'd just sort of…"

"Shrivel."

His grimace was apologetic. "Yeah. It sucked," he said with sudden vehemence. "I felt so guilty."

"There's no reason. It wasn't your fault. You

know that." She managed a kind of smile. "I'm only sorry I didn't have enough backbone to go out and get a tattoo and maybe a nose ring and dye my hair black."

Felix grinned. "It's not too late, you know."

"I think it is, because the truth is I don't care what she thinks anymore." Nell examined the concept and something settled in her. "I'm okay with who I am. If she doesn't like it, she can shove it."

That earned her a rakish grin from this brother who had inexplicably turned into a man. "You tell her, sis."

"I just might." She returned his smile. "Hey, how long are you here for?"

"Until Sunday. I ditched a few days of classes when Mom called to say you were home."

"Thank you." Blast it, she was getting teary-eyed again. "You, I'm really glad to see."

"Ditto." He looked over his shoulder. "Incoming."

"Can we do something one of these days?" she asked hurriedly.

"Tomorrow. We'll go cruise some old hangouts."

"I came to see why you two disappeared for so long," Helen said from beyond him.

"Just talking." Felix winked at Nell. "Long time no see, you know."

"I'd probably better get going," she said, but as she passed her brother she murmured, "I'll call you in the morning."

CHAPTER TEN

"WELL, ISN'T THAT interesting," Colin murmured, staring down at the key card Backpack Boy had apparently been carrying. A key card designed to open doors at Arrow Lake Lodge and Resort— owned by none other than Marc Dubeau. "If a kid disappeared during a stay at Arrow Lake," he said, "why wouldn't we have heard about it? Have him listed as missing?"

Duane shook his head. "Couldn't have been staying there. Maybe he'd snitched it and thought he could get into rooms to help himself to some valuables."

Colin could think of half a dozen other possibilities without even trying, none of which explained the young man ending up dead and buried in the park. "It's something," he finally said. "We can show the picture to Dubeau and any longtime staff."

He was only half-listening as the rest discussed the eight-by-ten photo. Protected from the elements by frame and glass, it was the first item from the backpack Colin had looked at. The damage around the edges hadn't spread to the subjects, a dark-eyed, dark-haired woman and boy. From the resemblance, they had to be mother and son.

Jane Vahalik, part of the huddle that also included Ronnie Orr, her trainee, volunteered to contact the studio whose stamp appeared on the back. It was located on the west side of the mountains in Eugene.

"Good," Duane said. "No guarantee that boy grew up to be our victim, but it's worth a try. If we can identify the woman, she may be able to tell us something."

Jane tapped her finger on the table, dragging Colin's gaze from the key card and photo, lying side by side. "Here's something interesting, too."

A Purple Heart, he saw, startled. The ribbon was in bad shape, but Linda had cleaned up the medal.

"Damn," Colin murmured, hit hard by his sudden understanding. "The kid was carrying around his memories of his parents. Why would he do that?"

Linda indicated the remnants of a few items of clothing. "Briefs, T-shirt, socks. A change of clothes, minus the jeans, which are maybe too bulky to carry all the time?"

Homeless. Shit. Colin didn't like the thought that was taking shape in his mind. He couldn't dismiss it, though. Homeless guy, sixteen, seventeen years old, probably good-looking—if he were the cute kid in the photo some years later. Killed, or at least buried, a stone's throw from where Maddie had very nearly also been killed.

Say something? Or keep what he was thinking to himself until he could talk to Nell?

"This is all very interesting," Duane said, "but here's what I brought you down to see."

Colin followed him to a brightly lit magnifier. Beneath it was a bank deposit slip, and his puzzlement became sharp interest when he took in the amount—$30,000.

"It survived," Linda said, "because it was in a plastic bag, the kind you put green beans in at the grocery store. There were a couple of photos in there, too. I'll see what I can do to restore the second one, but it may be hopeless."

The better of the two suffered from smeared and faded color, but Colin could make out enough to feel a chill. The photographer had been standing a distance away and had nothing like a telephoto lens, but Colin was easily able to recognize Police Chief Gary Bystrom, talking to another man Colin didn't know. Their expressions were intense. In the background... He leaned closer. "Isn't that the airfield at Arrow Lake?"

Marc Dubeau's resort was one of the few around Angel Butte that allowed small plane owners to fly in and out. The resort included some timeshare condominiums and cabins, and a few larger, fancier ones leased year-round. An Oregon senator used one of the more impressive homes, a massive log structure, to host parties, offer getaways to staff and for vacations for himself and family. His passion for hunting didn't help his cause with the Sierra Club crowd.

Duane was right beside him, staring down at the same photo. "I think so."

"Anyone traced that deposit slip?"

"Yeah, that's why you're here." Duane glanced at the others. "Linda, is that everything so far?"

She gestured toward a wad of papers that appeared glued into a block. "I'll work on separating those, but what little I've seen so far appears to be class notes, quizzes. This kid was in school somewhere."

That information didn't tie to the rest of Colin's speculation. If the kid were in school, damn it, *where?*

Duane nodded. "Good work, all. You know what to do."

Vahalik and her sidekick took their cue and headed for the door. Duane glanced at Colin. "Let's step outside."

Colin raised his eyebrows but went. They stopped under the overhang of the building.

"This is a political hot potato," Duane said bluntly. "The account number belongs to Bystrom's wife."

Forgetting this wasn't shirtsleeve weather, Colin gazed, unseeing, across the parking lot, his thoughts racing. It wasn't so much the amount deposited. The Bystroms' lifestyle suggested they were loaded. This amount could have been from a small inheritance, money moved from a CD that had come due, who knew what. The bigger question was why a murder victim thought the deposit slip held any significance.

"You want me to get a warrant."

"Can we justify it?"

Colin rolled his shoulders and thought some more. This could be career suicide. Duane waited.

"I'll need a copy."

"Linda already emailed it to you."

Colin grunted. "Coward."

Duane gave him a puckish grin. "This is why you have the office with the best view."

Colin laughed, thinking of the brick wall he looked out at. "That's gotta be it."

"What are you going to do?"

He shook his head. "I don't know."

Not exactly the truth. Of course they had to pursue every lead in a murder investigation. If he were going to step out on a limb already cracking under his feet, though, he needed some backing.

It was no stretch to decide the time had come to find out where Mayor Noah Chandler stood and what he was made of.

WITH COPIES OF the photograph and the deposit slip folded and tucked in the inside pocket of his suit jacket, Colin waited outside the mayor's office a few hours later.

He knew Chandler in a superficial way. As he'd told Brian Cooper, he had gained the impression that the new mayor wasn't all that impressed with his police chief. Which didn't mean he'd give Colin the go-ahead to rake through Bystrom's financial dealings.

Colin managed a surreptitious look at the time by checking for messages on his phone. Nothing from Nell. At least today she wasn't alone. Her brother was supposed to have picked her up at ten and they were spending the day together. He wished that let him feel easy about her, but it didn't. She was still out and about. Vulnerable.

Despite his best intentions, last night Colin had opened the front door the instant he'd heard Nell's car, and she'd come in for a cup of tea. The scrape on her cheek had scabbed over but served as a graphic reminder of her close call. She'd admitted to having a few panic attacks on the drive from her parents' house when she thought one set of headlights was behind her too long, but she'd followed his advice and realized after a turn or two that no one was following her.

Her face had momentarily glowed when she told him that her brother had come home to see her. The glow dimmed when she repeated the highlights from the private talk she and Felix had had.

Her perplexity made him ache with self-doubt.

If he'd let her go on the way she had been, her life wouldn't have been threatened.

Except he wasn't so sure that was true. *He* had stumbled on her. Someone else could have just as well. All he had to do was remember her terror the night he confronted her to know that she carried that fear with her at all times. Answers might allow her to let go of the fear.

And what? Go back to her life as Nell Smith? He was having trouble imagining that. Maddie—Nell, damn it—had filled his world since he'd caught that fleeting glimpse of her on television. Look at him, nerves jumping under his skin only because he didn't know where she was or what she was doing right this minute.

At least she'd agreed to let him take her out to dinner tonight. He had a plan for afterward he thought she'd like.

"Captain McAllister?" the assistant said pleasantly. "The mayor will be glad to see you now."

Colin nodded his thanks and stood. No one had exited Chandler's office. Colin hoped keeping him waiting hadn't been some cheap power play.

The mayor's office was more stripped down than Colin had expected. A couple of impressive paintings by local artists decorated the walls. The desk was a nice one, but it didn't appear custom-made the way the desk installed by Chandler's predecessor had. When Noah Chandler himself stood and came around the corner of it to greet Colin, he wore black slacks and a roll-neck sweater rather than a business suit. Heavy boots, too, which bore traces of dried mud.

Seeing the direction of Colin's glance, Chandler grinned ruefully. "I was inspecting possible sites for a new sewer treatment plant. The ground's a mess today."

"I noticed."

They shook hands and measured each other.

The guy had one of those faces that was too crude to call handsome. *Thuggish* came to mind. He had longshoreman shoulders, too, and hands that looked as if they should be wielding a sledgehammer or maybe drawing beer for a living. No rings, his watch was utilitarian. The ponytail might be gone, but well-cut hair hadn't succeeded in giving him a glossy veneer. Blue eyes were intelligent and guarded. Noah Chandler wouldn't be an easy read.

"Sit down." He gestured toward several leather chairs grouped around a coffee table.

Colin chose one and waited while Chandler did the same.

"I assume this isn't a let's-get-acquainted meeting." Bluntness seemed to be his style, which Colin liked.

"No. I'd like your backing to do something that could get ugly."

Chandler's mouth quirked. "That sounds interesting. Explain."

"Are you aware of the bones found in River Park when the contractors hauled a stump out of the ground?"

Chandler leaned forward, his elbows braced on his knees. "Sure. Have you identified the victim yet?"

"We were stymied when the ground was frozen. Once we were able to start digging again, some more bones turned up right away. With them was a backpack."

That sharp gaze didn't waver.

"Techs are still trying to peel apart papers that look like schoolwork. For now, though, they've found a couple of interesting things."

"Which is where I come in, I take it."

Colin's jaw muscles flexed. "Yes. The kid was carrying a key card for a room at Marc Dubeau's resort. These were also in the pack, sealed together in a plastic bag." He removed the folded sheets of paper from his pocket and handed them over. "Copies, of course."

Chandler unfolded them and studied the picture in silence for a minute. His eyebrows momentarily climbed when he saw the amount on the deposit slip. At last he looked up. "You do have a problem," he said. "I assume the account number is your boss's?"

"His wife's."

"And you believe these items are in some way connected to the murder."

He'd been right; Noah Chandler wasn't giving much away.

"I wouldn't go that far," Colin said, choosing his words with care. "At this point, however, we have to pursue what few leads we have. We have no missing persons listed who were staying at Arrow Lake Lodge, nor from any resorts in the close vicinity. The medical examiner is sure the bones belong to a young male, likely between about sixteen and twenty years of age. Given that we have the jaw, we've been able to compare teeth with X-rays from a couple of young men who are listed as missing in the right time frame, one from Bend, the other from Klamath Falls. Neither matched. Who was this guy? What was his connection to Dubeau's resort? And why was he carrying that photo and the deposit slip? Packaged together, no less."

The mayor mulled that over. "Did you consider asking Chief Bystrom?"

"I did. If it had been only the photograph, I'd have done so."

"What is it you intend?"

"I want to look at his bank records. Find out who wrote the check, if it was one, deposited on that date. Make sure there isn't a pattern of unexplained deposits."

"Do you expect that there will be?"

For the first time, Colin hesitated. "I can't answer that," he said at last. "Chief Bystrom and his wife live very well, clearly beyond his salary. I've always assumed there was family money. I have no idea. I will tell you that this would be part of our investigation no matter who it was."

"All right," Chandler said abruptly, folding the two pieces of paper and laying them on the coffee table. "Unless you already had a judge in mind, I'd suggest you go to Tenney. I'll give him a call." He rose to his feet. "And thank you for the warning." Amusement glinted in his eyes. "I like to know before the shit hits the fan."

"Chief Bystrom is going to see this as an attack. You may not be aware that he and I don't have an entirely cordial working relationship."

"He's said things." Chandler gave the faintest of smiles. "Chief Bystrom and I don't, either. Do what you have to do."

They didn't shake hands again. Colin left, fully satisfied.

Half an hour later, he had his warrant, which included bank and investment accounts in the names of Gary Bystrom and/or Marcia Bystrom.

It didn't take long to determine that Gary Bystrom and his wife had deposited over half a million dollars over a period of about fifteen years, distributed over a number of different bank and investment accounts. Many amounts were small enough not to catch anyone's attention, but there were too many of them. A decent supplemental income. Colin was going to have to ask his boss what the source of that money was, and then bring a forensic accountant in to verify the truth of his answer.

If it turned out a trust account had been paying out, Colin was up shit creek without a paddle—unless Mayor Noah Chandler chose to hand him one.

DELIGHT BLOSSOMED IN Nell the moment Colin turned into the parking lot of the Wolf Creek Resort that evening. The elevation was higher than the town of Angel Butte, which meant the ground was still white from the last storm. The outdoor ice-skating rink was surrounded by a two-foot bank of snow. More snow weighed down the branches of small evergreen trees scattered throughout the grounds. The ones around the rink were strung with tiny white lights. The restaurant he escorted her into looked out onto the rink.

They were seated by a window, and her gaze kept being drawn to the winter wonderland outside.

"You are planning to take me skating?" she murmured, as she closed her menu, decision made.

Colin laughed. "There's a reason I told you to wear pants."

"Oh! That's going to be so much fun." Her gaze strayed to the window again, and the sight of a man crashing to the ice made her wince. "I think."

"You said you knew what to do. I'm counting on you keeping me on my feet."

She laughed at him. "You're kidding, right?"

His expression was appropriately surprised. "Why would I be kidding?"

"Because you outweigh me by just a teensy bit. Like sixty, seventy pounds? You do know what would happen if we were holding hands and you started to go down?"

"Huh." A smile crinkled the skin at the corners of his eyes. "I'd take you down with me."

"Yes!"

"I've never been ice-skating, but I do cross-country ski. How hard can it be?"

Thus spoke a man arrogantly certain of his prowess. Nell rolled her eyes. "Maybe we won't hold hands."

His smile deepened. "Oh, we'll hold hands." His voice had deepened, too.

She couldn't look away. The velvety rough tone of his voice gave her quivers and she found herself squeezing her thighs together to try to contain them.

"I'll sue you for any bruises," she said lightly.

He chuckled. Both were distracted then by the waitress, who took their orders. When she was gone, he asked Nell about her day.

"It was fun." She made a face. "First time you've ever heard that word out of my mouth, isn't it? But I really like Felix, and we did have a good time. He told me this was my trip down memory lane.

Mostly, it was *his* memory lane, but that's okay. I found out where he went skinny-dipping, where teenagers in Angel Butte park to make out—" At Colin's expression, she mock-glowered at him. "So okay, you could have told me that." Her voice softened. "He showed me places we rode our bikes, where Mom and Dad took us on picnics. We went out to Arrow Lake. I don't know if Dad was there or not—we didn't ask for him. I got to sit on this rock that sticks out into the lake. Wrong time of year, of course, but I remember lying on it for hours at a time watching the minnows and dreaming. When there's so much I don't remember, visiting a place I do made me feel…anchored, I guess." She shrugged, probably a little awkwardly.

"I'm glad." He reached across the table for her hand. "That you had a good day, and that some of your memories are happy ones."

She squeezed his hand, hoping he couldn't tell that her reaction to his touch was a whole lot more than friendly. "Thank you."

They'd been served their entrees when he became quiet. A couple of lines between his eyebrows made his expression brooding. Beginning to feel apprehensive, Nell waited.

When he met her eyes, he looked troubled. "Something came up today I'd like to talk to you about, see if it awakens any memories. If it does, they probably won't be good ones. Damn," he muttered. "What am I thinking? We can do this later."

The too-familiar band around her chest tightened. "Sure, like I'm going to be able to think about anything else now. Tell me."

His reluctance was obvious, but finally he dipped his head. "You know some bones turned up in River Park." He explained how and when it happened, and that the continued search for both evidence and more bones had paused until the freeze let go of the ground. "You heard Detective Vahalik yesterday."

"Yes," she said, trying to hide her sense of foreboding.

"Here's what we've learned so far." He explained that they knew the victim was male and likely in his late teens. The exciting part for investigators was the recovery of a backpack with contents preserved well enough they knew the young man carried what might be items deeply personal to him, including a photo of a woman and boy and a Purple Heart. Oddly, he also had a change of clothes in the pack.

The foreboding had swelled until it hurt to contain. She managed a choppy nod.

"The clothes could have been because he'd just been to the gym." He paused. "But the framed photo? The military medal? My first thought was that he was homeless. Carrying what he absolutely needed with him, and some mementos of his parents. Things he wouldn't have left even if he had a temporary place to stay. The schoolwork complicates that explanation, though. I don't know what to think now."

"You're asking if he was my boyfriend," she whispered.

Regret darkened his eyes to charcoal. "Yeah, that's what I'm wondering. He was buried so close to where you were assaulted, the coincidence has been nagging at me."

She pushed against the darkness that separated her from all the things she *should* be able to remember, and was paid back by pain stabbing through her temple. Thinking at all became a struggle, but she made herself.

"I was wearing a shirt that I don't think was mine when I came to in the trunk." *Filthy. Bloody, but still comforting even though she didn't know why. It was the only thing she'd had to hold on to...something. Someone.* "The sleeves come down to here." She held her hand six or eight inches from the tips of her fingers on the other hand. "The patch on the shoulder says 'Airborne' and has a feathered wing holding a sword. I looked it up online and learned it's from the 173rd Airborne Brigade Combat Team. They took heavy casualties in Vietnam."

"Which means lots of Purple Hearts were awarded," he said slowly.

She nodded.

He let out a heavy breath. "It's not sounding good, sweetheart."

Her heart took a little hop. Did he realize what

he'd just said? The way he'd reverted to brooding made her suspect it was a slip.

The moment of hope was only a blip in the dark cloud of anxiety that had her clasping her hands on her lap to hide her shaking from Colin.

"I have the shirt with me. I mean, back at the apartment. It's…" Precious? No, that wasn't right. "I wore it a lot those few first years. It meant something to me. I just don't know what."

"If your parents didn't know you had a boyfriend, you wouldn't have dared wear that shirt where they'd see it. Or run it through the wash at home."

"No. He might have let me wear it sometimes." The pain in her head splintered until she saw black spots before her eyes. "That night…" Her voice broke.

Colin leaned forward, his intensity a force field. "Maybe you weren't running to Emily. You were running to *him*."

Nell had to close her eyes. She pressed fingers to her temple, pushing hard, harder. A whimper escaped her.

The next thing she knew, a big, warm hand captured hers and lowered it. Then he began to massage, far more gently, almost a caress. Her temple, her forehead, her cheekbone. The pain subsided slowly, ebbing like a tide sweeping all debris with it.

The tension gradually left her neck and shoulders, until she felt so weak her head fell back. But not far—it rested against *him*. His belly, rock-hard but moving with each breath he drew. He was standing behind her, she gradually came to realize, both hands now squeezing her shoulders until she moaned softly.

"Ma'am?" she heard someone ask. "Sir? Is there a problem?"

"Migraine." Colin bent forward so his lips had to be close to her ear. "Do we need to go home?"

She felt weirdly relaxed, and she wasn't sure she could stand. The relief was huge. Somehow she shook her head slightly and slitted her eyes open. People at neighboring tables were watching them. Belated self-consciousness had her straightening.

"No, I...feel better." To her astonishment, she did. The pain had to have been purely psychosomatic. *Am I just a little crazy, or a lot?* She blinked a few times. "Thank you, Colin. You saved me."

His worried gaze not leaving her, he returned to his seat. "God, I'm sorry, Nell. That was entirely my fault."

"No." Her head still felt a little wobbly when she shook it. "I've...had that happen before, when I tried too hard to remember. It's one reason I quit trying."

His frown deepened. "Does it happen only when you try to remember certain things?"

Nell bit her lip. "I think so. Not school or friends or Felix. Not even my parents," she admitted. She stared at him, wide-eyed. "Oh, my God. You don't know what a relief that is. It never was them."

"You did remember their faces."

"Yes!" Her ebullience didn't last long. "I can't picture Beck at all, if that was his name. When I try, I get filled with this…this horrible pressure that makes me think my head is going to explode. The minute Emily mentioned him, I had this ominous feeling and I didn't want to talk about him."

"Because he hurt you?" His jaw flexed. "Or because you saw someone hurt *him*."

She stared at him, hating this sensation of dread, hating whatever blocked her from remembering.

At whatever he saw on her face, Colin half rose to his feet, then closed his eyes and sat again. "Okay, that's it," he said, voice raw. "No more, I promise. Thank you for trying, Nell. We're not doing this again tonight." The strength of his concern for her made her tremble.

"It's okay. Really." Seeing his expression, she reached for his hand. "I came back to Angel Butte to remember. I have to keep trying. So I want you to tell me what else you found in the backpack. If any of it was important."

His expression closed. "I wanted you to have a good time tonight."

"I will, once we get this over with."

They conducted a silent battle, gazes clashing. At length his breath gusted out. "Fine. There was a framed picture of a woman and a boy, maybe nine, ten years old."

"What did they look like?"

"Dark hair, brown eyes."

"Can I...can I see it?" Inside she recoiled. *I don't want to. Please don't make me.*

"Damn it, Nell!" Colin said explosively.

"Please." She would not listen to the fear.

He groaned. "Maybe. Probably." After a moment he continued. "A couple of other odd things. He had a key card from your dad's resort. Looked like he or someone else was taking snapshots there, too. There was one of two men at your dad's airfield."

"That...sounds like something I would have done."

"What?"

"I think..." This didn't make her head hurt. "I went through a sort of Nancy Drew phase. Why do I remember this?" There wasn't any answer to that question. "I had a camera, not a good one, but I remember sneaking around spying on guests. If he'd caught me, my father would have killed me." Appalled, she stopped.

Colin's expression remained gentle. "You don't mean that literally."

"No, but..."

He shook his head. "You know that's not what happened, don't you?"

Nell sucked in a deep breath. "Yes." She couldn't

picture any more of that evening than ever, but… she knew. "Yes. It was someone else."

"Okay." He smiled at her. "Now we're going to let this go."

He was careful to keep conversation light while they finished eating. When he asked if she wanted dessert and she declined, he took care of the bill. Then they walked out, hand in hand, going to the open window by the rink, where rental skates were handed out.

After they'd both donned theirs, Colin produced fleece hats from his parka pockets. She snatched the navy blue one so he had to wear the white one with a small pom-pom, laughing at his expression.

Either he'd lied about never having ice-skated, or he was right that expertise at Nordic skiing translated well, because he moved with reasonable assurance on the blades. The rink wasn't huge—nowhere near the size of the indoor one in Seattle where she'd skated before. But she loved this, with the black arch of sky above them, the smell of snow and pine needles in the air, the sparkle from strings of white lights the only illumination except for the golden windows of the resort and restaurant.

Nell didn't let herself think about anything except this moment. Her mind muted the voices and laughs of the other people on the rink with them. Mostly she heard the scrape of blades on ice. Felt the comfort of that big gloved hand holding hers, even as she half wished for skin-to-skin contact.

Colin laughed when he faltered, pretended he was going to fall, coaxed her into showing him how to skate backward. He kept her on her feet when she tried a leap.

Inevitably, his blade caught on a rough spot and he went down. He tried to let go of her first, but she didn't let him. Which meant she crashed to the ice next to him, their legs tangled, both laughing as they slid to thump against a snowbank.

He rose on one elbow to look down at her, flat on her back.

"Told you," she teased.

"You did." His expression was utterly intent, as if the rest of the world didn't exist. Only her. Slowly he lowered his head.

Nell's heart pounded hard as she waited.

"I shouldn't do this," he said.

"I wish you would." She hoped she didn't sound as if she was begging. *I want to know what it's like.*

Shock and understanding transformed his face.

"Oh, no," she whispered. She'd said it out loud.

"I want to know, too," he said, low and rough. And then he kissed her.

CHAPTER ELEVEN

HER LIPS WERE cold. As cold as his. Each breath either of them released hung in a white cloud. He loved the quiver of her lips as he brushed one soft kiss against them after another. Once he had to lift his head to look at her again. In that moment, with her eyes closed so that her lashes fanned above those extraordinary cheekbones, she was so beautiful he felt awe.

This time, when he lowered his head, he nibbled at her plump lower lip, drinking in the small, ragged sound she made. Then, smiling, he made himself roll off her.

Nell squeaked and began to scramble to her feet. He gripped his hand and stayed her.

"Give me a second."

"You can lie there as long as you want." Her voice was stiff. Affronted—or was she hurt? "My butt is freezing. I can skate a lap while you stargaze."

"There are too many people here for me to kiss you the way I want to."

"Oh." He hadn't thought her cheeks could get

any redder, but they did. She sneaked a sideways look at a mother with two giggling children who were passing. "I'm sorry. I thought..."

"I know what you thought," he said, angry that she had so little confidence in her appeal. "You were wrong. I've wanted to kiss you since you showed up in Angel Butte." He levered himself into a sitting position and decided to be honest. "Maybe before that. I'm not sure. I was fixated on you being Maddie even when I watched you in the library that night and loved the way you smiled at people. But from the minute you got here, I've had more trouble seeing the kid. You're Nell," he finished simply.

She lowered herself to her knees in front of him. "Thank you." Her voice was small and husky. "Thank you. Everyone else sees Maddie. I hate it. I'm not her! Except sometimes, and then...I don't know if I want to be."

He nodded. He'd seen her conflict, which was more heavy-duty than his. "I understand," he said. "You *are* both, Nell, and my guess is you'll get more comfortable with it as you integrate the returning memories."

"What if I don't remember much more?" Her shadowed eyes beseeched him. "What if I'm stuck?"

"Then you are," he said practically. "You're a full and complete person, sweetheart. Now you know where you came from. That's got to settle something in you."

Her head bobbed after a moment. "Yes. Of course it does. But complete—I don't know if I am."

"Sure you are." He grimaced. "And now if you don't mind, I think my entire backside has gone numb."

She giggled, a happy ripple of sound that made *him* happier than he could ever remember being. "Okay," she said. "Need a hand?"

"Remember what happens if I'm going down and have hold of you?" If his voice was a little hoarse, he hoped she didn't notice.

"Trust me," she said, the smile still playing on her mouth.

In answer, he laid his hand in hers.

COLIN ACCOMPANIED JANE Vahalik to the police chief's office. Out of respect for Bystrom's dignity, he asked her not to bring her trainee. Out of respect for *her,* he'd have let her go alone if this had been anyone but their boss.

No one was in the outer office to stop them. Colin knocked briefly, and when he heard a growled "Who is it?" he opened the door and gestured Jane to go ahead of him.

Bystrom didn't even seem to see her. His furious gaze was pinned on Colin. "You," he snarled.

Clearly, the bank had called him. Colin was surprised he'd come into work this morning rather than staying away, lawyered up.

Vahalik drew herself up. "Sir, I'm Detective Vahalik. I have some questions I'm hoping you can answer."

The glower swung to her. "I presume this has something to do with the goddamn *warrant* to intrude on my personal finances."

"In part, sir." She walked to the desk and laid a copy of the snapshot in front of him. "Can you tell us who the other man is?"

Choleric color crept up Gary Bystrom's neck and onto his cheeks. "I have no idea. When was that taken?"

"In the neighborhood of ten or twelve years ago," she murmured.

He shoved it away with an impatient gesture. "And you expect me to remember some guy I happened to exchange a few words with *years* ago? Sorry."

"The conversation doesn't appear to be casual."

He stared incredulously at her. "You're reading something into a piss-poor photo taken by who the hell knows? I might have been giving him some tips on where to go trout fishing. I'll say this once more." He leaned forward, his tone belligerent. "*I do not recognize the man in the picture.* Is that clear enough for you?"

Hard to imagine a guy with as much to lose as Bystrom assaulting one of his own detectives, but violence filled the air like a too-heavy cologne. Colin took a few unobtrusive steps closer. Not unobtrusive enough, apparently, as the movement drew another vicious look from his boss.

Jane didn't even look at Colin. "I have further questions," she said, voice steely. "Concerning your finances."

"You owe me an explanation first," he snapped. "What is this concerning?"

"This deposit slip—" she set the copy in front of him, beside rather than on top of the picture "—was in the possession of a murder victim."

"What?" The single word was almost soundless.

"You are aware, sir, of the bones we've turned up in River Park."

"Yes. A few scattered bones. Aren't you making some big assumptions, *Detective?*"

"And what would those be, Chief Bystrom?"

Trying to stay impassive, Colin had trouble not letting his eyebrows climb. Jane Vahalik was good. Better than he'd realized. Interviewing and all but accusing the chief of police would intimidate anyone in the department, and she wasn't so much as flinching.

"What makes you think murder was involved?" Bystrom asked, his voice dripping with skepticism and contempt.

"The fact that the body was buried in an overgrown part of a city park seems suggestive to me." She paused. "The M.E. already believed a gunshot likely explained the way a rib had shattered." She flicked an apologetic glance at Colin. "The bullet found this morning during further excavation seems conclusive."

A nice tidbit she should have told him during their walk upstairs.

Bystrom seemed stunned. "I don't understand. I know nothing more than I've been told or read in the newspaper about these remains. There is no connection to me."

"And yet," Vahalik said, "the young man carried these two items that very much point to a connection."

He shook his head. Colin didn't want the SOB's bafflement to be genuine, but was unwillingly beginning to believe. There was definitely something wrong about the money—but maybe it really *didn't* have anything to do with the murder of a teenage boy.

Except, goddamn it, the kid was carrying the evidence for *some* reason.

He tuned back in.

"You understand why we have no choice but to ask questions regarding the circled deposits to these accounts in your name and your wife's name." Vahalik walked around the desk to lay a folder in front of Bystrom.

Unmoving, he stared at it as if it were a coiled rattlesnake. "This makes no sense."

He kept repeating that. Shaking his head frequently as the tip of Jane's pencil moved from one line item to another. He had no explanation for any particular deposit. Why would he remember them? He insisted that he and his wife regularly bought and sold stocks and bonds.

"We are aware of that," Vahalik said, slick as a patch of ice meant to take the chief's feet out from under him. "These deposits don't seem to correlate to any of those sales."

He got quieter, more surly. Jane informed him that she would need copies of his income tax returns. The purple color in his face faded until, beneath the deep tan, he was turning gray. Colin began to worry about the possibility of a stroke or heart attack.

In the end, Jane straightened. "This copy is for you to study. I assume you have an accountant or tax advisor? Perhaps a broker? We'll need to schedule a meeting with you and perhaps your wife. Bring whoever will be most helpful. Tomorrow at three o'clock?"

He mumbled something she took as assent.

"Thank you for your time, sir. I have every hope we can clear this up then so it won't distract us from the investigation."

Bystrom lifted his head and watched her walk across his office and out the door that Colin held open. Then he looked at Colin, hate glittering in his eyes.

Hair at his nape prickling, Colin eased himself

out of the office without turning his back and closed the door. The assistant's desk was still unoccupied and the two of them were able to quietly walk out and to the stairs.

The corner of Jane's mouth turned up. "I've never interviewed a cop before."

"If his hands had dropped out of sight behind the desk, I'd have been on him." Not knowing where Bystrom kept his service weapon had kept Colin vigilant. Now, alone in the stairwell, he grinned at Jane. "You did a damn fine job, Detective. You didn't need me."

She blushed. "Thank you, Captain. But you're wrong. Having you for backup gave me confidence."

He could only shake his head. She'd scared the shit out of their not-so-respected police chief, and now she was blushing at a compliment.

NELL HADN'T TOLD Colin what she planned for the next day. She might have, if he hadn't kissed her again after walking her to the apartment door.

This second kiss had been deeper, slower, so sensual that remembering it still made her shiver twelve hours later. His tongue had traced the seam of her lips until she parted them and let him in. Even then he hadn't been aggressive. Instead of grinding his mouth against hers, he teased and stroked, his hands rhythmically squeezing her upper arms. Stunned by these new sensations, she hadn't been able to think at all. Finally he'd gentled the kiss further, nuzzled her cheek and murmured, "Sleep tight."

Dazed and robbed of her voice, she couldn't do anything but turn, fumble with the key until the door opened and escape within. She knew he hadn't gone anywhere until he'd heard her turn the dead bolt.

Sleep was a long time coming. She did spend *some* of that time thinking about her plans. Felix was spending the morning with some friends, so she'd decided this was the perfect time to catch her mother alone.

When she reached the house, though, no one answered the doorbell. Turning and looking up and down the quiet street, she thought, *Well, that'll teach me not to call ahead.*

Dad, then, she decided. Maybe he would give her the answers she needed. If not…she'd come back by the house later.

The drive to the lodge felt increasingly natural. *I drove out here a few times once I had my permit.* As always, the memory was unpleasantly visceral. *These* memories were whole-body experiences. She felt her death grip on the wheel, the way she had to remind herself to check the rearview mirror. Dad snapping, "Watch it, Nell!" when she wandered toward one line or other. She desperately wanted her driver's license because it would give her independence, but oh, how she wished there were someone else to teach her. *If only Beck...* .

Oh, God, oh, God. Nell steered to the side of the road and braked, breathing hard, needing to close her eyes and gather herself. Having his name slip so effortlessly into the recollection shook her. *He's* there, *so why can't I remember him?*

If only Beck...what?

At the hint of a headache, she let go of the question. Both questions. A door had opened, though, and he was on the other side of it. The crack could only widen. *When I know,* she thought, *I'll know everything.* The certainty was more unnerving than anything that had so far happened since she'd come home.

Except maybe Colin, she corrected herself. He was something she had never in a million years expected. She knew in theory what these feelings were, but didn't yet know how far she dared let herself go with them.

The fleeting thought about Colin, confused though it was, calmed her. He had a way of doing that. Ever since she'd found his picture on the internet, then printed it and hung it on her refrigerator where she could see his face whenever she needed to. The idea of going home to Seattle and *not* seeing him anymore, having only the picture—that scared her.

Nell gave herself a shake, glanced over her shoulder and, when she found the road to be empty, started toward Arrow Lake again.

When she arrived and went into the main lodge to ask for her father, she first had to endure half a dozen people marveling over her reappearance.

"It's really Maddie!"

She distracted herself from her discomfiture by surveying the lobby with its open beams and massive fireplace. She'd already known what it looked like, down to the peeled ponderosa log furniture.

At last she escaped to the office suite. The assistant's desk was at least momentarily unoccupied, and her father's door stood partially open. The murmur of voices told her he wasn't alone—and it was her mother in there with him.

Oh, boy. Two for one. Nell didn't let herself hesitate.

Her father was behind his desk, her mother standing, looking out the window. Marc's head came up, and Helen swung around to see who'd come in.

"Maddie." Her father rose. "It's good to see you. Why didn't you let us know you were coming?"

"This was…something of an impulse." Which was only sort of true, but she thought a white lie was justified. "I actually stopped at the house first hoping to see you, Mom."

"We're refurbishing some of the lodge rooms," Helen said. "Your father leaves that kind of thing in my hands." Maybe she was here to get down and dirty, but she still wore wool slacks, a cashmere sweater and tiny gold-drop earrings. She looked as stylish as ever, leaving Nell chagrined at her jeans and sweater.

Nell nodded. She didn't remember her mother being very involved with the resort, but it made sense.

Her parents exchanged a glance she didn't understand. "According to Felix, you two had a good day together," her father said.

"Yes. I'm really glad he was able to get home right now."

"Would you like the grand tour? See what's changed?"

"Actually, Felix and I wandered a little yesterday." She smiled. "I remembered how many hours I used to spend on that rock poking out into the lake."

"Daydreaming." Instead of being amused, her mother sounded disdainful enough to renew Nell's discomfiture—and her determination. "You did a great deal of that."

"You sound as if I should have been doing something else." She kept her voice pleasant with an effort. "According to my teachers, I was a straight-A student. Emily says I babysat regularly, so I wasn't lazy. Why was daydreaming a bad thing?"

Her father made a sharp gesture her mother didn't see.

"You weren't involved in a single school activity," she said, the slightest edge in her voice. "I begged you to do something about your appearance, but you simply couldn't be bothered."

Nell met her eyes. "Maybe because you had made it so clear my looks were hopeless."

"What *are* you talking about?"

Just say it.

"I'm asking why I was never good enough. Why you weren't proud of your straight-A daughter. Why you aren't glad to find out I'm alive."

Her mother flinched. From a face that suddenly looked older, her eyes burned. "How can you say that?" she whispered.

Suddenly, Nell had had enough. "Because it's true. In every memory that's come back, I'm feeling inadequate and miserable. Not good enough, not pretty enough, not anything! Felix was the star in our family." Nell kept her head high and included her father this time. "I'm asking why."

"Then you lied about your amnesia?" Helen sounded shocked.

"No. But being in town has made quite a bit come back to me. One of the things I always wondered was why, even when I couldn't remember my own name, I knew I couldn't go home. That whatever was wrong that night, no one at home would believe me."

Her mother's nostrils flared in outrage. "You sound like a spoiled teenage girl, and I don't have to listen to this." She turned to her husband. "Marc, you can find me when you're ready to go back to work." She swept past Nell as if she weren't there, closing the door quietly behind her.

Her father's expression was harsh. "You hurt your mother. Does that make you feel better?"

She shook her head. "No. I'd feel better if I got answers, but I won't, will I?" She nodded and left, too, going straight to her car.

Once she got in, she didn't reach for the ignition and instead sat for a few minutes to be sure she wasn't going to fall apart. The odd thing was, she didn't feel much of anything. She poked and prodded a little to be sure she wasn't numb—numbness would wear off, after all—but she finally concluded that wasn't the case. She just didn't care, not enough to be upset. It seemed she had already dealt with her disappointment about the parents who hadn't loved her all that much.

I already knew, she thought. She'd hoped, but really she'd known. Was it some lack in her, or in them? No, she thought. *Some lack in my mother.* Instinct told Nell her father was typical for a busy, ambitious man whose family was as much for show as anything.

And there it was. His wife showed well. His athletic, handsome son did, too. His gawky, plain daughter with her head in the clouds didn't.

So simple, so sad.

And she still didn't feel more than regret.

Well, then, what else could she do today?

Explore some more, she decided, starting her car.

When she reached the main road, on impulse she turned away from town. She could at least circle the lake, see some more of the outskirts. Maybe drive all the way out to the new Nordic Center, if the highway remained bare of snow that far.

The resort on the lake just beyond her father's looked familiar. With a niggle of memory, she thought it had been upgraded. Oh, and there was the campground. She'd walked that far along the lakeshore sometimes, although she wasn't supposed to. When she was lucky she found other kids there to play with. Dad never noticed she was gone, as long as she was back by late afternoon when he was ready to leave for home.

Ahead, a road turned off to the right, away from the lake. Feeling…something, Nell squinted to see the road sign—253rd. There was no indication what, if anything, of interest was that way. The road was just a road. And yet, her heart had begun to thud in her chest.

She slowed and put her turn signal on. Apprehension morphed into dread.

I've gone this way. Not with Mom or Dad. So… how? Why?

Feeling nearly sick, Nell kept going. She lifted her foot to slow at the couple driveways she reached, but neither seemed to mean anything so she went on. Through the trees she glimpsed newer homes. Half a mile on, a county sign pointed to Bear Creek Picnic Area. A temporary sign had been added:

Closed for the Winter. Whatever force had compelled her to take this road knew she wasn't looking for the picnic area, either.

She had wound a mile and a half when she saw a falling-down sign. Letters had been burned into wood. She had to tilt her head to read it. Bear Creek Cabins. Across the sign, the word *CLOSED* had been spray-painted.

Here. This was it.

The pressure in her head made her want to keep going. Or turn around and drive back to town. Home. *Except it's not home, I'm only a guest.*

No, she had to know.

Low-growing shrubbery pressed close. Branches scraped the sides of her car. The resort might be totally abandoned. But surely the driveway would be grown entirely over if no one ever used it. Her breath came faster and faster.

She emerged into a clearing to see a run-down log lodge—really more of a large house, never fancy like her father's—and a string of primitive cabins stretching along the bank of the creek in each direction.

The resort might be closed, but *someone* lived here. More than a few someones. A couple of teenage boys had their heads under the hood of a car that had to have been as old as the resort. One of them banged his head when he straightened to look. Out of the corner of her eye she saw a whirl of movement by one of the cabins, as if someone were hiding.

I almost remember.

Nell coasted to a stop in front of the larger building. Once she turned off the engine, she sat very still, feeling as if more eyes were on her than the two teenage boys'.

Everything she hadn't felt during the confrontation with her parents crashed down on her like a wave that would snatch her off her feet, tumble her, pull her into an undertow. She wanted desperately to leave.

Instead she got out. Thirty feet away, the boys stood frozen, staring. One had a wrench in a hand marked with black grease. Neither called hello or asked what she wanted. She couldn't tell if they were alarmed or hostile.

She turned when the door opened. A woman stepped out. Unlike the boys', her expression was pleasant and inquiring. "Can I help you?" she asked.

She looked like a modern-day hippie, graying hair braided nearly to her waist. She wore what appeared to be a man's shirt over well-worn jeans and work boots. A few steps down from the porch, she stopped, her expression morphing into astonishment. "Aren't you Maddie Dubeau?"

"You know me?" Nell asked, filled with sudden hope.

The woman became cautious. "Only from the news. Your face has been everywhere."

Nell drew a shaky breath. "I've been here before. Back before I disappeared. Today, I just…drove here." She could do nothing but be honest. "You know I lost my memory."

"Yes."

"Some of it has come back. Only snatches. I don't know what this place is. I had a boyfriend back then. Is it possible… Could he have lived here?"

The woman hesitated for a very long time. "Why don't you come in," she suggested finally.

Nell nodded dumbly and accompanied her. The interior, she saw, was homelike, but on a huge scale, as if this were a summer camp, or a family of thirty people or more lived here. A number of shabby sofas and chairs with sagging cushions were grouped around a large-screen television. Bookcases held DVDs and books. Lots of books. The sight comforted her. By the window stood an enormous Christmas tree, decorated with a motley assortment of ornaments. On the other side of the large, open space, long tables were ranged in rows, a combination of benches and mismatched chairs providing seating. Nell could see through a doorway into a kitchen that was equipped with a commercial range and refrigerator, a contrast to the lack of money spent on the furnishings.

Something inside her relaxed. It was all familiar, but not because Nell remembered being here.

"My name is Paula Hale. We—my husband and I—take in teenagers," the woman said awkwardly.

"This is a youth shelter," she said with delight.

"In a manner of speaking," Paula agreed, but with restraint. "Please. Sit down. Can I get you a cup of coffee? It's always on here."

"I— Yes. Thank you."

A minute later they sat across one of the tables from each other, each conducting a cautious survey.

"You understand," Paula said at length, "that we operate somewhat under the radar here."

"Back home, in Seattle, I'm an active volunteer at a shelter called SafeHold."

Her face brightened. "I've heard of it. It's one of the best."

"Thank you. I think so."

"We're...somewhat different here." She hesitated. "This is a last resort for these kids. They have been returned repeatedly to abusive homes. If we didn't take them in, they would be living on the street in constant fear of authority. I'm sure you're aware how poor the outcome would be for them."

"Yes. Of course. I see." A sense of urgency pushed back her momentary pleasure at realizing what this place was. Her head hurt, and she knew how strained she must look. "You must wish I hadn't appeared. But what I'm here to find out is important. I was attacked.... You know my story?"

"I do." Paula sounded sympathetic.

"Some bones have been found in the park."

"I read about that," she said slowly.

"Along with the bones was a backpack. Things

in it suggest the boy might have been a runaway. Detectives are puzzled, though, because along with family mementos and a change of clothes he was carrying schoolwork."

"We do homeschool here." She sounded even more reluctant now. "I and another woman have teaching certificates with secondary certification. Of course we can't issue diplomas, but we prepare the kids to take the GED."

"You've been doing this a long time."

"Eighteen years."

"Could the boy in the park have come from here?"

She sighed. "Of course it's possible. Kids don't always tell us when they're leaving. We're sorry when they just disappear, but if we made inquiries it would alert authorities and jeopardize what we can do for the kids who remain."

"His name was Beck. I don't know if that was a first or last name."

Paula gazed past Nell, her eyes momentarily unfocused. "That's…familiar. It's an unusual enough name to have stuck." She didn't move. "You place me in a dilemma."

"I know. I shouldn't ask, but…I don't know where else to go." She hoped her sincerity showed. "I'll do my best not to reveal what you do here."

After a moment she nodded. "I do keep some records. If you're willing to wait…"

"Please." She was clutching the coffee cup as if it was a life buoy. "I think what happened to him might have been the same night. It might be linked to my disappearance."

When Paula returned, Nell's gaze locked compulsively on the thin manila folder in her hand. She wished fiercely that Colin were here, but she couldn't have brought him. Given his position, he might not be able or willing to turn a blind eye to what went on here, and being responsible for destroying this refuge was something she didn't want to have on her conscience.

"There's no photo, I'm afraid," Paula said apologetically. "Not all that much information, either. He was here only about six months."

Nell sat, her knees refusing to hold her up. Paula slid the folder across the table. Nell kept staring at it.

Please don't let me pass out.

"Unless he assumed a new identity when he left, or is dead, it ought to be possible to trace him from this information."

Nell stared at the top sheet, a court order. She'd seen plenty of them. This one remanded custody of one Beckett Spencer to an uncle, Kurt Jarvis, giving the uncle's address in Eugene—here in Oregon but on the other side of the mountains.

"After his mother's death," Paula said, "he was forced to live with his uncle, who was an abusive drunk. Unfortunately, the uncle was also a cop. Despite documented bruises and broken bones, he convinced the court that he was a caring guardian of a troubled youngster."

Nell turned pages and saw notes. Grades. A couple of essay tests and one that she thought was calculus.

"He was very bright, a fine student." The woman's voice was soft, regretful. "Certainly ready for college. He was also nearly eighteen, at which point he would no longer need to stay here."

"Did he drive?" Nell knew she sounded ragged.

"Yes. My husband teaches the kids who are old enough, but we do so on empty roads. None of them can afford the risk of applying for permits or licenses until they turn eighteen and family courts no longer hold sway over them."

Yes. That was why Beck couldn't teach me.

"We always have several mountain bikes here available for the kids to use. Some ride them into town. If they make friends, we discourage them from bringing those friends back here."

"Yes. But he did."

"It happens. We try to stay casual, as if the kids here are in conventional foster care. I don't think we met, or I'd have remembered you when I saw your face in the news."

"I...wish I knew."

Paula touched her hand lightly. Nell sensed that

her compassion came naturally. "You can take the file if that would help. I only hope…"

"I won't tell Captain McAllister where this place is."

The worry in her eyes remained, but she nodded.

"Thank you." Nell pushed herself to her feet. "I can't tell you how much this means to me."

Paula held her gaze. "Don't make me sorry."

"I won't. I'll try not to. It's going to be hard," she admitted, "with this a murder investigation."

"I understand. If it's true one of our kids was murdered, we have to support an investigation."

Aware her welcome had expired, Nell thanked Paula again and went out to her car. The two boys had vanished. In fact, the place might have been deserted but for her and Paula, who stood on the porch.

After setting the file on the passenger seat by her purse, Nell started the car. The drive circled so she didn't have to back up or maneuver. She had reached the tree line and was taking a last look in her rearview mirror, wondering how many people besides Paula were watching her go, when she heard a *crack*. Simultaneously, something stung her cheek.

Branch… But she saw the tiny hole in her window and dived sideways to the sharp sound of another gunshot.

CHAPTER TWELVE

COLIN ANSWERED NELL's call on the first ring.

"Colin?" Her voice was very small. "Somebody shot at me."

"What?" He shot to his feet, his desk chair rolling back and spinning.

"I don't think I'm hurt," she said, sounding as if she weren't sure.

He left the office at a run, ignoring his assistant who called after him, bounding down stairs instead of waiting for the elevator. "Where are you?" he demanded.

A different woman's voice came on the line and gave an address out in the boonies. "We've already called 911," she said. "Maddie is inside and safe. We're locked down. My husband has his rifle and is standing by the front window."

Lights and siren cleared the road in front of him. In the grip of fear, Colin drove with reckless speed. Goddamn it, he should have asked more questions. Who were these people and why was Nell at their home? But he wasn't sure he'd have taken it in if Nell or the strange woman had told him. His brain had stuttered and stopped on the unendurable realization that she could be dead.

He passed her father's resort without slowing. The turn onto 253rd took him out of his jurisdiction and into Butte County. He'd driven out here at some point in the past, but didn't remember why. County park on the right—yeah, he'd known that was there.

The black mailbox at the head of an overgrown driveway had the right street number hand-painted on it. Colin turned off the siren and slowed to navigate the narrow track. Within moments he emerged into a clearing and saw that he was the first responder. Nell's car had been left at an angle next to a battered pickup truck with the hood propped open. Her driver's side door stood open. To avoid contaminating a possible crime scene, he parked a distance away, then, hand resting on his weapon, got out and started toward the main building. His gaze swept the surroundings ceaselessly. Forest in three directions, too many buildings. He felt incredibly exposed, uneasy with the isolation and silence so complete it seemed unnatural. He saw no movement whatsoever.

His fear and fury soared when he saw two perfectly round, splintered holes in the driver's side window of Nell's car, two more, he saw, bending over, on the passenger side. Entry and exit. Two holes in the windshield, too. A tear and hole punched in the headrest. The rear window was intact. They'd be able to recover at least one of the bullets.

How had she escaped alive?

He guessed at sequence and trajectory, trying to calm himself before he went in to talk to Nell. He was aware that the front door of the main building had opened and that an armed man stood there. The possibility existed that he had been lured out here. The smart thing to do would have been to wait out at the road for the sheriff's deputies, who had to be on their way.

He hadn't even seriously considered doing so.

He kept his hand on the butt of his Glock as the man nodded and started down the steps. His head kept turning, too, as he stared uneasily toward the woods.

"Captain McAllister?" he asked when he got close enough.

Colin nodded at him. "You are?"

"Roger Hale. This is my place."

"Nell's inside?"

"Nell?" His eyes narrowed. "We have a woman in there, but that's not her name."

"Maddie," he corrected himself. "Maddie Dubeau."

"That's her."

"Damn." On a tsunami of emotion, he squeezed the bridge of his nose. "I need to talk to her."

"I think he's gone," Hale volunteered as they walked side by side. "Haven't been any more shots.

It's been damn near fifteen minutes." He cocked his head. "Sheriff's department."

Colin, too, had heard the distant siren. He couldn't imagine the shooter was still in the woods, but by God they were going to comb every square foot until they found out where he'd stood and how he'd arrived and left.

Hale gestured for Colin to go ahead of him into the big log building. Scanning the interior he felt momentary surprise before his focus locked onto Nell, sitting on a bench in the dining area. He was only peripherally aware that another woman was with her. The bearded man kept talking.

"Place used to be a summer camp. We foster kids off and on, have family that comes and goes. Works for us."

Nell had to be in shock. She held a wad of tissues to her cheek—the same place where the scrape had barely healed. Her face was too pale, her eyes glassy. Freckles stood out sharply.

Colin squatted in front of her and took her free hand. The part of him that still could assessed her. The other part choked his voice. "You just took ten years off my life," he said.

She gave a funny, choked laugh. "Who needs to jump out of airplanes for an adrenaline rush?"

"How are you?" he asked, voice pitched for her ears only.

"Just shaken up. I was…" Her voice wavered. "I was lucky the Hales were here."

All he wanted was to hold her. But, damn it, the wife was standing only a few feet away, and the husband had gone to the door as the siren was silenced outside.

"Can you tell me what happened?"

She did. She was driving around, thought this resort looked familiar and turned in for a look. She'd talked briefly to Ms. Hale, gone back to her car and started down the driveway when she heard a gunshot and realized bits of glass had struck her face.

"I threw myself sideways, thinking, I don't know, that it was a hunter out there, although this isn't the right season, is it?"

He shook his head.

Behind him the woman said, "We have our land posted 'no hunting.' Lots of signs."

"There was another shot. And…and I hadn't put my seat belt on. I never forget! But this time… Thank God. The belt might have gotten in the way." She had to stop to breathe.

Colin squeezed her hand.

"I've never been so glad not to drive a manual. I managed to reverse and push on the accelerator. I guess I just went hurtling back. I think—" she shivered "—I think that's when a bullet came in through the windshield."

Two bullets. He nodded encouragement and didn't correct her.

"I'm lucky I didn't smash into something." She directed an apologetic look at the woman. "I managed to brake when I could see the buildings and the hood of the pickup still raised. I thought I was sheltered behind the pickup. I threw open my door and fell out. I started to crawl. Mr. Hale came rushing out, bent over, I guess, to make a small target, and together we got back in here. And then he called 911 and I called you."

He heard voices on the porch but didn't so much as turn when feet stamped and cold air and a couple of deputies entered. To their credit, they hung back as he coaxed Nell into telling him where she was on the driveway when she heard the first shot. She knew it had come from her left, which he could have guessed now that he knew she was departing rather than arriving when she was ambushed.

He left her with Mrs. Hale and a cup of cocoa—apparently he wasn't the only one who thought of it as comforting—while he stepped outside to talk to the Butte County deputies.

Their initial prickles about his presence subsided quickly when he explained who Maddie was and that this was the second attempt on her life this week. They set out to case the woods while he returned to ask her some more questions.

Could she have been followed here?

"I...I don't think anyone was behind me." Chagrin tinged her cheeks with color. "I wasn't really paying attention. I mean, I was just wandering, not going home. Not even planning to stop anywhere."

"Nell, where had you come from? Any previous stops this morning?"

Her parents' house, where no one was home, then her father's resort. Turned out both her parents had been there. He didn't ask what was said, but could tell from her expression it wasn't good.

"You parked in front at Arrow Lake, went straight into the lodge, then straight back to your car."

"Yes."

He mulled that over. "Not a good place to set up for a shot."

"There were quite a few people around," she agreed.

Her eyes were aware now, the glassy look gone. She was scared, all right, but thinking again. "You believe somebody spotted me in town, followed me to Arrow Lake, then decided to stick behind me in case an opportunity arose?"

"That's what I think." As empty as the roads out this way were, Colin figured sooner or later the guy would have taken his chances and roared up beside her little Ford as if he planned to pass. With electronic windows, he could have rolled his down, pumped some bullets in her and kept going, nobody the wiser. Goddamn. He wasn't letting her out of his sight. "Seems unlikely we have a random nut wandering around in these woods." He rolled his shoulders and stood. "Have you had any problems before, Ms. Hale?"

She shook her head. "Never."

"You'll stay with Nell while I go outside?"

"Of course I will."

Colin asked for permission to have Nell's car towed to the Angel Butte P.D. impound yard. The deputies exchanged a glance and agreed.

The search turned up some trampled vegetation and a fresh wound on the trunk of a lodgepole pine. If snow had stayed on the ground out here, they might have found a good footprint or tire print. No such luck. None were clear enough to be worth taking a cast of. They didn't find any cartridges; whoever he was, he didn't believe in littering. A couple hundred yards beyond the Hales' driveway was a gravel road that led to a cabin. When Colin jogged back, Roger Hale said it was a summer place. He didn't think anybody had been there in months. The shooter had pulled in, probably knocked on the door to be sure no one was home and left his vehicle there, nicely out of sight of passing motorists as well as anybody at the Hales', while he trekked through the woods and found a perfect blind to set up for Nell's departure.

Colin suspected the first shot was the one that carved the groove on the tree trunk. Missed Nell. The shooter had corrected immediately, but she'd had time to react. He pulled the trigger a few more times, but likely knew people were at home at the Hales', so he beat a retreat. By now, he could be anywhere.

Hale said he thought he had heard a vehicle about the time he was escorting Nell into the small lodge, but it was far enough away he didn't think about it at the time.

The deputies agreed to wait for the tow truck. Nell thanked both the Hales half a dozen times and then allowed Colin to lead her out to his 4Runner. They were almost there when she broke away.

"I have to grab a couple of things from my car."

Once he had her belted in and started forward, her gaze roved ceaselessly over the undergrowth pressing so close.

"He's gone," Colin said quietly.

"I know." But he could tell she wasn't convinced, and he couldn't blame her.

He accelerated onto 253rd and left the former Bear Creek Cabins behind. Nell sat beside him, silent.

Colin waited until he'd reached the highway to ask his questions.

"Why the Hales' place, Nell?"

She jumped. "I told you. It seemed familiar."

"So you drove all the way in."

"Yes."

"Did anything there nudge your memory?"

She bowed her head and stared down at her hands. "Not exactly."

"Evasive maneuvers 101."

She shot him an angry look. "What's that supposed to mean?"

"You know what it means, Nell. You're hiding something. Why?" When she didn't answer, he contemplated what he'd seen out at the Bear Creek property. Ten or twelve cabins—he hadn't counted. Run-down enough, they probably wouldn't appeal much to vacationers, but they weren't falling down, either. Glass sparkled in windows. He'd noticed the raw look of new wood on a couple of the cabins where porches had been replaced. Someone was doing maintenance. Room in the dining hall for as many as thirty people to eat together, if he had to guess. He hadn't really been paying attention to what Roger Hale was saying, but was able to pull it out of his memory banks.

Place used to be a summer camp. We foster kids off and on, have family that comes and goes. Works for us.

Voice elaborately casual. The guy had felt the need to explain the unusual.

"Runaways."

Nell turned an alarmed look on him.

"The place is a shelter, isn't it?" He braked at a red light as they came into town. Home Depot on the right, Staples on the left. Colin was able to turn his head and see the worry and guilt and who knew what else in those big brown eyes. "Did you already know about it, Nell?"

Her shoulders sagged finally, about the time the light turned green and he was able to start forward. "No. Colin, I'll tell you about it, but I want you to promise you'll leave them alone," she begged. "Please."

He wanted to give her the moon, but knew better. "I can't promise until I know what you're asking."

After a moment she swallowed and nodded. But then she looked out the window, lost in thought, and stayed silent. Knowing how much she'd been through, he let her stay that way.

Colin kept an eye on his rearview mirror as he drove through town toward home. Nobody stuck behind them for an unreasonable length of time. In fact, they had the road to themselves when he turned into his driveway. He used the remote to raise the garage door and parked inside. Nell got out and stood waiting for him, her body language awkward and even rebellious. For a flicker he saw Maddie. She would have looked just like that, waiting for one of her parents.

The brew of anger and fear in him kept Colin from feeling as sympathetic as he might otherwise have.

"Come on up to the house," he said. "Have you had lunch?"

She shook her head.

He didn't ask if she were hungry. He knew what she'd tell him, but by God she was going to eat.

Inside, he nudged up the thermostat, then shed his parka as she did the same. He headed to the kitchen, and saw her set her bag on the table.

As he put soup on to heat and began assembling sandwiches, he said, "Talk to me, Nell."

"I told Paula I'd try to keep what they do there to myself."

"Paula?"

"Hale."

"What is it they do?"

She told him, every word reluctant. A runaway shelter that, for all practical purposes, didn't exist. Kids who refused to go home no matter what the courts determined. An underground referral network, he imagined.

"Kids can be damn fine con artists," he said. "How do these people know they aren't falling for sob stories and hiding criminals?"

"We didn't get so far as to discuss how they screen the kids they take in. But Beck's file..." She stopped, as if just realizing what she'd said.

Colin turned slowly from the stove. "Did you just say what I think you did?"

"Yes." She lifted her chin defiantly. "I was going to show it to you."

"But not tell me where you got it."

"I was going to tell you about the shelter, just not where it is or who runs it."

He swore under his breath and faced the stove again. The soup had reached a hard boil and with a frustrated motion he yanked the pan off the burner.

"You think I don't trust you," she said, sounding timid and diminished in a way that made him even madder.

He was overreacting and knew it. A man whose rigid self-control was so integral he never had to think about it, he didn't like discovering he could be knocked off center so easily. This wild swing of emotion threw him back to his youth, to a time he didn't want to revisit.

Dishing up the soup and carrying it to the table gave him a minute to regain a semblance of his usual calm.

Even that was shaken again at the sight of her face, pinched and anxious, turned up to his.

"Shit." He set down the bowls, bent over and kissed her. The taste and scent and feel of her soaked in, giving him the reassurance he'd so far lacked. Arousing him, too, but he tried not to think about that as he ran his fingers over her cheek and into her hair. For an instant she stayed completely still, not pulling away but not responding, either. Then her lips softened and she pushed herself up enough to deepen the kiss.

Satisfied, he was able to straighten. Her cheeks were flushed, her hair tousled by his fingers. "I meant it when I said you scared me," he told her.

She gulped and nodded, her eyes huge.

Maddie.

No...Nell. All Nell when she kissed him.

He returned to the kitchen for the sandwiches and drinks.

Sitting down, half a sandwich in his hand, Colin watched as she picked up her spoon but made no move to start eating.

"Nell," he said, "I know you have good reason to sympathize with what the Hales are doing. If anybody had recognized you during the years you were on the run, you'd have been returned to your parents, no question. Nobody would have listened when you said you were afraid to go home."

"I suppose I was thinking that."

In that moment, he made up his mind. "I'll do my damnedest to keep the Hales out of this as anything but kind folks who helped you."

"Thank you." She seemed to be battling emotion. Not tears, he hoped. "Paula—Mrs. Hale—gave me the information she had on Beck even though she knew she was taking a risk. She said if one of their kids had been murdered, they'd do whatever they had to."

Colin nodded acknowledgment. They'd seemed like good people to him. Officially, he couldn't approve of an operation designed to thwart the law he upheld. But he'd been abused himself. He knew how often courts sent kids back for more, in part because quality foster and group homes were scarce.

"Did she remember Beck?"

"Yes. Mostly because his name is unusual. He'd only been with them about six months when he disappeared. She said kids sometimes just leave.

That's what they assumed he'd done. She gave me the entire file on him, which isn't much."

She dug in her bag and produced it. Colin flipped through the few pages. Beckett Spencer. Birth date included. He would have been seventeen when Maddie knew him. The uncle's address in Eugene matched up with the address of the studio where the photograph had been taken of mother and son.

"Now you can find out if he's alive, can't you?" Nell asked, an entreaty in her voice.

"I can." He spoke gently, because they both knew the boy hadn't lived to turn eighteen. "He must have taken you out to the shelter."

"Yes. Paula said they discourage kids from bringing friends home, but don't forbid it. She's sure she never met me, though, or she'd have remembered me when there was all the coverage after I disappeared." She huffed out a breath. "It makes me crazy. I can drive straight to a place I probably only went to once or twice, but I can't see his face."

"You're protecting yourself."

She dropped her spoon. "I wish I'd quit."

"It's coming back, Nell, you know it is. Dealing with those memories in increments has got to be easier than being slammed with all of them at once."

She nodded, but her expression said she was frustrated and angry. Colin didn't blame her. He hated having his own emotions fluctuate. How would he handle feeling as helpless as she must?

Not well.

"Eat," he said.

She made a face at him, but complied.

She'd finished half her sandwich before she said anything else. Then she fastened her gaze on him. "Do you think he hurt me, and that's why I blocked him out?"

Although still a possibility, it was a remote one in Colin's opinion. There must have have been a confederate. Somebody had dumped Maddie in the trunk of that car and then driven north to dispose of her. Somebody had shot Beck and buried his body.

"We can't rule it out, but…no. That's not what I think happened."

"Then *what?*" she exclaimed in frustration.

He could only shake his head.

NELL OFFERED TO load the dishwasher while Colin studied the scant information in the file and then made a call. She couldn't hear everything he said, just enough to know he was talking to the woman detective Nell had met. He gave the basic facts about the attempt on Nell's life. Hearing anyone, but especially Colin, discuss it so coolly upset her for reasons she couldn't pin down. She'd been trying to keep herself from remembering, and the matter-of-fact recitation made it flash in living color behind her eyelids.

She blinked hard, trying to obliterate the images,

and became aware that, even as he talked on the phone, Colin's gaze rested on her.

She turned her back and squirted soap into the saucepan.

Behind her there was a pause. Then... "Beckett Spencer." Colin spelled the first name. "Yeah, that's right." There was a pause before he gave the date of birth and uncle's name and address. "If the uncle doesn't know Beck's current whereabouts, it would be helpful if he can point us to dental records. After this many years, it's not likely he kept something of the boy's we might be able to get DNA from, but you never know." He said "uh-huh" a few times before ending the call.

"Nell?" He'd come up behind her silently.

She took her time hanging up the dish towel before turning, her face carefully composed. "Are you heading back to work now?"

"I'm not going anywhere."

There was something in his voice and in the way he was looking at her. Her whole body seemed to flush, and then did it again. She wanted to back away, even as she longed to throw herself into his arms.

"I might go take a nap." She *couldn't* back up, with the counter behind her.

"For my peace of mind, will you nap in here?" His voice had a noticeable rasp. "You can have my bed."

"I... You don't think...?"

"No. But right now, I need to keep you close."

"Are you going to stand there staring at me while I sleep?" she joked, wishing her voice hadn't wobbled in the middle. She could not imagine lying down and closing her eyes with him watching.

"I won't do anything you don't like," he said gently.

Nell let herself look into his gray eyes. It was like falling down the rabbit's hole, tumbling and tumbling. She *couldn't* look away.

She knew what she wanted, but…was it what he wanted, too?

He took a step closer and cupped her cheek in his hand. "Nell?"

A little sound escaped her. Tears burned her eyes, and she couldn't do anything but step forward, almost as close as she wanted to be.

"Nell," he said again, this time sounding raw. The next minute, he was kissing her, devouring her, and she lost herself in a kind of pleasure she had never even dreamed she could feel. She flung her arms around his strong neck. He gripped one buttock and lifted her against him even as his other hand cradled her head. She was shaking, and thought he was, too.

He tore his mouth away at last and looked down at her, the gray of his eyes now molten. "Nell, the last thing I want is for you to feel pressured. I'm here for you, no matter what. Tell me you know that."

"I know that." She rose on tiptoe and pressed

kisses along his hard, scratchy jaw. "I know you wouldn't abandon me."

"I want you."

A chill chased away some of her body heat. "I want you, too, but…I have to tell you something first."

His fingers sifted with exquisite gentleness through her hair. "Are you infected with HIV? Something else?" He sounded impossibly kind.

A little shocked, she stared at him. "No!"

"Then what, Nell?"

She closed her eyes, feeling such shame. Wanting to hide from the expression she feared to see on his face. "When I first got to Portland…I was afraid to ask for help, or go to a shelter. Some older kids sort of took me under their wing. They thought I was even younger than I really was." She opened her eyes. "I did, too."

"I know what you're going to say, Nell." His hand slid around to lift her chin. "Those kids told you how you could make enough money to buy food, maybe pay your share of a room, didn't they? They probably told you where to go and what to say, how much money to ask for."

Her face wanted to crumple, but she nodded.

"What were your options? Begging, stealing or selling yourself."

"I couldn't make myself steal. I just couldn't." She gave a broken laugh. "Letting a man do…do *that* upset me less than shoplifting. What does that say about me?"

For a moment something hard and dangerous crossed his face. "You're honest," he said finally. "That's what it says."

She shook her head even though she wasn't sure she wanted to know what had passed through his mind. "You were thinking something else."

He looked at her for a long moment. "All right. I'll tell you, but first let's go in the bedroom. I'll tuck you in, and then you can invite me...or not. Completely optional."

After a moment she nodded, wanting to believe she was courageous enough to take a step so monumental.

CHAPTER THIRTEEN

WITH COLIN'S ARM around her, Nell felt brave. Besides, the worst was behind her, wasn't it? She'd told him, and he really didn't seem to mind.

As he guided her toward the back of the house, she caught a glimpse of an office. The other room, the one he steered her into, had a huge bed with a comforter covered in patterned ivory and navy blue flannel. She had trouble taking in anything *but* the bed. She made herself glance around, however, pretending if only to herself that accompanying a man to his bedroom was at least a seminormal occurrence for her. She liked the few furnishings, the simple Shaker-style. Closet doors were closed.

He sat her on the bed and knelt to untie her shoes.

"Oh!" Nell tried to stand. "You don't have to…"

He smiled at her, so much tenderness in his expression she came close to crying. "I want to." When she sank back down, he removed first her shoes then her socks before rising to his feet. "Do you want to take off your jeans?"

"I…suppose so." Feeling the heat in her cheeks, she stood and shimmied out of them quickly, pulling back covers and climbing in before she dared look at him again. Then she lay back against his pillow, comforter tucked under her arms.

"Scoot over." When she did, he sat beside her. "Have you done any reading about repressed memories?"

Her breath came faster and she quit worrying about where she was or that she was already half-undressed. "Yes."

"Then you know that a common theme is sexual abuse. More than children who are physically battered, ones who are sexually molested learn to distance themselves. Go away in their head, so whatever is happening to them feels unreal."

"But *who...?*"

He shook his head. "I don't know. Your brother is too young. Your father leaped to mind, but you don't seem to react to him as if you have that kind of history with him."

"I wish I knew for sure," she said, troubled. "Could it have been Beck?"

"You associate him with something traumatic, but if he made sexual advances you didn't like, why wouldn't you just have said no? He didn't have any hold over you. You could have avoided him."

"That's true. And then there's his shirt. It was comforting to me, not scary."

"Were there any other adults you spent a lot of time with?"

"I don't know. I can ask Felix. I'd say my parents,

but they're pretty mad at me right now. I asked why I was such a disappointment to them."

"Didn't go well, huh?" he said sympathetically.

"No. I probably shouldn't have bothered. Mom said I was acting like a spoiled teenager and stalked out. Dad was mad because I had upset her." She shrugged. "No great insights shared."

"I'm sorry." He sounded as if he really meant it.

"I wasn't as upset as I thought I might be. I guess I didn't expect anything else."

His jaw set. He seemed to have trouble speaking. "I'm really starting to hate your parents," he finally said, then shook his head. "And I shouldn't have said that."

She smiled and touched his hand, lying on the cover temptingly near hers. "Why not? I appreciate the sentiment."

His hand captured hers, not letting her draw back. "It occurs to me we should talk to your uncle Duane. As far as I know, he didn't spend that much time with you, but it won't hurt to ask him."

Why didn't she remember this uncle at all? Her puzzlement didn't last long; why didn't she remember most of the kids she'd gone to school with, or her teachers? Why didn't she remember most of her life?

"Ask Felix, too," Colin continued. "You may have been involved in some activity. Debate, Knowledge Bowl? There could have been overnight trips to competitions."

She shook her head. "I don't think so, but…" She felt a spurt of temper. "Oh, do you know how tired I am of having to say 'I don't know'?"

"I can imagine."

Both were silent for a moment, and her thoughts jumped back to her confession. Maybe she wasn't done with what she had to say.

"I feel dirty when I think about what I did." The burning pressure in her sinuses was different from her "trying to remember" headaches, but just as bad. "I don't see how anyone else can not despise me."

He shook his head, and she could see only tenderness and understanding. "I hate that it happened for your sake. I kept a picture of you where I could see it for twelve years. You looked so young, so innocent, and yet also so sad. It's hard for me to imagine that girl enduring what you did."

She blinked hard to keep herself from crying. "I only did it a few times. I thought I could stand it, but I couldn't. I got by after that for a couple more months by hanging out in fast-food restaurants and snatching food out of the trash when people threw it away. They had clean bathrooms, too, and nobody paid that much attention to who was hanging around."

He closed his eyes. "God, Nell."

She remembered him saying, *You're breaking my heart,* and wondered if she could. If he felt that much for her, and why.

"You really don't mind."

He looked at her again. "For your sake," he repeated. "Not mine."

She waited for him to tell her she really should sleep and they could talk about this later. Under the guise of caring, it would be easy for him to leave her without overtly rejecting her. But when he didn't move, her heart felt as if it were swelling painfully in her chest.

"The thing is," she said in a husky voice, "since then, I've never…"

Heat flared in his eyes, but he seemed to deliberately bank it. "I don't suppose you associated men with anything good."

"No." She hadn't consciously thought, *I don't like men,* but knew now that it was true. She kept her distance from them. Her friends were all women. She exchanged as few words as possible with their husbands and had certainly never gotten to a hugging or kissing-on-the-cheek stage with any of them. She was cautious around men who came into the library. Not afraid, just…not letting them get too close. No wonder, now that she knew what her relationship with her father had been like. She'd had no basis for trust.

So how was it she had trusted Beck? *If I actually did,* she reminded herself.

"Were you a virgin the first time, Nell?"

She stared at Colin, shocked. "Of course I was!" Then she realized how illogical she was being and shook her head. "That's a dumb thing to say. But it means I wasn't sexually abused, doesn't it?"

He was shaking his head even before she finished. "The abuse didn't have to involve penetration. It could have been no more than touching. That's plenty traumatic when you know it's wrong and nobody will listen to you." He kept his tone matter-of-fact, although a thread of strain told her it was taking him some effort. "There could have been oral sex. A man could have been grooming you for later, when you were more physically mature."

She knew all those things happened because at SafeHold, she'd heard stories that gave her nightmares.

So why was it that, beneath her surface calm, pain gathered in her head, as bad as when she tried to remember Beck? Worse. She was so close to remembering this. Touches. Commands. Affection disguising something horrible. *It happened to* me. *I know it did.*

"Nell," Colin said sharply. She blinked and discovered he was shaking her lightly, his hands on her shoulders. His face was creased with worry.

"I'm okay." The sight of him brought her back to the here and now. The anxiety diminished. "I almost knew something," she whispered. "I think… it did happen. What you said."

"But you don't know who."

She shook her head quickly. "It was almost there, but...not. My head started to hurt."

"Like at the restaurant." He groaned. "My fault again. I'm pushing you."

Nell stiffened. "*I'm* pushing me. I won't be safe until I remember. I have to remember."

"It'll come."

"When?" she cried. "When?"

"I don't know." His guilt and discouragement weren't hard to see. "Maybe I should leave you. Let you get some rest."

It was only what she'd expected, Nell reminded herself. She didn't blame him. She lifted her chin to be sure he didn't know he'd hurt her. "If that's what you want."

"Damn it, Nell, you know it's not what I want." He glared at her. "I want *you*. But you've had enough today. We have time."

Did they? She had come so close to dying today, she knew better. She sucked in a fortifying breath. "I'd like it if you would stay." Uncertainty kicked in. "If...if you really mean it."

His eyes blazed. "You're sure?"

She nodded, even if she was also afraid of the unknown.

"Uh...give me a minute." To her surprise, he stood and went into the bathroom. A drawer opened and closed, then another one. What on earth...? But when he came back, she thought, *Oh*. He had something in his hand.

He bent and unlaced his shoes and kicked them off, tossed his socks on top of them. He hesitated and unbuttoned his dress shirt, leaving it dangling over a rocking chair. Nell's breath caught at the sight of his broad, naked chest. Over strong muscles, dark hair formed a triangle ending in a line that disappeared inside his slacks.

"Too much?" he asked, in a deep voice.

She gave her head an emphatic shake.

His mouth quirked in an almost-smile as he unfastened a narrow black belt and the button at his waist, then eased the zipper down. Beneath he wore snug-fitting navy blue knit boxer shorts that did nothing to hide the extent of his arousal. She desperately wanted him to shed those, too—and yet it was a little bit of a relief when he didn't.

He grabbed the duvet, said for a second time, "Scoot over," and slid into bed beside her. Rolling onto his side to face her, he smiled wryly, probably at the sight of her near-panic.

"Your first time."

That made her stomach dip. "It's not." Had he not *believed* her?

"What you did wasn't making love."

"Is that what you call it when you want to have sex?"

"Yeah, but it's usually a euphemism. A way of prettying up something that's really just physical." The timbre of his voice vibrated her senses. "What we're going to do, though, Nell, it will be making love."

"Oh." Her cheeks felt as if they were flaming. "Have you…?"

He shook his head. "I've had sex. I've never felt like this before, though."

If she'd been standing, she would have melted like candle wax. As it was, her fear melted away. *Oh, please,* Nell thought, *please let him mean it.* She reached out tentatively and laid her hand on that lovely bare chest. He tensed, and she felt a thump as if his heart had thrown in an extra, hard beat.

"Explore all you want," he murmured.

For a few minutes, he only watched, groaning a few times, as she did exactly that. She kneaded, curled her fingers in his chest hair, followed it down to the elastic band of his shorts and chickened out there. That was okay—she reveled in what she could see. Eventually she got brave enough to lean close and kiss his neck and even lick the hollow at the base of his neck, loving the salty taste of his skin. No ugly memories surfaced, to her relief. Maybe she could do this. She drew circles around his small, flat nipples, then daringly kissed them, too. That groan was especially guttural. His hips seemed to lift from the bed momentarily.

She drew back. "Is that okay?"

"Yeah." He sounded breathless. "Nell? Can I do a little exploring, too?"

She bit her lip and nodded.

"Is it okay to lose the shirt?" When she nodded again, he said, "And the bra?"

"Yes. I don't, um, actually need it, you know."

"Sure you do." He smiled at her. "It's armor."

It was. She wore lots of armor, she realized.

She sat up and let him pull her shirt over her head, then watched his face as he took her bra off and looked at her. She was barely a B cup, but the dark flush that ran over his cheekbones and the glow in his eyes convinced her he liked what he saw.

"You're beautiful," he said, low and rough, then bent his head, first to kiss her. It was deep, passionate, fueling her rising tension. But he didn't linger; instead, his mouth moved down her throat, then her chest until he kissed one nipple.

The sight of his dark head bent over her was erotic, but even so she hadn't imagined how it would feel when he drew her nipple into his mouth and sucked. She squeaked and her hips bucked and he slowed enough to slide his tongue in a slow, sensual circle around her nipple. Then he moved to her other breast and did the same.

By the time his hand slid inside her panties, she was past feeling shy. She needed his touch, first pressing, rubbing. When one finger slipped between her folds, she moaned and opened to him.

Every so often, he lifted his mouth from her body long enough to talk. He told her over and over how beautiful he thought she was, how sexy, how he loved the way her hips rocked and her nipples peaked and how she blushed.

After coming back to her mouth for another slow, hungry kiss, he lifted his mouth and just looked at her for a minute. "Your eyes have always gotten to me," he said, his voice transformed by hunger.

Nell ignored the twinge of unease that gave her. Right now, it didn't matter what he meant by *always*. She was savoring the sight of his eyes, too, almost black with need and tenderness. The muscles in his back and upper arms were rigid, and instinct told her the deliberately slow pace of his lovemaking was costing him. But, oh, it was wonderful. So like him. He'd never been anything but patient with her. There was none of the groping, ugly urgency she remembered, only that patience and…love. It felt like love.

Her panties were gone, and suddenly, so was *her* patience. She wanted to feel, to see…. She curved her hand over the thick, hard ridge barely contained by fabric and squeezed gently.

His laugh was closer to a groan. "Let me…"

"Yes, please," she said politely, and he laughed again, more genuinely, if still strained.

The shorts went flying and he lay, rigid, letting her stroke him, cup him, tease him. And then he made an inhuman sound, growled, "Enough," and reached for the packet he'd set beside the bed. He had to push the covers back, giving her a chance to see his thick, pulsing penis before he sheathed it. The sight was the first to awaken something unpleasant in her head. She'd seen...

Colin noticed that she'd frozen. He caressed her face. "We're making love," he whispered, and began to kiss her and touch her again, until that glimpse of a memory was forgotten and hunger to merge her body with his swept away any doubts.

Once he'd spread her legs and moved over her, he held himself completely still. "You okay, sweetheart?"

"Yes." She wriggled her hips. She wanted...no, *needed* him to move. "Please."

He rested his cheek against hers and thrust. There was no pain at all, only pleasure. She heard herself make sounds that should embarrass her but somehow didn't. He rocked into her, out, and she couldn't have stopped herself from pushing up to meet him if someone had put a gun to her head. This desperation to feel him deeper, harder, faster, grew until it felt like... She didn't know. A spring winding tighter and tighter in her belly. It couldn't take any more tension. It couldn't. It couldn't...

And then it sprang loose, flooding her with unimagined pleasure. She could only hold on to Colin and stare in astonishment at his face, stark with his own release, as he pulsed inside her and his body jerked.

He tried to half roll off her as his weight came down, but she wouldn't let him. Nell wrapped her arms around him, and she squeezed her eyes shut and rested her cheek against his as he buried his face in the crook of her neck. Tears stung her eyes.

So this was what real happiness felt like.

REGRET, OR AT least worry, brought him down fast once he'd gotten dressed and left Nell sleeping.

Making love with Nell—Maddie—might have been a huge mistake. No, it was the timing that stank. Colin didn't know how he felt, she couldn't possibly know how she felt. She'd been scared and needed reassurance. He groaned and rubbed a hand over his face. Yeah, he'd been scared and needed reassurance, too.

But he didn't want to feel too much for her if she intended to return to Seattle as soon as her leave of absence was up. Why would she want to stay in Angel Butte? Was he willing to quit, start over somewhere else, when he was so damn close to getting Bystrom out of office and maybe having the chance to develop a truly effective police force?

Even thinking things like that was so uncharacteristic of him, it set him on edge. And yet—he was in love with her. He knew he was. There was a reason he hadn't been able to help kissing her several times before. What he feared was that his fascination for Maddie had morphed into the emotion that was giving him heartburn now. He couldn't deny the power her face, her eyes, had always held for him. If that were the case, what did it say about him? What if Nell had come to town and he'd recently met her? What if she wasn't Maddie? Would he feel the same?

He swore under his breath.

What if, in his confusion, he hurt her, a woman who had been hurt too many times?

He knew he'd never forgive himself.

Colin sat at the table, his laptop open in front of him although he hadn't gotten any further than turning it on yet. Twice he'd stood up and walked silently to the bedroom to make sure Nell was still there. Still sleeping, not tossing in the grip of a nightmare. He'd meant it when he said he didn't want to leave her this afternoon. Couldn't leave her.

But he also itched to know what was going on with the various investigations. Had accountants turned up any answers about where all that money deposited into Bystrom's account had come from? What about Beck? Jane would have been—

His phone rang and he reached for it quickly. Who else? "Jane," he said.

"The uncle isn't a very nice guy," she announced without preamble. "The first time I called he said, I quote, 'Why would I have kept anything of his? I was done with him.' He did grudgingly give me the name of the family dentist."

"And?"

"We have confirmation, Captain. No question."

"Oh, hell," he said, bowing his head. So much

for any hope those bones had nothing to do with Maddie Dubeau.

"Opens a can of worms," she agreed. "Means he can't be the one who attacked her and abducted her."

"No. It's more likely he was protecting her."

"That seems to be the likeliest scenario."

Had to be, he thought, even knowing there were other possibilities. Maybe she'd shown up to meet him and he was already dead or she saw him killed. But why would anybody have wanted him dead? Because he was dealing...? Colin shook his head without finishing the thought. The Hales thought Beck was a great kid. Colin had seen the kind of student he was. Maddie had been shy and innocent, not the kind of girl to be attracted to a bad boy.

And then there was her memory block to account for. The headaches confirmed Colin's belief that they weren't talking memory loss from the physical injury, even if it had contributed. She was afraid to remember, even now.

He heard her say, *I think it did happen.* The look on her face, when she just...went away, that had scared him.

What worried him was that there would be no answers until she did remember. And in the meantime she'd be in danger.

Jane also reported having sent her trainee out to Arrow Lake to show the photo of mother and son around. He'd gotten only head shakes. The dentist in Eugene, though, remembered the family. Beck and his mother both looked Eastern European, pale, with dark hair and eyes.

"It has to be them."

"There's some connection to Arrow Lake, damn it. But what?" Colin growled.

"Maddie," she said tentatively.

He only shook his head. In November, Maddie was in school full-time and unlikely to be going to work with her father much or at all. The weather would have been too cold for her to enjoy wandering at will the way she did in the summer.

Except, it occurred to him with a jolt, the proximity of the resort to the Hales' place was suggestive. If her father didn't pay any attention to where she was or what she did all day, she could have gone with him on Saturdays or Sundays, then walked as far as the Hales'. Or Beck biked to meet her. She probably knew how to program key cards for a particular room. She could have chosen a vacant one and let herself and Beck in. Of course, she'd be risking an uproar if a maid walked in on them. Daddy Dubeau wouldn't like his little girl being found in a lodge room or cabin with a seventeen-year-old boy.

Where else could they have hung out for the day? he wondered. Did it matter? Even if they found out, would that tell them anything?

Probably not, he thought, scowling, but he didn't like loose ends.

Right now, something else was on his mind. "Jane, you were on the Drug Enforcement Team."

There was a moment of silence. "Yes?" It sounded wary.

"I want you to crop out Chief Bystrom from that picture and show it around. You don't have to tell anyone the context. I don't want to be thinking this, but I am. The combination of a private airfield, substantial, unaccounted-for payments and the photo of Bystrom talking to a man he doesn't want to admit he knows…"

She mumbled something he suspected was profane.

"Go for people who were working drug enforcement then. They might remember the face."

"Do I tell the lieutenant?"

Colin hesitated, feeling reluctant. "No reason not to," he said at last. He trusted Duane, of all people. Duane wasn't a gossip. "We don't want word to spread, that's all. You know how touchy this is," he ventured. "If you'd rather, I'll do it. You know there's a risk here."

"Of finding myself unemployed?" Her brashness was part of what made her good at her job. "I console myself with knowing that if I am, you will be, too."

He laughed. "Misery loves company."

They ended the call with him thinking, *If Bystrom fires my ass, there won't be any reason not to move to Seattle.*

And he'd be close to Cait, too.

He was making a big assumption. What if Nell wasn't thinking beyond tomorrow, or next week?

Trying to settle himself down, he checked email, responding to several messages that had nothing to do with the investigations that had him on edge.

His thoughts spun in circles. The glory of making love to Maddie. Nell. His confusion. The gray cast to Gary Bystrom's tanned face as he stared at his downfall, neatly highlighted in yellow. The picture of the dark-eyed boy with his mother. Maddie again—the knowledge of what she'd gone through, and the terror that had driven her to do anything at all to avoid authority in any form, because she would be sent back where she came from. The headaches, so far triggered by thoughts of Beck, and of the possibility she had been sexually molested. But not her parents, however unsatisfactory the relationship with them had been. Not her brother.

He had a hell of a headache by the time he heard the soft sound of a door closing and then the toilet flushing. A minute later, Nell appeared, looking shy. Knowing he couldn't let her see his doubts, he smiled and rose. "Hey."

"Hey," she responded.

She came to him and he kissed her, sinking into the rightness of her in his arms. He had to figure out what held him back. He didn't think he could bear to lose her. He hadn't known how lonely he was until he saw Maddie in that television clip. From that moment on, he'd been waiting, hungry for those phone calls.

And that took him back to Maddie. Because he couldn't deny she *had been* Maddie to him, until she arrived in person and he got to know her better.

Finally he held her away from him and studied her face. Despite the nap, purple shadows underlaid her brown eyes. Several tiny clots of dried blood decorated her cheek where she'd been struck by flying bits of glass. He could still see the healing trace of the scrape from the icy street on the same cheek.

Whatever else he needed and wanted, seeing her happy, relaxed, contented, rose to the top. There was an ache at the realization of how protective he felt, because it hadn't gone so well the last time he felt like this. He'd have done anything to keep his little sister safe, and instead he might have played a role in driving her away. He'd used violence to try to protect her, and had long since realized that probably wasn't the best tactic. Maybe bringing Maddie home hadn't been any smarter.

"You look worried," she said, and he realized she was studying him as thoroughly as he was her.

"There's something I have to tell you," he admitted.

Her face went still. "Beck?"

"We identified him. Detective Vahalik called the uncle, who gave her the name of the family dentist. She says there's no question."

Nell sank into one of the chairs at the table. "I knew it was him," she admitted in a small, tight voice. "Otherwise, wouldn't you think he'd have come forward then? Told the police if I'd confided anything to him?"

"He had reason not to." But Colin had a feeling she was right. The young Maddie had loved, or at least liked, Beck Spencer, which said a lot about him. His choice of mementos, the fact that he kept the photo of his mother and the evidence of his father's service and sacrifice in a war—that said something about his values. "Yeah," he said, for Nell's sake, "I think he would have come forward, too."

She nodded. "So we know something."

"Something that doesn't seem to take us anywhere else." He hesitated. "There's something I haven't told you. I probably shouldn't, but it might conceivably spark a memory for you."

Nell tilted her head and watched as he returned to his place at the table. "What's that?"

"We found one more thing in Beck's backpack. A deposit slip." He explained, and saw comprehension darken her eyes.

"That must be a hard question to ask."

"We asked anyway. I don't think the answers are anything Chief Bystrom wants to give us. I know damn well nobody in the department will like finding out what he was doing to earn those payments."

"Do you think this has anything to do with *me?*" She looked as bewildered as he felt.

"I don't know," he said honestly. "You were fifteen years old, damn it!"

"But if I was getting nosy. If he realized he'd dropped the deposit slip but couldn't find it and maybe remembered seeing me snapping pictures…"

"That's a possibility we have to consider. Jane told him where the deposit slip was recovered from, though, and I don't think he had a clue who Beck was or how he came to be buried in the park. I could be wrong—but I hope I'm not."

She gave a smile that had a quirk to it. "Imagining the police chief you've been working for all these years doing something illegal is bad enough, but the idea of him murdering a kid must be worse."

"You're right." He detested Bystrom, had for years. But he'd despised him for his lack of work ethic, his choice of appearances over substance, his unwillingness to support his officers in favor of making nice with his buddies on the city council and in city hall. However bitter his dislike, Colin had never considered the possibility that the chief was crooked. He had such a bad taste in his mouth, he understood why he wasn't rejoicing in circumstances that would inevitably mean Bystrom's dismissal.

Good riddance, yes; pleasure in the way it was happening, no.

He had a feeling Nell wasn't going to like what

he had to say next. "I don't want you wandering around on your own anymore."

She stiffened. "What *do* you suggest? That I stay in the apartment by myself?"

Colin wanted to believe no one knew she was living here, but he couldn't be sure. And no, he didn't like the idea of her being alone.

She wasn't done. "Or here's an idea. Maybe you have a free cell in the jail?"

She suggested it so nicely, he had to grin. "Actually, that's not a bad idea."

"Of course, even there I might be vulnerable to someone who works for Angel Butte P.D."

He stared at her. Either she was being snippy— or she'd taken a jump he hadn't wanted to.

If Chief Gary Bystrom were on the take, how could he possibly be alone?

"We'll think of something," he said, feeling unexpectedly grim for a man who'd only a couple of hours ago had the best sex of his life, and was hoping to have more as soon as bedtime arrived.

CHAPTER FOURTEEN

COLIN FINALLY CONSENTED to release Nell into the custody of her brother the next morning. He drove her to her parents' house and waited until Felix came to the door. After the briefest of introductions, he then issued instructions and extracted a promise from them both to meet him for lunch.

In bemusement, her brother watched Colin stride back to his SUV. Shaking his head, he shut the door. "What's got him hot and bothered? I know he's the guy who found you, but why are you still hooked up with him?"

She peered cautiously past him. "Is Mom home?"

He looked troubled. "Yes, but she went back upstairs when I told her you were coming. Neither she nor Dad said a word about you last night. Does that have anything to do with what's got your cop stirred up?"

"Uh...no." She sighed. "Yesterday was eventful."

"Well, *I* haven't had breakfast. Why don't we go out?"

"Please," she begged, stealing another furtive look up the stairs at the still-empty hall.

He took her to a Pancake Haus and wolfed down a truly enormous breakfast while she nibbled on toast and sipped coffee. He listened, his expression still worried, as she told him about her talk with their parents.

"Mom is excellent at denial" was his only comment.

He reacted with predictable alarm to the rest of her story. "Maybe you should buy a gun." He shook his head. "No, you don't have to say it. Dumb idea. Maddie…maybe what you should do is leave. Go back to Seattle."

He was the one person besides Colin she had told about her life in the past twelve years. If nothing else good came out of this journey back in time, finding her brother made the trip worth it. Now she had family. He'd even talked about job hunting in Seattle once he completed law school. Her flicker of pleasure at the idea of having Felix near had been drowned by grief at what she'd lose when she went back.

But…maybe that wouldn't happen. Colin hadn't said he loved her, but he had implied.

What we're going to do, though, Nell, it's making love.

Unless he were only trying to make her feel good about it. Distinguish between the act that shamed her and an honest sharing with a man who cared.

The look on his face yesterday when he walked toward her at the Hales' had stunned her. She had good friends, but no one had ever looked at her like that, as if his world would end if she died. That was more than caring, wasn't it?

Now, she told Felix what Colin had pointed out—that if he could find her, so could other people. It would be easier now. The publicity about her return might well have reached Seattle. Chances were good she'd find herself a minicelebrity when she went back to work at the library. Too many people would know plain Nell Smith was also Maddie Dubeau.

"That makes sense," Felix agreed, his forehead still creased. "What if you come home with me for a little while?"

She smiled tremulously at him. "Thank you, but I'd have to resume my life at some point, and then what would happen? I'm here to try to remember what happened."

"And if you can't?"

Nell didn't answer. Somebody wanted her dead. Recovering her memory and finding out *who* might be her only hope.

His phone rang and Colin glanced at it impatiently. Considering he planned to take a whack out of his day for Nell... And then he saw the name of the caller.

He picked the phone up. "Cait?" he answered in disbelief.

"It's me," his sister said. "I, um, just called to say hi."

"To say hi," he repeated. It had been years since she'd called for any reason, never mind to chat.

"I'm sorry we didn't get more time when you were in Seattle. Blake wanted to come with me, and then you and I didn't get much chance to talk."

"No, we didn't," he said.

"I shouldn't have told him I was meeting you."

She couldn't have simply told the guy she was getting together with her brother and she'd rather go on her own?

"He wanted to meet you," she added, as if reading his mind.

"I see." He frowned. "Cait, are you okay?"

"Of course I am," she said hastily, but for the first time he realized how soft and uncertain she sounded. Not okay at all.

To get her to open up, he asked how her Ph.D. dissertation was going, and her voice gained some animation. She hoped to have it done by summer, which meant she'd be job-hunting in the not-too-distant future. She asked about his work, and they talked superficially about their lives for maybe five minutes. Colin relaxed some, but didn't lose his worry that something was wrong. Whatever that something was, it became apparent she hadn't called to tell him.

"I'd better go," she said finally, even though

neither had said anything very important. "I love you, Colin."

A stab of emotion made his voice gruff. "I love you, too, Cait. You know, I'm here if you need me."

"I do know." She said that so quietly, he barely heard. "Goodbye."

She was gone, leaving him to continue brooding about why she'd called. *My sister, the stranger,* he thought.

All he could think was, Cait had felt lonely. She'd needed a connection, and he'd gotten elected. Maybe she'd had a fight with their mother. Or with the boyfriend. Or both.

He didn't like to think of her lonely, but didn't see what else he could have said.

Disconcerted, he realized that a month ago he'd have been as lonely as she sounded. Now he wasn't.

He looked at the clock, wishing it was time to meet Nell.

"THE KID BROTHER," Hailey said with a grin when Nell and Felix arrived at the bistro. "And *so* much better-looking than you were back then."

He snorted. "You were the fat girl then."

She only laughed. "Now I'm the fat chef."

"Nah." One eyebrow rose as he appraised her. "Now you're pleasingly plump. A peach."

Watching the flirtatious byplay, Nell found herself laughing, too. Her brother must have women lined up. As if she'd ever see him if he did move to Seattle.

"As it happens, I have a lovely peach tart available today. I think you've earned a freebie," Hailey told Felix. "In a manner of speaking. Ah. Here comes Captain Sexy."

Nell turned as she heard the creak of the door and felt a rush of cold air. He appraised the room in one sweep, as he always did new surroundings, then had eyes only for her. She suspected that, despite the brevity of that survey, he could have described every single person in the room down to the color of nail polish or the tattoo peeking out of one shirt collar. Her heart drummed at the sight of him, tall and strong in one of his well-cut suits, today's a dark gray.

"Safe and sound," she informed him.

Menus in her hands, Hailey was already heading for a table at the back, Felix following. Nell basked in Colin's smile as the two of them trailed behind.

"Did he have to throw his body between you and danger?" Colin asked.

"No, but he did whisk me out of the house before Mom came downstairs," she confessed with wrinkled nose.

"Good enough," he murmured in her ear. She thought he nuzzled her slightly, the contact still enough to send electricity through her sensitized body.

Too late, she saw that Felix had turned and was watching quizzically.

He didn't comment, though, and once they were

seated she and Felix described their morning—a drive out to the Nordic Center, then some shopping downtown.

Not until they had ordered did she ask about Colin's morning.

"I did some wandering at your dad's resort."

"Why?" she asked, puzzled. Felix, too, she saw, was looking at him in surprise.

"It just seems the resort is at the center of too much. I've been out there, but not really taken a look around. Somehow, I hadn't quite realized how sprawling it is. I think it's expanded since the last time I was there."

Felix told them both about the stages of expansion, starting with the airfield not long before Maddie disappeared. "That was pure genius," he said, admiration in his voice. "It's an attraction for people with real money. They wanted more luxury, so Dad tore down some of the old cabins and added the monster places. That's when he decided to go time-share with them and, later, some of the smaller cabins. Brought in solid capital and the yearly maintenance fees besides."

Hailey herself delivered their lunches and bantered with Felix again. Nell might have thought they were interested in each other, even though he was three years younger. But maybe, it occurred to her, the difference in age didn't matter much now that both were in their twenties.

JANICE KAY JOHNSON

307

She was still thinking about the spark her friend and her brother had as they all dug in to their food.

Colin and Felix had continued to talk about her father's resort.

"I'm surprised your father didn't talk Duane into ditching law enforcement and going to work for him," Colin commented. "He'd have made a hell of a lot more money."

"Uncle Duane moonlights as security out there sometimes." Felix grimaced. "Who'd *want* to work for Dad full-time?"

Colin frowned at Nell. "You still haven't seen Duane, have you? He took it as hard as your parents did when you disappeared. Harder, maybe, because he insisted on taking charge of the investigation and then felt like a failure when we didn't find you."

She shook her head. "I've been a little busy, you know. And I haven't been in town very long." She thought back. "Nine days?"

"That's true," Colin agreed, but the creases remained in his forehead. "Duane told me he bowed out of the dinner because Felix had showed up and he didn't want to get in the way. Listen, why don't I have him to the house for dinner?" He raised his eyebrows at her brother. "Maybe you can join us?"

"Sure." Felix sounded pleased. "I saw Uncle Duane at Thanksgiving, but not since I've been home this time. I have to head back to Salem on Sunday, though."

"Tomorrow night, then." Colin's eyes glinted with amusement. "Here comes your peach tart."

"Both kinds," her brother murmured, then winked at Nell's astonishment.

COLIN STOPPED BY the detective's division to pick up Jane Vahalik before the meeting with Bystrom. Once again, he was accompanying her only to provide the authority of someone in a senior position. *Backup,* he thought, with a small grin.

She was waiting for him with news. A sergeant on the Bend police force who had served for ten years on the Drug Enforcement Team had immediately known the man in the picture, the one engaged in an intense conversation with Angel Butte's own police chief.

"James Lewis, although that may be an alias. He's a pilot who the DEA had been watching for years. They know damn well he was ferrying drug shipments. Before they were able to make an arrest, he dropped off everyone's radar about five years ago. The assumption seems to be that he's dead. Bend had gotten a tip about him, but by the time they caught up with him and his plane, it was clean and he had insisted he was only flying some skiers in from Southern California. A rich couple backed up his story. Nobody believed him, or them, but what could they do?"

"So our police chief just happens to have been

conversing with a likely drug trafficker at a private airfield."

"Right about the time he started pocketing some nice payments."

Duane had joined them and heard the update. "Would you prefer I step in for Jane this afternoon?" he asked.

Colin shook his head. "She's doing a good job. And me, I've already got a bright red bull's-eye painted on my chest. Best if some people with seniority around here keep their heads down when the bullets start flying."

Duane chuckled. "You know me. I like nothing better than hunkering down."

"I wanted to talk to you." Colin stepped to one side, his lieutenant joining him. "You still haven't seen Maddie."

"Things have been happening…." He grunted and rubbed a hand over his thinning hair. "Hell, I can't lie to you. I think I've been making excuses to myself. I'm not kidding myself about what kind of reception she's probably getting at home, and that makes me feel guilty. I knew she wasn't very happy back in the day. My sister…" He hesitated. "She's got problems. Reasons for 'em, but I'm not sure that excuses her for being as hard on Maddie as she was. All I've been able to think all these years is that maybe I could have made more of a difference if I'd tried harder."

"You never said any of this."

"Helen is my sister," he said simply. "With Maddie gone, there was no point."

"I'm sorry," Colin offered. "I didn't realize. I expected you to be first in line to greet her."

"Honestly—I think I've been holding on to the memory of her as a little girl," he said gruffly. "I really loved her. I don't know the adult she is now. I guess I don't want to find out she's changed too much."

Colin had no trouble understanding that. He was having enough inner conflict himself over the girl she had been and the woman she was now. Explaining that, though, would give too much away. Something told him Uncle Duane wouldn't like finding out Colin was sleeping with his little Maddie.

"She would like to see you, though," he said. "Any chance you could come to dinner tomorrow night? Felix will be there, too."

Duane's face worked, as though he were struggling to hide too many emotions. "Yeah," he said finally, clearing his throat. "Yeah, that sounds good. Have her let me know if she wants me to pick her up. Felix, too."

"I'll do that." Colin didn't know why he was hiding the fact that Nell was living at his place, even from Duane. It was better if no one at all knew, he told himself. Saved him from admitting how much time they were spending together. "Six o'clock?"

"Sounds good." Duane glanced at his watch. "You'd better be on your way."

Five minutes later, Jane and Colin walked into the conference room to find only their accountant present. Ten minutes later, a Bend attorney Colin had encountered in courtrooms before arrived to say that his client was angered at this intrusive investigation and had chosen not to cooperate. He saw this as a political attempt to get rid of him. He would be speaking to Mayor Chandler and possibly filing a civil suit against the city, in particular naming Captain McAllister.

When he left, the three of them looked at each other. Colin nodded after a minute, resigned.

"I'll call the mayor." He looked at the accountant. "Anything you can tell us?"

"The questionable payments are from two sources, both corporate holding companies that consist of nothing but some named officers—all attorneys—and a post office box. Going deeper is beyond my means. I've got to tell you, though, entities like this raise obvious red flags."

"So, since explaining is problematic, he's decided to see if he can get by with *not* explaining." Colin nodded again to them both. "Thank you for coming. I'll let you know what we need to do for follow-up."

The two left him alone to make the call.

He stood at the window looking out at the river as he dialed. He was put through to Noah Chandler right away. Colin explained what he knew.

The silence felt reflective, and he waited patiently.

"I think this investigation needs to get bigger," Chandler finally said. "If he'd cooperated, I would have been willing to keep this confidential until we had answers. As it is, I'll let him know that any hope of keeping his job is conditional on that cooperation. If he won't give it, I'll ask for his resignation. Give me a day before you take any further steps."

"All right."

"What do you want to do next?"

Like most cops, Colin didn't love bringing in the feds, but the time had come.

"We need to bring the DEA in on this." He told the mayor what the accountant had reported. "They have the resources to dig deeper into the source of that money than we can." He hesitated. "I think it's important that, for both our sakes, we avoid the appearance of this being some kind of coup."

There was a moment of silence.

"I've heard a lot of gossip about drug shipments moving through this area," Chandler said bluntly. "What I haven't heard about is the number of arrests you'd expect. Not a lot of shipments seized, either."

Colin had given up being anything but blunt. "Detective Vahalik is currently coordinating with the members of the Drug Enforcement Team in an attempt to find out whether these payments coincide in any way with failed raids."

"Good. What worries me is that he couldn't act

alone. If he warned about raids, who gave him the information in the first place? You know we're heading toward an internal investigation. Who else has been paid off?"

Colin swore under his breath. "Every officer in this department is going to feel unfairly targeted. Morale is already poor. This may be the killing blow."

"You're suggesting we let it go?"

"No." He squeezed the back of his neck. "No, of course not. It has to be done."

"All right. Let's hold off for a day or two, see where we get with Bystrom. Then I think we can't afford to wait."

They talked for a minute more about the whys and hows. A minute later, Colin ended the call and growled a few words he didn't usually allow himself.

Before he knew it, the finances of colleagues and friends within the police department would be under intense scrutiny. These were men and women he had trusted and would need to trust again in the future. But he knew as well as Chandler did that, if the police chief had been on the take, there had to be others.

Goddamn it. He would have liked to warn Brian Cooper, his counterpart in Patrol Services, a straight arrow if he'd ever known one. And Duane. Blindsiding a longtime friend like Duane didn't sit well with him. But he also knew he wouldn't say a word to either.

This wasn't how he'd anticipated accomplishing his longtime goal of cleaning up the Angel Butte Police Department. He wouldn't be a popular man by the time he was finished. He would be traveling a dangerous road, and essentially doing it on his own. *His* only backup would be a man he hardly knew, the political outsider who had become mayor.

CHAPTER FIFTEEN

COLIN'S MOOD WAS grim the next day. He wouldn't tell Nell much, only that the police chief had "lawyered up"—his words—and that he was having to expand the investigation. When she asked how, he said, "Better you don't know."

The conversation was taking place in his kitchen. Felix had taken her grocery shopping and she had cooked dinner for Colin again. Her reward was the relief on his face when he came in the door and saw her, and then smelled Hungarian goulash cooking.

"Is this all happening because of me?" she asked, turning from the stove.

"No." He kissed her lightly. The lines on his face were deeper than she'd seen before. "Can I do anything?" he offered, checking out her dinner preparations.

"I already have a salad made. Dinner will only be a few minutes. Relax."

He disappeared to his bedroom and came back having shed his suit coat, tie, badge and weapon. He was rolling up his sleeves when he walked back into the kitchen.

"What do you mean, 'no'?" Nell asked. "If Beck was killed because of me…"

"He might have been, and he might not. I may turn out to be wrong, but I really don't think whatever Bystrom got himself involved in has anything to do with you, unless you're the one who took the picture of him talking to someone he shouldn't have been associating with."

"And maybe picked up the deposit slip."

"Yeah." His smile eased the strain on his face. "Nancy Drew."

After dinner, while they were clearing the table, he asked if she'd stay at the house with him.

"Because you're worried about me being alone?"

"A little bit." He tugged her to him, then rested his forehead against hers. "Mostly because I want you in my bed."

Happiness blossomed in her. How long he'd want her in his bed—well, that was something she'd worry about later, when she had to.

Suddenly she laughed.

Lifting his head, Colin quirked an eyebrow at her.

"Felix says Mom is a master of denial. It just occurred to me that I've got her beat in that department. Refusing to think about anything that's uncomfortable? That's for amateurs. Me, I can *really* put things out of my mind."

His rich, husky laugh sent shivers of reaction

through her. Colin noticed—and somehow the dishwasher didn't get loaded that evening.

THE NEXT MORNING, Colin dropped Nell at Emily's house. It was Saturday, and they'd arranged to spend the day together. He wanted to issue all sorts of protective orders again, but resisted.

"You should be safe enough with her," he said finally, unsatisfied but resigned to the fact that this was the best they could do.

He'd have been embarrassed if Nell had known how relieved he was to find her in one piece and even cheerful when he picked her up at five. He liked her friend, who was such a contrast to Hailey that he'd been surprised by her. Emily was class, Hailey irreverence. Somehow Maddie had attracted both as friends.

"You sure you don't mind cooking again?" he asked during the drive. "And for company?"

"Which happens to be my family. And no. I bought what I need yesterday. I might as well at least make myself useful."

He frowned at her. "I don't want to take advantage of you."

Nell laughed. "Admit it. You love having a break from cooking."

He gave her a crooked smile. "You're right. I do." He liked even better not having to say good-night to her at the foot of the stairs to the apartment. That first night after she arrived in Angel Butte, he'd taken comfort in seeing the light on in the window up there. Now he didn't want to be standing alone, looking out and seeing that light again. Tomorrow morning, he was going to suggest she move the rest of her stuff to his bedroom.

He might still be confused, but he sure as hell wanted her with him no matter what. The idea of going back to his solitary existence held no appeal whatsoever.

Nell kicked off her boots and padded around in stocking feet while she put dinner together. Tonight it was purple socks with big, splashy red flowers. A green stem twined around the toes on each foot. Every day he looked forward to seeing her socks. She admitted they were something of a fetish.

Tonight was to be sweet-and-sour chicken on brown rice, he learned. As Colin worked on the salad, he couldn't help noticing that she was getting quieter and quieter.

"You okay?" he asked.

She barely glanced at him. "Sure. I'm just feeling a little anti-family right now. With the exception of Felix, of course. But he says he likes Uncle Duane, so I'm sure it'll be fine."

"I don't know how close he is to your mother, except that he told me once he did move to Angel Butte because she was here. He said she was the only family he had."

"I assume he isn't married or you'd have invited his wife, too?"

"Never has been, as far as I know. I suppose he could have been before I knew him. He's got to be mid-fifties. Pretty much a loner. I think he's got a lady friend over in Portland. He gets over there regularly."

The doorbell rang. "I'll get it," he said, kissed her cheek and left her in the kitchen.

Felix was on the doorstep, Duane just pulling in. Felix and Colin waited while he parked his car next to Nell's small red one and crossed the yard.

"Felix," Duane said as the two shook hands. "Bet you're glad to see your sister."

"Yeah, having her back is pretty amazing." It was obvious her brother meant what he was saying.

"You two don't look much alike," Colin observed.

Felix shrugged. "Never did. She got her looks from Mom, I got mine from Dad." He cocked his head and studied Duane as the two divested themselves of outerwear. "Come to think of it, you don't look much like Mom, do you?"

"Same deal as you two, I imagine. Then there's the fact that your mother colors her hair...."

Felix elbowed him. "You mean, she's *kept* her hair, don't you?"

They all laughed.

Nell came from the kitchen to meet them, her gaze on Duane although she first hugged her brother. Duane held out his arms and, after an almost infinitesimal hesitation, she let him hug her.

Her reluctance wasn't obvious, but Colin saw it. No wonder, he thought—hugs probably weren't plentiful in her childhood.

She crossed her arms in front of herself when she stepped back. "You're Mom's brother."

"That's right." Duane seemed shocked. "You really don't remember me."

"I'm afraid not. There's…a great deal I still don't remember."

Colin wished she hadn't put that *still* in there, with its implication that her memory was coming back.

"Damn," Duane said, shaking his head. "Colin told me, but I guess I didn't believe it." He searched her face. "He said you remembered Helen and Marc."

"Only flashes. But I must have spent a lot more time with them than I did with you."

His expression darkened. "I knew your mother was hard on you. I tried to give you some extra attention to try to make up for it. You and I were good friends. I thought seeing me might bring that back."

Nell shook her head, something panicky in the tight movement. "I'm afraid not."

Colin stepped closer to her, laid a hand on her back. "Do we need to work on dinner?" he asked, keeping his voice relaxed, easy.

Her eyes flashed to his, grateful, he thought. "Oh, no! The rice is probably boiling over. Excuse me for a minute."

She fled. He offered drinks and ended up getting beers for all four of them. He paused in the kitchen. "You okay?" he asked her quietly.

"Yes," she said. "Just…" She didn't finish. He waited a moment but she didn't continue.

As the evening progressed, he worked damn hard to keep Felix and Duane from noticing how withdrawn Nell was becoming. Something was going on in her head, but he had no idea what. She didn't blank out the way she had a couple times, which was his only consolation.

At first he thought Felix was oblivious, the way he kept teasing her, trying to make her laugh, but then Colin began to wonder if her brother wasn't trying as hard as he was to keep conversation ongoing and light.

Duane, in contrast, kept trying to dig out memories that weren't there—or were burrowed deep and unwilling to lift their heads.

Half a dozen times, he started questions with, "Do you remember when…?"

"I'm sorry," Nell kept having to say.

Understandably enough, Duane wanted to know about her life since she'd disappeared, too, and she answered some questions and was politely vague about others.

"What part of Seattle? Oh, like most renters I move every so often. Rent goes up, I shop around."

Duane asked for another beer, and then another. His bafflement and hurt were plain, giving away enough to make Colin feel sorry for him. As long as he'd known Duane, the man still kept his private life just that. Colin had guessed he didn't have much of a life off the job. He hunted and fished with some buddies his age, neither activity interesting Colin. Colin had been to his house and seen how bare it was. For twelve years, Duane had mourned Maddie, but now she was here and he meant less than nothing to her. Yeah, that wouldn't feel good.

Dinner was excellent, as were the tarts topped with cream Colin thought he recognized. Especially when she set a plate in front of Felix and murmured something in his ear that made him laugh.

His own was cherry, but when he glanced across the table as Felix took a bite, he recognized peach and hid a grin.

"I hope you like blueberry," she said politely to Duane. "If not, I'd be glad to switch. Mine's apple. I confess I bought these. I went for a variety."

"Either's fine," Duane assured her. "Dinner was a treat. I'm ashamed at how rarely I make a real meal for myself. Your mother is a heck of a cook, too, you know."

"I'd kind of forgotten." A frown crinkled Nell's forehead. "She was out at the lodge the other day," she offered. "She said they're refurbishing some cabins, and Dad leaves things like that in her hands. I wonder if she gets bored?"

Felix and Duane began to speculate on what Helen actually did most of the time to fill her days, their ideas growing wilder by the minute. Colin would have expected Nell to be laughing, but her smile looked forced. They were still at it when she excused herself to refill coffee cups, then to clear away dessert plates, declining offers of help. Colin began to wish their guests would notice that their welcome had worn out.

He'd barely finished the thought when Felix drained his cup and stood, stretching. "Time for me to get going." He flashed a smile at his sister. "Happens I have a date."

Her eyes narrowed. "Anyone I know?"

He grinned. "Yep. Sometimes things look different when you come home. People, too."

She rolled her eyes. "I can't decide whether to be disapproving or not."

"Not." He kissed her cheek. "We're just having fun." Colin was pretty sure he was the only one who heard the addendum. "*Lots* of fun."

Their byplay went right by Duane, but he pushed himself to his feet, as well. "I'd better be off, too." He frowned at Colin. "You're not going to hold my niece hostage so she cleans the kitchen, are you?"

Colin laughed. "No, but we have some things to talk about."

"You mean, while I'm slaving over the dirty dishes?" she retorted pertly.

The two of them walked Felix and Duane to the front door. Duane was beginning to look a little suspicious, but, to Colin's relief, chose not to ask questions about where she was sleeping. At least, not in front of her.

On the doorstep, he faced her. "I can't tell you what it means to me to have you home, Maddie." He sounded choked up. "I want you to know, anything you need…" He labored to a stop, finishing with a harrumphing sound.

Nell gave him a small, polite smile that failed to disguise her discomfiture. "That's kind of you. You've been more welcoming than Mom and Dad."

"Having you stay away on purpose, that may be hard for them to swallow."

"It…wasn't exactly like that," she said, stilted.

"Either way." He looked as if he wanted to envelop her in a hug again, but recognized from her tightly held posture that she would be happier if he didn't. "Good night," he said, nodding at Colin. "Call me tomorrow if you can tell me what's happening."

Colin had dodged him yesterday afternoon.

"I'm…in a holding pattern. It'll probably be Monday before I know what comes next."

"Good enough."

Felix kissed Nell on the cheek, and the men departed together, talking until they separated to get in their vehicles.

Colin closed the door and took Nell in his arms. She made a little sound, wrapped her arms around his waist and leaned as if she needed him to hold her up. He rubbed his cheek against her head and reveled in the feel of her body, fitted against his. As tough as this homecoming had been, she had rarely seemed as fragile as she did right now.

She finally sighed and straightened. "That was really hard. I don't think I handled it very well."

"You weren't comfortable with Duane." He hadn't seen her so stiff with anyone, not even her parents.

"No." Uncertainty filled her eyes. "I don't know why. At first I was really freaked-out."

"Like when you tried to remember Beck?"

"I don't know." Her frustration was obvious. "It felt like that, but…I really *don't* know. Part of it is meeting someone who has all these expectations of me, but who feels like a total stranger to me. I could tell I was really hurting his feelings."

"I noticed. I'd warned him, but I guess he assumed once you saw him all those beautiful memories would come swooping back."

"Wouldn't you think I'd have *some?*" she exclaimed, tension vibrating through her body again.

"Hey." He tugged her close again, kissing her forehead, her nose, the corner of her mouth. "I keep saying this—"

"It'll come back." She made an awful face at him. "But I also distinctly remember you telling me that the day of the assault might not."

Was she associating her uncle Duane with that day? His alarms pinged. Damn it, Duane had implied she'd spent a lot of time with him, something Colin hadn't known. Duane fit the pattern in some ways—never married, apparently not dating women his age unless you counted the possibly mythical woman in Portland. Colin felt sick at even so vague a suspicion.

"I've changed my mind," he told Nell. With a nudge, he started her toward the kitchen. "It's not gone, it's buried. I think Beck had something to do with that night, and you know it. You're resisting the memory because it's so painful, but it's there."

Her expression was bleak when she met his eyes. "Even if it is, I *need* to remember."

He wanted to reassure her by saying, *There's no hurry,* but it would have been a lie. He felt a sense of urgency that wouldn't let go. The assault on Maddie that long-ago night wasn't as simple as they'd believed at the time. It sure as hell hadn't been chance—a predator seeing a teenage girl alone on a dark path. No, it was all about Maddie. Maddie's boyfriend, too, and in some way her family. Her intense fear all these years of returning home meant something. The pieces weren't fitting together yet, but they would. The churning in his belly increased at the idea of Duane as one of those puzzle pieces.

Damn it, no! He'd worked closely with the man for twelve years. Colin knew how much Duane cared about the people they sought to protect.

But he found he couldn't dismiss the possibility

that Duane had sexually molested Nell, however much he wanted to.

"Pushing doesn't seem to work," he pointed out. "All it does is give you a headache. Maybe what you need is a long soak in the tub."

A tiny smile rewarded him. "Actually, that sounds lovely. And I did cook."

He swatted her lightly on the butt. "Go. I'll take care of the kitchen. And I promise not to start the dishwasher until you're out of the bath."

"I don't suppose you have bath salts? Or some bubble bath…?"

He slanted a look at her. She was giggling as she went down the hall.

His mouth quirked as he watched her go, but Colin's mood wasn't any lighter.

NELL STRUGGLED OUT of sleep, crying out as she surfaced. Hands were on her, and she thrashed wildly.

"Maddie!" Somebody was shaking her. "Damn it, Maddie, wake up!"

She kept fighting, some of the nightmare hanging on. *I won't, I won't.*

I won't do what? she asked herself in bewilderment, halfway between states.

"Maddie."

She opened her eyes to darkness. Heard herself breathing in gasps that rasped like skin over gravel. For a moment she had no idea where she was or whose hands were on her.

"Maddie," he repeated, patient, gentle now that she'd quit fighting.

"Colin. Oh, God. Colin." She threw herself at him, felt his arms close securely around her. Either his chest was wet or her face was.

She was crying. In her sleep?

"It was a nightmare. That's all, love, a nightmare. You're safe here with me. I promise." He was moving slightly, as if trying to rock her.

She wasn't close enough. She wriggled and scrambled until she was lying on top of him and she felt him from where her toes curled against his shins to the heart slamming beneath her to his breath moving her hair.

He kept talking; she hardly made out words. Crooning. It had to be five minutes before her frantic need to climb inside him eased. Her muscles gradually went slack, leaving her utterly drained.

"Are you all right?" he murmured, and she nodded, although she wasn't sure she was.

Somehow she knew the nightmare had been a familiar one. This was the first time ever she hadn't been alone when she woke from it, though.

"Angel," she whispered.

He went still. "What?"

"Angel. Somebody called me angel."

"Has anybody since you got here?"

She shook her head as well as she could without removing her cheek from his shoulder.

"Okay," he said. "Do you remember the rest? Do you want to tell me?"

His hands were moving up and down her back, the patterns soothing. Here and there he'd stop to knead, seeming to find every knot.

"No," she mumbled. "Can't remember." Not entirely true. *I won't, I won't,* still whispered in her head.

She'd hated whatever was done to her then. Through the murk of her memory she knew it had been a man. Still, she'd somehow been able to respond positively to Beck, and now to Colin.

Colin was different than anyone she'd ever known. His gentleness extraordinary for a man who had admitted to a capacity for violence, who had tried hard to close himself off emotionally.

I love him, she thought, this time with no doubt but plenty of misgiving. *You're safe with me,* he kept saying, but for how long?

He was here now. Now mattered. The turbulence inside coalesced into a desperate need for the ultimate closeness. She needed to feel him deep inside her, to know that moment when he came, when she was his whole world—if only fleetingly.

Nell lifted her head enough to kiss the taut skin stretched over his powerful pectoral muscles. Encountering dampness from her tears, she licked it.

He went absolutely still, not even breathing. But he couldn't control his reaction to her. She felt him swelling beneath her belly.

When he did move, it was to yank her up so their mouths could meet. No gentleness now, only hunger and urgency. His tongue stroked deep. So fast, she wanted more. She straddled his body, squirmed until she rode atop the long, hard length of his penis.

He wrenched his mouth away. "Wait! Condom."

The words blurred, scrambled. She didn't care, only wanted him. She fought to get in position even as he rolled them sideways and somehow reached around her into the drawer.

"Sweetheart, lift up." With his help, she did. A brief tearing sound, then his hands gripped her hips. *"Now."*

He slid into her, as deep as she'd craved. Being on top, in control, obliterated the helplessness she'd felt in the nightmare. The sense of helplessness that had ruled her life for so many years.

Her climax came in a blaze of triumph: body, mind, heart.

With a guttural cry, he thrust up into her, deeper yet, and let himself go.

Let himself feel helpless, so I can be triumphant. Colin was a man confident enough to do that.

All the strength left her, and she seemed to melt over his solid body. Nell's happiness was profound. It prickled behind her eyelids like tears that weren't.

"Maddie," he whispered, drowsy and sated, and she froze.

He'd called her Maddie before, too, she remembered in shock. When she came out of the nightmare.

While she had been reveling in her newfound belief in the woman she'd become, *he* had soothed and made love to the lost girl he'd saved. To Maddie, not Nell.

Nell scrambled off him in instant, horrified reaction. "I'm not Maddie!"

"What in hell?" He reared up.

"You called me Maddie." She all but fell out of bed, suddenly feeling naked in a way that made her ashamed of herself. She swooped to grab something light on the floor and realized it was his shirt. Hands shaking, she put it on and began buttoning as he turned on the lamp. Nell turned away to protect her eyes, and herself, too. She was buttoning the shirt askew, she realized, but didn't care. The tails came almost to her knees.

"It was…unconscious."

She spun to face him. "I know it was! That makes it worse, don't you see?"

"Nell." His voice was insultingly calm, although his gray eyes were as stormy as she felt. Angry, confused, regretful? "You *are* Maddie, too."

She knew she was overreacting, but couldn't seem to help herself.

"You said you understood."

"I do. It slipped out, that's all. Felix and Duane

were calling you Maddie all evening." The words were okay, the tone not.

She felt patronized. "I thought you were the one person here who saw *me*...." Her voice broke. "But I was wrong." She headed for the bathroom, where she'd left her clothes earlier.

Colin got out of bed and started forward to cut her off. "You weren't wrong." Now his voice had an edge, as if he were getting irritated because the whole pat-her-on-the-head, soothe-her thing hadn't worked.

Call her irrational, but now anger supplanted hurt. She spun to face him. "Maddie was a kid, and I still don't know her very well. What's more, I'm not sure I like her. How she handled her problems. What she let happen to her. She's inside me, but I'm not her. And I'm beginning to think you still see me as that poor, pathetic girl whose picture you had up all those years. What is this all about, triumph because you found me? Isn't sex how men celebrate victories?"

Looking stunned, he fell back a step. His Adam's apple bobbed. "It's not like that." His voice was quiet, as shocked as his expression. The uncertainty she heard in it was more than she could bear.

"I'm going back to the apartment."

"Don't do that, Nell. I'll sleep on the couch."

"I need to be alone." She shoved her feet into her shoes, gathered up her things and even stormed into the bathroom to grab her toothbrush. "I should never have..."

"Don't say that." He sounded devastated, the confidence she'd believed so entirely in shattered. "Nell, it was a slip of the tongue."

She shook her head hard. "Don't lie. You know it was more than that. And maybe I'm making too big a deal out of this, but…I can't help it."

She rushed from the room before she could start crying. She didn't stop for her parka, only her bag. She groped and found her keys, then sprinted down his porch steps and across the yard, hardly feeling the cold.

Even so, she was shivering by the time she climbed the steps to the apartment. Instead of adjusting the thermostat, though, she simply dropped everything and climbed into bed, huddling in a ball until her body could create a cocoon of warmth beneath the heap of covers.

She felt so much hurt, so much confusion. Grief even.

I made a fool of myself, she thought, but then pictured his face when he'd claimed she'd misunderstood. He'd tried to hide guilt, but it was there.

He wanted, maybe even loved Maddie Dubeau. And Nell knew that, even if she recovered every last memory, she would never be Maddie again. She didn't want to be! After being born again, she'd defined herself. She *was* Nell.

And she wished, more than she'd wished anything in her life, that Colin loved *her.*

CHAPTER SIXTEEN

SLUGGISH AND HEAVY-EYED, Nell dragged herself out of bed late in the morning. It was nearly eleven before she checked her phone and discovered she had a couple of messages.

The first was from Colin. "Nell, we need to talk. I think you misunderstood last night—but I admit to moments of confusion," he said gruffly. "I wish we could have that talk right now. Bystrom has just resigned, though, and I've been appointed acting police chief. I need to meet with the mayor and city attorney, then bring myself up to speed with whatever was sitting on Bystrom's desk. Will you stay home? Or at least, if you're going anywhere, call and let me know your plans? Whatever you do, don't let yourself be alone with anyone but maybe your mother. And Hailey or Emily, of course." There was a pause. "Damn. I want to see you, not be leaving a message." His voice was suddenly explosive, frustrated. "I don't know if I'll always be able to answer the phone today. Text me if it's important."

Beep.

"Maddie, this is your mother. I'm hoping you will come to dinner tonight. Whatever you may believe, we *are* happy beyond words to have you home." There was the tiniest of pauses in the stilted speech. "I regret giving you any other impression. Please let me know if you can make it."

End of messages.

Nell listened to both again. To Colin's just to hear his voice, to realize he sounded as ragged as she felt. To her mother's in disbelief.

Acting police chief. Despite her turmoil, she was glad for him. She knew he was smart, kind, fair and ethical, capable of the necessary dispassion as well as being stern and even hard, but he'd have to be, wouldn't he?

He wasn't dispassionate where she was concerned, and she was glad of that. *We need to talk.*

Apparently her parents wanted to talk, too, which surprised her. As wretched as Nell felt, another uncomfortable get-together with them was the last thing she wanted to do, but of course she had to go. Spending time with them was part of her quest to remember. Besides, while she was obviously never going to have an ideal relationship with them, they were her parents. The family she'd envied her friends having. And surely dining with her parents would be on Colin's list of approved activities.

What was more, it might get her out of having that talk with him tonight. She didn't think she was ready.

After having a stiff little conversation with her mother, Nell texted Colin to let him know her plans. An hour later, she got one in return, demanding details. Rolling her eyes, she told him what time she was expected and that she planned to drive herself. All right, he responded. Don't know how late I'll be tied up.

Midafternoon, Felix texted to let her know he was back in Salem. He suggested she come over to visit him for a few days. The idea sounded extraordinarily appealing except for the fact that she'd lose some of her limited remaining time with Colin.

Assuming they were going to be spending time together.

She was even more embarrassed today. She could see why he'd slipped; he might have even called her Maddie over dinner, because the other two were, and she hadn't even noticed. *She* had trouble sometimes distinguishing between Maddie thoughts and Nell thoughts. And yet…she did need to know why he was attracted to her. Whether it was mostly Maddie he felt compelled to protect. What he meant about being confused.

Tomorrow, she thought, but knew better. When she got home tonight, his porch light would be on, and he would step out, waiting for her to cross the yard to him. And she wouldn't be able to resist going. She didn't even want to resist him.

She spent half an hour browsing job openings in Angel Butte and neighboring towns. Just out of curiosity, she told herself. Salary ranges in the libraries tended to be lower than in Seattle, but not by much. She looked wistfully at an opening for a librarian—master's degree required—but then spotted one for Deschutes Public Library for a supervisor in a branch library that didn't require the degree but was essentially the same work. She had the qualifications they were asking for, and the commute wasn't impossible from Angel Butte....

And you are crazy, she told herself flatly as she closed the website, *to even let yourself think you might have a reason to stay in Angel Butte.*

She showered and changed into decent pants and a sweater, and used a couple of clips to pull her hair back in wings to each side. A touch of makeup, and she decided she looked respectable enough for her mother.

Nell hated the fact that it was already dark. Even at home she didn't like leaving work in the dark. The world felt a lot scarier at night.

Because whatever bad thing happened had been in the dark.

That made sense—but human instinct in general was to be more cautious after nightfall, and for good reason.

She locked the house carefully. Just as she got to her car, headlights turned into the driveway. *Colin,* she thought with hope and relief. Until that moment, she hadn't realized how alone she'd felt today.

The headlights blinded her. She squinted, trying to make out the shape of the vehicle. It didn't seem quite right. On a niggle of apprehension, she turned and tried to get the key in the lock of her car, but she was still seeing stars and kept stabbing metal. If she could just get in, lock the doors, then she could roll the window down a little to greet whoever this was....

It was a car, she saw as it pulled in, blocking hers from backing out. She got the key in just as the driver's side door of the sedan opened and someone stepped out. "Maddie? Good, I caught you."

That sounded friendly. She hesitated, recognizing the man who came toward her. "Uncle Duane?"

"I thought I could drive you to your parents instead of both of us going separately."

The motion-activated light lit his face harshly. Her apprehension deepened into something stronger: fear that wanted to become panic.

"I'm meeting Colin after dinner," she said. "Why don't I follow you?"

"I'd rather you come with me," he said, closing on her fast.

She wrenched open her car door, then felt shattering pain.

SUNDAY OR NOT, he'd been trapped in meetings for hours. Now Colin sat at Bystrom's desk trying to get a handle on the urgent issues. He'd long since lost the ability to concentrate, though.

Nell would be at her parents' by now, he told himself. Rushing home wouldn't do him any good.

This state of distraction wasn't normal for him. If a month ago he'd had the right to take over this desk, he'd have been immersed until midnight and been up at 6:00 a.m. and ready to go again tomorrow. He was capable of sustained, intense focus— usually.

Instead, here he was staring without any understanding at the coming week's calendar presumably maintained by the assistant to the police chief. His intention was to cancel anything unnecessary; he'd need to start the week by making the rounds internally. Brian Cooper first thing tomorrow morning, then lieutenants, sergeants, heads of support departments. *So decide what can be put off.*

A split second later, his mind had jumped sideways. *Damn it, I should have cut out soon enough to drive Nell to her parents'.*

She should be safe enough. Hardly anyone knew she was staying with him.

Duane did.

He was staring blankly at the monitor again. Colin groaned, squeezed the bridge of his nose until the cartilage protested, then closed the calendar and logged off the computer. Enough, damn it! There was nothing he could accomplish now that couldn't wait until morning.

He'd phone Nell and insist she not start home until he was there to follow her.

He tried to call during his walk down to the parking lot. Again as he drove through downtown, clogged with tourists trying to find parking. Voice mail each time. She'd probably put her purse with her phone somewhere she couldn't hear it.

But then his rang. Was that the Dubeaus' number? He pulled to the curb and answered.

"McAllister?" It was Marc. "We expected Maddie for dinner and are concerned because she hasn't showed up. She's not that late, but… Do you know where she is?"

His blood ran cold. His gaze flicked to the dashboard clock—6:11 p.m. Late enough that she should have called.

"No," he said. "I'll find out and call you. Let me know if you hear from her in the meantime."

He ended the call without waiting for protest or comment. Except for the few blocks closest to her old home, he was driving the same route Nell would have. If her car had broken down…

Why wouldn't she have called either her parents or him?

Don't think that way.

He'd spotted no small red car before he reached his own driveway. He turned, wound through the trees—and there her car was, in its usual spot. He wanted to be relieved, would have been if lights had been on in her apartment or his house. But both were dark.

Something on the pavement beside her car

glinted in his headlights. Colin slammed on his brakes and leaped out. The motion-activated light came on, and he was already swearing viciously when he crouched to pick up Nell's keys.

NELL MIGHT ALREADY be dead. If she weren't, she would be soon if he didn't find her quickly.

Colin shoved his fear down deep and capped it. She needed him to think calmly and logically, not to let his emotions make him act stupidly.

His first call was to Duane.

"Where am I?" Duane sounded surprised. "Portland. I left this morning, plan to come back tomorrow night. Do you need me? What's up?"

"Maddie's missing."

"Jesus. How? When?"

Colin explained.

"It won't take me ten minutes to throw everything in the car," Duane said, sounding stricken. "I'll start out right now."

"Thanks," Colin said, hating the sickening certainty that sat on his shoulders like some grotesque horror with razor-sharp teeth.

The first thing he was going to do was have Nell's cell phone traced—and Duane's.

It took almost no time for Nell's phone to be traced to River Park.

The location filled Colin with dread. It wasn't chance. She was supposed to have died there. He mobilized a search team. Officers with flashlights fanned out, each in a carefully laid out section of a grid, all of them knowing it was quite possibly her body they were looking for.

It didn't take any special intuition to know where he was going to look first. Colin set out down the same path he'd followed that night twelve years ago. Tonight was bitterly cold, and the park nowhere near as quiet as it was then. The thrashing to each side and an occasional call gave away the clumsy presence of the searchers. Flashlight beams glanced off tree trunks and crisscrossed.

With each step, he swept his light in a careful arc, determined to miss nothing. He couldn't let himself think about what it might illuminate. They'd gotten here fast. She might still be alive.

He hadn't gone ten feet when he saw something. A heap of cloth. Sick with apprehension, he pushed aside stiff branches of snowberry and saw the cloth amidst low-growing ceanothus, just as Maddie's small, whisker-faced coin wallet had been. But this—

Colin crouched. It was her handbag. Swearing, he swung his flashlight beam in increasingly frantic circles. He yelled for help. Picked up her bag and groped in it, his fingers closing on her phone.

He stood and stared back toward the road. Somebody could have pulled over, maybe gotten out, maybe not, and given the handbag a good heave. Sent a message, and eliminated the threat her phone represented all at the same time.

His knees almost buckled. And yet, he didn't recognize relief in the stinging pain. She wasn't here, thank God. Thank God.

But she could be anywhere in the vast empty country comprising forests and high mountain desert that stretched in every direction from Angel Butte. They might never even find her body.

SHE AWAKENED TO darkness, pain and nausea.

One of her recurrent nightmares always began the same way. But this didn't feel right. Nell struggled to understand why, and finally did. In dreams, the physical sensations were never so real. The sharp edge of metal beneath her hip, that roiling nausea with the taste of bile.

And, oh, her head hurt.

Panic welled up, momentarily paralyzing her as she panted for breath. This had to be her greatest terror, to be trapped in the trunk of a car, knowing when it was opened she'd be facing her death personified.

Breathe, she ordered herself. *Slowly. In. Out.*

Somehow she kept the nausea at bay as she tried to *think.* Why would she feel so awful?

The surface beneath her was vibrating and her heart clenched with fear. This was real. She had to be in the trunk of a car again. She groped above her and found the angular metal lid she'd expected. And beneath her was slick plastic, but when she pulled it toward her, her hand found—yes, there was a semistiff, carpeted surface. Underneath *that* was the rounding of a spare tire. Also underneath it was whatever sharp thing was poking her. A tire iron? Maybe.

Using touch seemed to clear the mists from her mind. Duane.

I'd rather you come with me. Nasty, sneering, revealing anger and even hate.

He had called her angel. As if a door had opened, she did remember. Her beloved uncle, whom she'd loved as a child, but who didn't seem to recognize she was growing up when she reached puberty. He kept taking her for overnights to his house, insisting she get in her nightgown and cuddle with him while they watched a movie. Then he'd give her a massage, and ask her to give him one. Tickle her, his hand sliding to places that made her painfully self-conscious.

She'd tried talking to her parents.

"Don't be ridiculous," her father snapped before telling her he was busy.

Mom froze her with one look instead. "Do you know how lucky you are to have family, including an uncle who loves you so much? How can you possibly imply there's anything wrong with that?"

She was never allowed to make excuses when he offered to take her. His touches, his kisses, grew more and more sexual. She had pretended none of it was happening. *He didn't just press my hand to him* there.... *Rubbing it up and down, as if absent-*

mindedly, except it wasn't, because he was swollen and hard. She worked hard at turning her mind to something else. Recite poetry, or think about the last time she'd spent the night at Hailey's and how silly they'd been. Yes, that was when she'd learned to go away in her head.

Curled into a ball in the trunk of the car, her body flushed with horror at the memory.

And Beck. She remembered him, too, a friend until the end. He'd treated her almost like a little sister. He'd known something was wrong, and teased and begged and waited patiently until she told him. His face had darkened, his hands knotting into fists.

"Run away," he told her. "I'll help you. You can come and live here, at the Hales'."

She had been so tempted.

But he scared her, too, when he said, "We could get married when you're a little older. I'd keep you safe. Kissing and all that stuff can be nice, Maddie. I promise. It's not like what *he's* doing to you."

And he'd coaxed her, saying, "Let me kiss you. I'll show you."

Stiff with apprehension, she had wanted to say no, but she liked Beck so much. He was the only person she could really talk to. And he was cute. So…maybe it wouldn't be the same.

It wasn't. She'd liked it.

But…that was when the terrible something happened.

The first terrible something.

HIS PHONE RANG. Marc Dubeau again. Colin didn't let him speak.

"We found Maddie's purse. It was thrown into the park, not far from where she was attacked the night she disappeared."

"But she's not there?" Her father's voice was stark with fear, enough that Colin felt sure the man did love his daughter even if it were in a limited way.

"No." Another call was coming in. "I've got to go, Marc—"

"No, listen," her father said, his voice threaded with urgency. "I keep thinking about something Maddie said back then."

Standing beside his SUV, unaware of the cold, Colin stared into the greater darkness of the park. "What was it?"

"I didn't take her seriously. After she disappeared... But, damn it, he was so upset, I couldn't believe—"

Colin had to unclench his jaw. "Tell me."

"It was Duane. She'd always loved him, but something changed. She quit wanting to go with him. She said—" His voice broke.

Colin felt as if his skin had been peeled away, leaving his nerve endings raw. How could he not have guessed sooner? Duane had tried so damn hard not to encounter Nell. The way she'd withdrawn even at the *idea* of him. More when he actually arrived.

When I let the son of a bitch hug *her, right in front of me.*

"She said he kept touching her. I thought…I thought Duane just didn't want to let himself recognize that she was growing up. That maybe he was being insensitive. And you saw him!" His voice rose. "He was so desperate to find her."

"He was," Colin said harshly. "Because he'd lost her. Finding her was life or death for him. He didn't even have to pretend."

There was quiet for a moment. "You really think?"

"I think." Choking on his rage, he ended the call. If only her father had said something back then. Said something since she'd come home. He'd known how vulnerable she was, stripped of memory.

Marc Dubeau had felt so guilty, he hadn't wanted to believe.

He'd kept his mouth shut, but he hadn't invited his brother-in-law to his home to see Maddie after she returned, Colin realized. It wasn't only chance that Nell hadn't seen Duane until Colin himself had committed the catastrophic mistake of bringing the two face-to-face while giving Duane reason to suspect where she was living.

Where she could be found and grabbed, in a horrific replay of the night she had saved herself.

And through his smug belief that he'd known what he was doing, that he could keep her safe, Colin was responsible for her coming home in the first place.

So I could feel good about finding her, he thought, sickened.

He circled the 4Runner and got in. It wasn't too late. He couldn't let himself give in to the fear that he and Marc were both wrong.

He had one chance to rescue Nell. Only one. He was throwing the dice, believing his friend and mentor was a monster. If they found Duane, and he had nothing to do with Nell's disappearance…

Colin held on to the steering wheel so hard it creaked. It was all that kept him from being swept away by the vicious, dark current of despair.

Finally, he was able to loosen his fingers and reach again for his phone. Go to "missed calls." Hit "reply."

BY SCRUNCHING HERSELF into the back of the trunk, Nell managed to pry up a corner of the mat. The ripping sound of velcro parting made her cringe, but the car didn't slow. She stuck her hand blindly into the hole. Almost immediately she felt a smooth surface that, when she wrapped her fingers around it, felt like…a can? Pop or beer, maybe? But it was too lightweight and yet didn't have the give of an empty aluminum can. Exploring, she discovered one end had a nozzle. *Oh.* She carried one of those in the trunk of her own car, to add air to a low tire.

She set it aside and kept groping. She'd just gripped hard metal when she caught the flash of red from taillights. Unable to brace herself in time, she was abruptly flung to one side, banging her head.

Her eyes burned with tears. The ride, she realized immediately, was rougher. The driver had turned off a main road. Earlier, she'd heard passing cars, but now there was only silence except for the rumble of the engine. Her sense of desperation increased.

Nell levered herself back to where she could reach the hole. Had to pull up the carpet again. This time, she closed her fingers right away on what felt like metal pipe. With tugging and maneuvering, she pulled the tire iron out.

"Yes," she whispered.

Then, despite the pounding in her head, she tried to reason out whether it would be better to pretend to be unconscious and let her assailant pull her out of the trunk...or to surprise him immediately by swinging the tire iron.

The car braked and came to a stop, but although she froze in dread, the engine remained running. The car door opened; were those footsteps she heard? A second person joining the first? Or...? No, the driver had gotten out. Now she heard him returning, getting back in. Had he picked something up? Dropped something off? All she knew was that the door slammed, and the car started forward again.

He opened a garage door—

No, she'd have heard the rumble of it on its tracks.

A gate?

She didn't have long.

"WHY DON'T YOU answer your phone?" snapped Jeremy Bronecki, the department's electronics whizz.

"I had another call."

"That other cell phone you wanted me to trace?" Clearly Jeremy didn't care what Colin's excuse was. "It's on the move. It was going north on 97, but it just veered off. East."

"It's not between here and Portland."

"Huh? No. Damn, I think it may be that road to Quail Butte."

Another volcanic cinder cone. Not as large as the better-known Lava Butte but possessing a modest interpretive center for visitors and a road to the summit. A field of rough lava stretched to the north. A few paved paths wound through it, one providing access to a lengthy lava tube, locked and closed off except during tours. A gate closed the road leading into the butte at night—maybe for the entire winter, Colin didn't know—but it could be smashed. Or Duane might not try to drive to the top at all. He could carry Nell's body far enough to bury her in the loose cinder cones. Shove her in one of the smaller, seldom visited lava caves that riddled the area.

Colin remembered the gruesome story the Crook County sergeant had told him, about the teenagers sliding down the side of Lava Butte. One boy's foot smashing a human skull.

He had to get a helicopter in the air *now,* and by God he was going to be on it.

He barely managed a "thanks." A few calls later, Butte County Sheriff's Department was tracking down a pilot for their search-and-rescue helicopter. Even as he made and took more phone calls himself, Colin used lights and siren to achieve maximum speed toward the airfield on the outskirts of the city where the copter was housed. Without even thinking it out, he chose Jane Vahalik to go up with him.

She listened. "I'll be there in five," she said, and was gone.

Quail Butte wasn't ten miles off the highway. Duane might already be there, while Colin was tediously assembling his team.

Hold on, Nell.

THE ROAD WAS rising, and seemed to be curving. She could tell from the steady force that pushed her one way. A never-ending curve.

Nell pictured the road rising to the top of Angel Butte. But that didn't make sense. They'd been traveling for a while. She doubted she'd regained consciousness immediately. So...surely not there?

There were plenty of other cinder cones in the area. She had no idea how many had roads leading to the top. Pilot Butte in Bend, and Lava Butte. But she thought there were others. Perhaps some within the Newberry National Volcanic Monument?

She would be completely on her own. Who knew when Colin would discover she was missing. Would her parents think to call him when she failed to arrive for dinner? But he would have no idea who had abducted her or where to look when he did find out.

She allowed herself a pathetic minute of regret. How stupid she'd been with her extreme reaction to him calling her Maddie. He might not love her, but...he'd made love to her as if he did. His kindness, his patience, his tenderness toward her. The way he looked at her and only her. Now he'd never know that she loved him.

Maybe it was better that way.

The ache in her chest seemed to crystallize into something much harder: determination. She might be alone—but she hadn't heard any voices, which likely meant she would be facing only one man when that trunk opened.

Undoubtedly armed.

Well, she just wouldn't give him time to reach for his gun. She would slash out, *hard,* with the tire iron. Nell imagined it striking his head, crushing the relatively fragile bones of the cranium. It would make a terrible sound, but she didn't care. *He* had hit her in the head twice now, with the intention of killing her. She wouldn't have to kill him, only incapacitate him so that she could grab the car keys and escape.

She wasn't a terrified fifteen-year-old this time. She was an adult, small compared to him, but in good physical condition. In a different way, she'd defeated him last time. So why not again?

The road seemed to be leveling off and the car was unmistakably slowing. A moment later, it came to a stop. This time, the engine went silent. The car door opened and closed, the sound sharp. Footsteps came around the side, the last soft scuff so close she shivered. The key turned in the lock.

Nell closed her eyes and played dead, her fingers gripped painfully tight on the tire iron hidden beneath her.

CHAPTER SEVENTEEN

THE HELICOPTER MOVED fast, staying low. Colin stared down at the bright glow of Angel Butte. In the midst of his fear, it seemed unbearable to realize he was looking at thousands of strings of Christmas lights, meant to convey cheer and hope. He was grateful when the city fell behind and below he saw only the headlights of vehicles traveling Highway 97.

Leaning forward tensely, he held a rifle cradled in his arms. Jane was likewise armed. He glanced to see her looking tight-jawed and as grim as he felt. Like him, she wore a bulletproof vest, hastily donned. Maybe he'd have been smarter to bring a SWAT member—but he knew and trusted her.

Down somewhere below, Butte County deputies were racing for the turnoff to Quail Butte, too. One unit had been close enough, it might conceivably beat the helicopter there. God, he hoped it would.

Every time he relaxed his guard, he pictured Nell sprawled, lifeless, in the trunk of a car. Blood matting her hair. Why wouldn't Duane have killed her before he put her in the trunk? Leaving her alive until he could dispose of her body was taking a risk, as he'd well known after his experience twelve years ago.

To block his fear for her, Colin thought about the bones of teenage girls that had been found in the tri-county area, the decomposed body of the girl found buried in cinders on the flank of Angel Butte, a death he had investigated himself. Had Duane murdered those girls? If he'd molested Nell, that made him a pedophile. She was unlikely to have been his only victim. But where had he found the others? Had he picked up street kids in Portland and brought them back here? Given them a place to stay at his house?

Colin swore under his breath. Was there any chance at all Duane was hooked up with the shelter the Hales ran? Did they take in girls as well as boys?

In the darkness below, he saw flashing lights. The Butte County unit turning off the highway, accelerating again.

"Coming up ahead," the pilot warned.

"We're ready."

Please, God, let her still be alive.

WHEN HANDS GRIPPED her, Nell let her body flop. The trunk light might not be bright enough for him to see that she was still breathing. Even if it was, she wanted him to believe she was unconscious, to fail to notice the awkward angle of her arm that disappeared beneath her.

With an impatient growl, he rolled her toward him. She used the momentum he was providing to add power to her swing. He shouted with surprise and fell back, but not in time. Unfortunately, one of the cross pieces of the tire iron had skimmed the rim of the trunk, causing her blow to lose force. Still, it glanced off his shoulder and gave her time to roll out of the trunk and—almost—get her feet under her.

She fell jarringly to her knees, but she took another hard swing and caught his knees. The *crunch* was satisfying but nowhere near enough.

"You *bitch*," he snarled.

Nell staggered to her feet and, backing away, brandished her weapon. She'd been in the trunk so long, her eyes were probably better adjusted to the darkness than his. The moon was nearly full, though, shedding a silver light against which he was a dark, hulking figure.

Where am I? But she didn't dare take her eyes from him. All she knew was that there was pavement beneath her feet, and that space seemed to drop away somewhere off to her left.

"Why didn't you die the first time?" he asked her.

Taunting him wasn't smart, but she did it anyway. "Because you were careless."

With another growl, he launched himself at her.

She swung and connected with his forearm, but he got a grip on the tire iron, too, and wrenched it away. Nell scrabbled backward until she came against the car. She inched along it.

He flung the tire iron away. Sparks skittered in its path. She spun and raced around the car. Behind her, Duane laughed.

Nell saw enough to know that they were on the summit of a lava cone, as she'd guessed. No city lights below, only darkness. The crater was greater darkness one way. A trap.

Ducking, peering through the windows, she saw he had something in his hand now. A handgun. He started around the car, and she ran. A dark building wasn't far away. Probably an old fire lookout. Duane wouldn't have brought her here if it was still manned, but getting past it bought her precious seconds.

Her feet slapped on pavement, then slid on the looser cinders. The gun barked and the bullet bit into the wooden side of the lookout inches from her head. She focused on a small stand of stunted trees growing on the crater rim maybe twenty-five yards away. Nell ran for all she was worth, zigzagging a little.

He fired again, then yet again. A blow struck Nell in her back and she almost fell, but somehow she kept going. Another bullet passed so close she felt the brush of air, but she was almost to the trees. Almost there. And then she plunged into them.

Small branches whipped her face and ripped at her parka and pants. She fell and went down once, landing on her wounded side. It hurt so much for a moment she wasn't sure she'd be able to get up, but she did.

Risking a glance behind her, she didn't see him for a moment. What was he doing? Then the headlights of the car came on, shining directly at her, followed by another powerful beam. He'd gone back for a flashlight.

With a moan, Nell plunged over the edge of the cinder cone, trying to keep on her feet as she half slid, half fell down the steep side.

JANE LEANED FORWARD. "I see headlights."

Colin, too, was staring until his eyes burned. He'd seen only darkness a moment before. The lights had just come on. Did that mean Duane had disposed of Nell's body and was about to depart?

Not a praying man, he found himself doing it again. *Please, God, no.*

The helicopter was rapidly closing the distance.

NELL CRASHED PAST small trees clinging to the steep side and the eroding cinders. She reached the road that spiraled to the summit, dashed across it, had to scramble over the guardrail and plunged once again into the safer darkness. A moment later she fell and rolled, bouncing off outcrops of rough lava. The precipitous descent into darkness was terrifying, but nothing like the man above, so desperate to kill her.

The sweeping beam of the flashlight found her and the gun cracked again. More burning: this time in her arm. Once again she fell, rolling, rolling until she was sickened and dizzy, but the shots were missing her. Even the flashlight couldn't keep up.

She thudded painfully to a stop on the paved surface of the road. *Again*. Oh, God. How many times did it circle the butte on the way to the top? She half crawled across it. This time the guardrail was almost more than she could manage. Her legs felt weighted with lead as she lifted them, one at a time.

There was a roaring in her ears, and suddenly a bright light shone from the sky.

"Drop your weapon!" The voice was deep, metallic.

She might be imagining it. She felt so unreal now, she wasn't thinking anymore. All she knew was that she had to keep going. Get away. Find someplace to hide.

The gunfire that broke out above was part of the nightmare, no more real than her pain.

She knew she'd reached the base when she fell onto her hands and knees on brutally rough lava.

THE SEARCHLIGHT SWUNG in arcs, briefly illuminating a dark figure plunging down the side of the volcanic cone. On the next arc, it found a man on the edge of the rim, holding a weapon in one hand and a big flashlight in the other. As the helicopter swung to take up position above him, he lifted his face. Unmistakably Duane, although the vicious expression was nothing Colin had ever seen on this man he'd thought he knew.

The handgun lifted and bullets began pinging off metal.

The pilot was swearing, a litany that rang through Colin's headphones.

"Hold it steady!" he shouted, and opened the door.

He knelt, lifting the rifle. The helicopter bobbed and he cursed, grabbing for purchase. The pilot was apologizing and swearing. A hand gripped Colin's belt.

"I've got you." Jane's voice.

Hoping she was well-braced, he lifted the rifle again, found Duane Brewer in his sights and fired. *Bang, bang, bang, bang.* He was distantly aware of the rotors spinning overhead. Earphones deadened his hearing. Another bullet pinged off the metal, close enough that he flinched. In his peripheral vision he saw flashing red, blue and white lights reach the top.

Suddenly the helicopter seemed to find an air pocket and was as still as if he were standing on a platform rooted to the ground. Narrowing his focus so that nothing and no one else existed, he sighted again and fired. This time his target dropped and stayed unmoving in the harsh white light. The flashlight had rolled away, its beam now pointing toward the crater. The weapon was visible a few feet from his outstretched hand.

My friend. The man who taught me so much.

A pedophile, and killer.

"Do you want me to bring us down?" the pilot asked.

"No, the troops have arrived."

Running, the two deputies emerged into the spotlight, both holding weapons out, arms braced. As one kept his distance, the other edged forward, first kicking the handgun farther away. He bent cautiously, then after a moment straightened, holstered his gun and waved at them.

"Find Nell," Colin ordered, backing away from the open doorway.

The helicopter swooped dizzyingly over the rim and pointed downward.

DESPERATE AND MINDLESS, Nell sought a place to hide from the white light sweeping across the lava field, hunting her. She staggered and swayed, barely keeping to her feet. She knew she was almost done; each step felt like her last. But she reached a taller outcrop of lava, and feeling her way around it found a concavity on the far side. She sank down, curling herself into the smallest ball possible.

Every part of her hurt. She felt like a wounded

animal waiting to die. She wanted to die alone, not with *him* standing above her in triumph.

The beam of light moved slowly over the lava field right in front of her. So close. Nell squeezed her eyes shut. If she couldn't see it, it couldn't see her, she decided with the irrationality of a child.

A wind seemed to be whipping her. She hunched tighter and covered her ears against the roar that filled her ears.

"Nell!"

It almost sounded like Colin's voice. *I'm dying.* The thought was the most coherent she'd had in some time. She shook in great shudders, hearing footsteps crunch on the lava.

"Oh, God, Nell." His voice again, this time breaking at the end. "He's dead, Nell. Sweetheart, I found you."

She almost believed that. She opened her eyes the tiniest bit but could only squint against the light that had found her.

"I think I'm dead," she told him.

"No. You're not. Thank God, you're not."

Very, very gently, she was lifted. There were too many hands to be only Colin's. And, oh, it *hurt* to be touched, so fiercely she decided she wasn't dead after all. People coming back from near-death experiences reported that following the white light was peaceful, and this wasn't.

"I'm sorry, so sorry," he groaned, and the hands

laid her on a flat surface that then lifted. She thought he was swearing.

"Love...you," she whispered, and the white light was gone.

NELL WAS TAKEN straight into surgery to remove a bullet lodged beneath her shoulder blade.

The wait was agonizing.

Jane hugged Colin and left to deal with some of the fallout of the night. Pacing the hall outside the waiting room, he did call Noah Chandler, telling him what had happened in a few terse words.

"What the *hell?*"

In a monotone, Colin continued with as much information as he had. Duane had sexually molested Maddie as a girl. The best assumption at the moment was that it was Duane who had abducted her back then. "We think there's more. He may have murdered the boy who was buried in the park, but we don't know why. I'm hoping when Nell wakes up..." His throat squeezed shut. After a minute, he managed to say, raggedly, "Maddie. When Maddie wakes up..."

"All right." Chandler sounded surprisingly kind. "Call me tomorrow when you can."

Maybe Angel Butte had gotten lucky with this mayor. More cynically, Colin thought, *Time will tell.*

As he ended the call, he saw the Dubeaus hurrying toward him. Marc looked distraught, his wife...

maybe worried. Either her face was incapable of expression, or *she* was incapable of emotion.

But when they reached him, she was the one to fix him with a surprisingly desperate gaze. "Maddie?"

"She's…in surgery." He hesitated. "The waiting room is right here. Why don't you sit down?"

Helen fumbled her way to a seat. Gripping one of her hands, her husband stayed on his feet. Both looked at Colin.

"Was it Duane?" Marc asked.

There was no way to soften it. "Yes. He's dead, Helen." Forming the next words was a challenge, but they had to be said. "I'm sorry for your loss."

A sob escaped her. She pressed her free hand to her mouth and stared at him with brimming eyes. "He tried to kill Maddie."

"He did."

"Oh, dear God."

Marc crouched and wrapped his arms around his wife. She leaned into him and cried silently, only the shaking of her shoulders betraying the tears. His anguish was painfully visible.

Only when she straightened and reached for the tissues on the table beside the chair did Marc look up at Colin. "This is my fault."

Helen shook her head vehemently. "No, it's mine. *I'm* the one who wouldn't listen to her. Who told you he would never…"

Colin gazed down at them from what felt like

a great distance. Most of him was attuned to the double doors leading to the surgical suite. Nell was in there. He'd have given anything to be with her.

He looked at Helen. "You had no idea."

"No," she said dully. "I think… No, I *knew* we were both damaged by our childhoods. I've never told anyone but Marc." Her face worked. "Sometimes, pride was all I had. But I never dreamed my brother would do anything like this. I swear." She ended in a whisper. "I loved him."

Her *pride* had been more important than her daughter? Anger roiled in Colin, mixing with the volatile combination of emotions he was already struggling to contain. He had no civility left in him. No sympathy for this woman.

"Tell me." His voice ground like the cinders had underfoot.

Both stared at him, alarm on their faces.

He leaned forward a little, vibrating with that anger. "You owe me—most of all, you owe Maddie—that much."

Her mouth opened and closed a couple of times. After a moment she nodded. "My father was navy," she said in a constricted voice, looking away. "He had long ship deployments. When he was home, our mother was the perfect wife. The house shone, dinner was on the table when he walked in the door, she helped us with homework…." Her laugh was caustic. "When he shipped out, she brought men home. A different one every night, sometimes. She wasn't…discreet. Both of us saw her…doing things with them. But how could we tell Dad? It would have broken his heart. Only…then he came home unexpectedly and walked in on her. It all came out. He wondered if we were even his children. He insisted on testing, and…" For a moment it didn't seem as if she could speak. "Duane wasn't," she said so softly, Colin had to lean toward her to hear. "Dad…rejected him. It was hideous. Duane ran away and…well, I didn't see or hear from him for years. I know he ended up in shelters."

Colin had known that much. Like Nell, Duane had gotten his GED and been able to go on to college.

"I'd already married Marc when Duane got in touch," Helen finished. "I was so glad to see him." Her face contorted.

"He called Maddie 'angel,'" Colin said, his voice harsh in contrast with hers.

"Yes." Tear-drenched eyes finally met his again. "He used to talk about how innocent she was. How pure. Nothing like our bitch of a mother. That's what he said. 'Nothing like our bitch of a mother.' And he was right. She was." Helen seemed to struggle for what she needed to say. "I spent years wishing I wasn't a girl, because that made me like *her*. I suppose…"

She didn't finish. Didn't have to. Colin could finish her sentence. She supposed she'd rejected her own daughter, because she was a girl. Helen

presumably despised herself on some level, rejecting her own femininity.

And he could imagine Duane worshipping everything that was pure and angelic in his niece
even as he corrupted that innocence. What had happened? Had she responded too sexually to something he did, disillusioning him?

Or had he discovered she had a boyfriend?

God. Colin rubbed a shaking hand over his face.
Yeah, that would have done it.

All he could do was nod at the two of them and
walk away. He couldn't bring himself to sit beside
them pretending they were all united in a common
fear for Nell.

They were here, and he supposed that was something. For him, it was too little, too late.

He loved Nell, and he'd almost been too late.

Had she really said she loved him?

Damn. Out of sight of the Dubeaus, he turned,
flattened his hands on the wall and bent his head,
trying to regain some semblance of control.

NELL UNGLUED GUMMY eyelids and raised them. A
monitor close by was beeping softly. Dim lighting
was adequate for her to see the rails on her bed,
the IV stand beside it, the pleats of a curtain that
mostly circled the small space, although a gap allowed her to see the head of the empty bed that
shared the room with her. Really, all of that was
only background. Mostly, she saw the man who sat

in a chair pulled up to the bed. Leaning forward, elbows resting on his knees, he was watching her steadily. She looked down to see that he was holding her hand.

She'd woken up several times before, first in recovery. Different nurses' faces had appeared above her. She'd been given ice chips to moisten her mouth. They'd asked questions that she thought she'd answered. She remembered being wheeled to a room and shifted to this bed. Later, she thought she'd even talked to Colin, but she'd still been so fuzzy.

Nell wriggled her fingers and his tightened. "I really didn't die," she whispered, and he laughed, low and husky.

"No. Why did you think you had?"

"The white light."

He nodded. "That makes sense. It was a searchlight coming from a helicopter."

"The heavens."

He chuckled again. "In a way."

"I hurt."

He stood to hand her the button she could use to administer pain medication. She squeezed it once, twice, and sighed in relief. He helped her sit up a little and sip water until her mouth no longer felt as if it had been stuffed full of winter-dead sagebrush.

"Better?" Colin asked, smiling at her.

"Yes." She wished she didn't have to breathe,

but at least now the pain was less sharp, more of a deep ache. "I was shot."

"Twice." He smoothed hair from her forehead, stroking so gently she closed her eyes and tried to nestle her face into his big hand. "A bullet entered your back and lodged under your shoulder blade. The other passed through the muscle on your upper arm. You had surgery to remove the one bullet and they cleaned up your scrapes and cuts. You were a mess. One ankle was so swollen they thought it was broken, but apparently it's only a severe sprain. You'll be on crutches for a few weeks, though."

She did an inventory and discovered she knew which ankle was injured. She could feel each and every one of those scrapes, too. "I suppose I ruined my parka," she said in resignation.

This laugh sounded helpless. "Parkas can be replaced."

"I bought it for this trip," she told him with some indignation. "It was expensive."

Colin let down the rail and sat on the bed next to her, his hip pressing against hers. "I'll buy you a new one for Christmas."

"You're laughing," she said suspiciously.

"No. Maybe." Now his mouth curved. "Yes. You survived, and you're worried about a parka."

She guessed it was silly. She was avoiding asking the important questions, like whether he expected to spend Christmas with her. But also…about the monster her mind had tried so hard to block from her memory.

No more hiding.

She didn't have to. She'd won again.

She heard the soft *shush, shush* of footsteps in the hall. They passed her room without hesitation.

"Is he…?" She fumbled and swallowed. "Did you arrest him?"

"Duane's dead, Nell. I shot him."

Absorbing that, she searched his face, seeing grief and relief and probably a hundred other things. "Have you ever had to kill anyone before?"

He shook his head.

"I'm sorry. Not," she added fiercely, "that he's dead, but that you had to do it. He was your friend."

"I thought he was my friend. I still can't believe—" His throat worked. "All those years. I'd have sworn he was a good cop, Nell."

She held on tight to his hand, and realized he was holding her as tightly.

"He never should have been allowed to be involved in investigating your disappearance. As green as I was then, I wondered. But he wouldn't take no from anybody." He shook his head in disbelief. "I have no doubt he was the one who talked to your friend Emily, then made sure no one else ever heard a word about your boyfriend."

"Beck was more of a friend," she said softly. "A really good friend. We met by accident and he… I don't know. Recognized something in me. I told him things I hadn't told anyone else. Except my parents. You know that." She waited for Colin's nod; saw the muscles tighten in his jaw. "Beck thought I should go to authorities. If I wouldn't do that, I could run away."

"In the end, that's what you had to do." He paused. "You remember."

She gave a tiny nod, not anxious to move any more than she could help. "Everything. Almost everything," she amended. "The night before, Uncle Duane took me to a movie and then to his place for ice cream. He kissed me and rubbed up against me and then he pulled down his zipper and asked me to kiss him down there. Usually I just…closed my eyes and let him touch me. You know. But that time I freaked. I yanked away from him and ran outside. He followed me and drove me home. The whole way, he kept saying, 'It's just a different way of kissing, Maddie. Of loving.' And then he said I shouldn't tell my dad, because he'd be jealous that I was more loving with him than I was with Dad. 'He'll be angry at you, Maddie. If he believes you. He never does, does he?'" She tried to smile. "He was right. I tried anyway, as soon as Dad got home from work the next day. But he wouldn't listen. He said, 'You're back to that again? Are you so desperate for attention?'"

Colin swore. "They were here tonight. Your parents. We talked. When you didn't show up at their house this evening, your dad called. He told me you'd tried to tell him about Duane back then. He'd always wondered, he admitted. And he overheard your mother mentioning to Duane that you were coming for dinner."

"That's what he said, when he showed up. That he wanted to drive me to Mom and Dad's. But he wasn't invited, was he?"

"No, I got the impression from your father that the uneasiness has stuck with him. Enough so he didn't want to put you and Duane together."

So finally he *had* believed her. Maybe she ought to feel some sense of satisfaction, but she couldn't. She'd needed her daddy then, and he had failed her.

"Duane came to dinner right after I had tried talking to Dad. I think maybe he guessed. I tried not even looking at him. The minute we were done, I excused myself and, instead of going upstairs, I got my bike out the side door of the garage. Beck and I had arranged to meet."

"So you weren't on your way to Emily's."

"No. I was thinking maybe I'd ask him to take me with him to the Hales. He kept insisting they'd help me."

"But Duane saw you making your getaway and followed."

"I guess he must have. Beck and I met near the river. He gave me his dad's shirt because I was shivering. He was trying to take care of me." She slid a shy glance at Colin. "He kissed me. It was the first time. He said as soon as I was old enough he'd marry me and then I wouldn't have to be afraid of anyone."

Colin bent down and brushed his mouth over hers, his tenderness like a salve on old wounds. Then he straightened and let her continue.

"Duane came out of nowhere. He was just…just there. He punched Beck and then he dragged him into the woods. I was screaming but there was nobody around. I heard a gunshot and saw him standing over Beck." The scene was as vivid as when it happened. She felt the old horror and disbelief, the terror that he was going to kill her, too. "My bike was right there. I jumped on and pedaled as fast as I could. It wasn't fast enough."

"No. Damn." He gathered her carefully into his arms and she leaned, taking comfort from the strength he was so willing to lend.

Eventually he shared some things her mother had told him, about her and Duane's childhood. And then she voiced one of her greatest fears.

"Do you think it was only me? Or…have there been other girls?"

"I called Paula Hale tonight. Turns out Duane stumbled on them years ago. Told them he'd lived in teen shelters, and the adults that volunteered were his salvation. The irony is, that might even have been true. He's been mentoring kids there for years. One at a time. Sometimes a boy, sometimes a girl." His face had a grim cast. "He'd take them fishing, hiking, whatever. They felt lucky to have a cop as a role model. Of course the Hales were grateful he'd kept his mouth shut about them. They never noticed anything was wrong with the girls, but several of them disappeared. Like they told you, it happens. Two were girls whose bodies have been found in the area, one buried in the cinders right here in Angel Butte. She was fifteen years old and pregnant."

"He found out she was pregnant," Nell said with great certainty. "That she wasn't an angel."

"That's what I think."

"Do my parents know?" she demanded.

"Not yet."

"If they'd listened to me, he could have been stopped."

"Yes."

What else was there to say? Nell closed her eyes briefly and thought of girls she'd known at Safe-Hold—of Clarity, so painfully young and pregnant, of Katya, who came and went, running from who knew what. Of so many others like them. And then she imagined someone like Duane preying on them, stealing their last bit of hope.

No, she wasn't sorry he was dead.

Colin didn't say anything, only waited. Patient, as he had always been with her.

"I'm surprised you were allowed to stay like this. It's so quiet. It must be the middle of the night."

"It is." He glanced at his watch. "Four thirty-seven, to be exact. And they probably wouldn't kick me out anyway—"

"Because you're an important man in this town," she teased, amazed that she could.

His grin flashed. "That's right. But just to be on the safe side, I lied." Was his glance the slightest bit wary? "I told them we're engaged."

That took her breath away. "I'm expected back at work, you know. I won't be here for Christmas. I mean, for you to give me a parka."

"Yeah, you will be." Dark with worry and something more, his eyes met hers. "Nell, I love you."

Her heart did a dip and roll. Speech was impossible. Was that vulnerability she saw on his face? Captain Colin McAllister?

"Don't ask me if I love Nell or Maddie," he said hoarsely. "I love all that you are. Maybe I felt something for that sad-eyed girl all these years. I don't know. Your eyes haven't changed." His thumbs caressed her cheekbones right beneath her eyes. "Now I've seen them happy a few times. I liked that. You were an amazing girl, and you're an amazing woman. A survivor." His smile was so crooked, it didn't distract her from the dampness in *his* eyes. "I was…content alone until you came into my life. I'm not anymore. I need you to stay with me, Nell."

With a muffled cry, she lifted her hand and touched his jaw, bristling with a day's growth of beard. "I do love you." Her voice shook. "So much. I kept wishing I'd told you, but then I thought maybe it was better that I hadn't, so you wouldn't feel so bad."

He gripped her hand and turned his face to press a kiss against her palm. "Nothing would have kept me from feeling bad if I'd lost you." He shook his head. "I can't believe you defeated him again."

"I guess I did." She thought about it. "With some help this time."

"I don't think he'd have found you where you were hiding. I think you'd have survived no matter what." Pride rang in his voice. For *her*.

"Marry me, Nell." His voice was low and urgent, gruff. "You probably don't want to stay in Angel Butte. I can't blame you. I'll quit and move to Seattle with you. Wherever you want. You can go to grad school. I can get a job anyplace we end up." He cleared his throat. "If you'll have me."

Tears welled in her eyes, but she didn't let them fall. "Of course I will. And…I think maybe we should stay here. Having all this about Uncle Duane come out will make everything worse in the police department, won't it? You finally have the chance to make things better. You're needed."

"I don't want you to give up anything."

She shook her head. "I've discovered I actually have friends here. Good friends. And I confess I went online and started looking at jobs. I found a great one, if they'll hire me. I can be happy here, Colin, as long as…" Her voice hitched. "As long as I have you."

"You have me," he said roughly. "You've had me since we came face-to-face. It just took me a while to admit what had happened to me."

"After that night at the library." She squeezed his hand. "I found a picture of you online and printed it. I hung it on the refrigerator where I could see it. I thought it was because you made me feel safe. But that wasn't all. You made me feel a whole lot of things I never had before. I want to keep feeling all of them."

"I do, too." He kissed her again, but gently, first on the lips, then her forehead. "I can tell you are hurting again. Push the button."

He was right. She fumbled for it and did.

"Now sleep."

"You should go home…."

He only smiled. "Not a chance. When they let you, you're going home with me. In the meantime, this is where I'll be."

She opened her mouth to argue, but couldn't make herself. Knowing he was here…she could sleep. "I love you," she whispered.

He stroked her face, his fingers whisper-soft. "You know I love you," he murmured in that deep, velvety voice that had riveted her from the first time she'd heard it.

However fuzzy she felt, she knew she was smiling. Her final conscious thought was, *Now I'm home.*

* * * * *

Look for EVERYWHERE SHE GOES,
the next book in
THE MYSTERIES OF ANGEL BUTTE
series by Janice Kay Johnson.
Coming in January 2014
from Harlequin Superromance.

LARGER-PRINT BOOKS!
GET 2 FREE LARGER-PRINT NOVELS PLUS
2 FREE GIFTS!

HARLEQUIN®

super romance®

More Story...More Romance

YES! Please send me 2 FREE LARGER-PRINT Harlequin® Superromance® novels and my 2 FREE gifts (gifts are worth about $10). After receiving them, if I don't wish to receive any more books, I can return the shipping statement marked "cancel." If I don't cancel, I will receive 6 brand-new novels every month and be billed just $5.69 per book in the U.S. or $5.99 per book in Canada. That's a savings of at least 16% off the cover price! It's quite a bargain! Shipping and handling is just 50¢ per book in the U.S. or 75¢ per book in Canada.* I understand that accepting the 2 free books and gifts places me under no obligation to buy anything. I can always return a shipment and cancel at any time. Even if I never buy another book, the two free books and gifts are mine to keep forever.

139/339 HDN F46Y

Name _____ (PLEASE PRINT)

Address _____ Apt. #

City _____ State/Prov. _____ Zip/Postal Code

Signature (if under 18, a parent or guardian must sign)

Mail to the **Harlequin® Reader Service:**
IN U.S.A.: P.O. Box 1867, Buffalo, NY 14240-1867
IN CANADA: P.O. Box 609, Fort Erie, Ontario L2A 5X3

**Are you a current subscriber to Harlequin Superromance books
and want to receive the larger-print edition?
Call 1-800-873-8635 today or visit www.ReaderService.com.**

* Terms and prices subject to change without notice. Prices do not include applicable taxes. Sales tax applicable in N.Y. Canadian residents will be charged applicable taxes. Offer not valid in Quebec. This offer is limited to one order per household. Not valid for current subscribers to Harlequin Superromance Larger-Print books. All orders subject to credit approval. Credit or debit balances in a customer's account(s) may be offset by any other outstanding balance owed by or to the customer. Please allow 4 to 6 weeks for delivery. Offer available while quantities last.

Your Privacy—The Harlequin® Reader Service is committed to protecting your privacy. Our Privacy Policy is available online at www.ReaderService.com or upon request from the Harlequin Reader Service.

We make a portion of our mailing list available to reputable third parties that offer products we believe may interest you. If you prefer that we not exchange your name with third parties, or if you wish to clarify or modify your communication preferences, please visit us at www.ReaderService.com/consumerchoice or write to us at Harlequin Reader Service Preference Service, P.O. Box 9062, Buffalo, NY 14269. Include your complete name and address.

HSRLP13R

LARGER-PRINT BOOKS!

HARLEQUIN *Presents*

PASSION
GUARANTEED
SEDUCTION

GET 2 FREE LARGER-PRINT NOVELS PLUS 2 FREE GIFTS!